LOCAL
GONE
MISSING

LOCAL GONE MISSING

FIONA BARTON

BERKLEY
NEW YORK

BERKLEY
An imprint of Penguin Random House LLC
penguinrandomhouse.com

Copyright © 2022 by figbarton productions ltd.
Penguin Random House supports copyright. Copyright fuels creativity,
encourages diverse voices, promotes free speech, and creates a vibrant culture.
Thank you for buying an authorized edition of this book and for complying
with copyright laws by not reproducing, scanning, or distributing any part of it in
any form without permission. You are supporting writers and allowing
Penguin Random House to continue to publish books for every reader.

BERKLEY and the BERKLEY & B colophon are registered trademarks
of Penguin Random House LLC.

Library of Congress Cataloging-in-Publication Data

Names: Barton, Fiona, author.
Title: Local gone missing / Fiona Barton.
Description: New York : Berkley, [2022]
Identifiers: LCCN 2021051387 (print) | LCCN 2021051388 (ebook) |
ISBN 9781984803047 (hardcover) | ISBN 9781984803054 (ebook)
Classification: LCC PR6102.A7839 L63 2022 (print) |
LCC PR6102.A7839 (ebook) | DDC 823/.92--dc23
LC record available at https://lccn.loc.gov/2021051387
LC ebook record available at https://lccn.loc.gov/2021051388

Printed in the United States of America
1st Printing

Book design by Daniel Brount

For
David Thurlow
February 19, 1932–January 12, 2021

As long as you live, there's always something waiting; and even if it's bad, and you know it's bad, what can you do? You can't stop living.

—TRUMAN CAPOTE, *IN COLD BLOOD*

LOCAL
GONE
MISSING

PROLOGUE

T HERE WAS SOMETHING BUZZING. A fly.

Unable to move, he could only listen to its whining drone and try to follow it round the small room in his head. Where was it? Near the sinks? The drain in the floor?

There was a silence and then it was flickering at the edge of his vision. He shook his head violently to stop it coming nearer but it waited and landed just below his left eye where sweat had pooled. It lifted off when he flinched but was back immediately. He was totally at its mercy. And the fly seemed to know, loitering like one of those sullen teenage boys who hung around the High Street.

The fly danced over the damp tea towel plugging his mouth and moved toward his nostrils, rising and landing, the light brush of its feet and wings a subtle torture. When it finally flew off, it headed straight for the window, the sole source of light. He turned his head slowly to watch it frenetically beating against the pane before falling exhausted to the sill.

It was a prisoner too.

He closed his eyes and tried to focus on how he was going to get out. He didn't know how long he'd been there. How long he'd got before they returned. It was getting darker in the room. The summer evening was fading and he struggled against his bindings one more time until his muscles screamed for him to stop. It was useless. Maybe he could work the gag out and shout for help? He forced his mouth open as far as it would go, feeling the gristle pop in his jaw, and stabbed at the material with his tongue as he rocked in the chair. It was working but the effort made the blood sing in his ears and he began to choke. He stopped and tried to slow his breath, whistling down his nose. Then bucked in his chair until it toppled over, crashing him to the floor.

As he lay, he was suddenly aware of the silence in the room. He strained to hear the fly's whining and its pathetic attempt to break the glass. But there was nothing.

Had it escaped? How?

Dread spread like a stain through his whole body, and his heart started to bang against his chest wall.

Someone must have let it out. While he was fighting to get free. Opened the door behind him. And come in. He tried to turn his head to see.

ONE

Dee

AFTERWARDS, PAULINE SAID SHE hadn't even noticed Charlie was missing until I woke her.

'The car had been in the drive but there'd been no sign of him when I'd let myself in to clean. I've got my own key and I'm often here before they're up. I prefer it, to be honest. I can just get on with my job. I'm almost done before they even realize I'm about. *The invisible woman,* my husband jokes sometimes.

But he's right. I can vanish when I walk through a client's door. 'Course, they hear me hoovering or moving furniture, but most of them act as though I'm not there. It's like on *Downton Abbey* when the servants materialize through hidden doors to dust the chandeliers while the family is discussing Lady Mary's latest scandal. But there are no secret doors or belowstairs at the places I clean. I'm at the other end of the scale. I mean, the Perrys live in a caravan.

"Luxury park home," Pauline had snapped the first time I called it that. "Travelers live in caravans, Dee. And this is only temporary until we finish the big house."

The big house. When you see it from a distance, it does look special. But close up, it's a different story. It's crumbling, one brick at a time. There are great big holes in the roof, and ceilings are coming down inside. It ought to be condemned, my husband says, but Pauline still makes me polish the brass knocker and letter box. I suppose it helps her kid herself that she'll be living in it soon. The things people do to make life bearable.

Front, that's what they all put on. The shiny outside that hides the filth. You should see what I see: the fat-caked ovens, the shit-streaked toilets, the stained mattresses. And hear what I hear—who has money problems or fungal infections. But you won't. Part of the job is not to tell.

"Charlie!" Pauline suddenly yells from her bedroom.

"Haven't seen him," I call back, and put my head round the door.

"Well, he's not here," she says, pulling his folded pajamas out from under his pillow.

"Right," I said.

"I took one of my pills last night—I must have been asleep when he came in. And when he got up," she says.

But I can't smell the lingering sour breath of Charlie's secret last glass. I've been opening the window in the tiny room as soon as I can when I do in here—and helping him hide empties from Her Majesty. This morning the bedroom is filled with the salty stink of sweat and sex. And they don't. Have sex, I mean. Charlie can't manage it, according to Pauline. But someone can. There's talk in town about Bram, the gardener, who's up here a lot. And does no gardening.

"He's supposed to be buying me a new dress in Brighton today. He promised," Pauline wails. "I've been stuck in this bloody caravan for days."

She's used the C word. She's properly furious.

"I'll get on with the kitchen," I say. She pulls a face and nods.

I should say something straightaway. That I saw Charlie last night. But there'd be questions.

Don't get involved, I tell myself. *It's none of your business. And you've got enough going on.*

I fill the bucket with soapy warm water while I try not to think about my own problems: about the rent that needs paying next week, Liam's lack of work. And my family creeping back into my life after all these years. Making me remember.

The bucket overflows and splashes onto my feet. *Come on, Dee. It'll all be okay,* I tell myself.

And Charlie'll turn up in a minute, won't he?

BEFORE

TWO

Seventeen days earlier

Charlie

H E COULD SEE HIS daughter through the window. Head cocked so that her hair fell over her face. Listening for the beep of his key locking the car door. She'd know he was there already, would have heard the car pull up, but he didn't rush. He watched as she moved slowly from the window to the door, steadying herself on surfaces, ready to welcome him. Charlie Perry levered himself out of the car and pressed the key fob. His daughter smiled and raised her hand. He went to wave—still an automatic gesture after all these years—and let his hand drop. Instead, he tapped his greeting on her window and marched up the steps.

"Good morning, Mr. Perry," the new woman on the desk cooed at him. He'd asked them all to call him Charlie at the beginning but they'd just smiled. It wasn't that kind of place. The staff at Wadham Manor didn't wear those awful carer tunics—all pink polyester. Here, it was crisp white shirts and smart trousers. And disposable aprons only when the need arose.

There were yellow roses on a central table in reception, replacing last week's fat pink peonies. Charlie breathed in the purified air overlaid with wood polish and allowed himself a smile of satisfaction. It was a façade—he knew that; of course he did. Wadham Manor was still an institution but he'd let five-star reviews—"more like a country house hotel than a residential home"—and fresh flowers sell it to him. And it was what his girl deserved. What he owed her.

"Good morning!" he sang back. He couldn't remember her name but he'd make sure he asked someone. Always important to get names right. "How are you? And how is Birdie today?"

"Good—she did brilliantly with the new physio yesterday. She'll be so happy to see you."

Except she can't, Charlie wanted to say. Birdie hadn't seen him for almost twenty years.

"I'll go through," he said.

"Of course. And I'll tell Mrs. Lyons you are here. There's a note that she needs to speak to you afterward."

BIRDIE HUGGED HIM CLOSE when she opened the door to her apartment. "Wow! Did you fall in a vat of aftershave, Dad?" She laughed and held her nose.

"What do you mean! Don't you like it? It's very expensive."

"I bet it is. Did Pauline pick it?"

"She said she was sick of my old stuff. I needed updating."

"I liked the old stuff. You smell like an airport duty-free now."

"Ha! Shut up and make me a coffee. There's a good girl."

He watched as she organized cups and milk in her kitchen area, tucking her beautiful dark hair behind her ear as she chatted. *You'd never know she can't see,* he found himself thinking. But he knew.

I'm lucky to still have her, he told himself. His mantra.

"So how was the new physio yesterday?"

His daughter's sunny smile clouded over.

"Physio?" she muttered.

"You had a session in the morning." *Gently, gently. Let her cover if she wants to.*

"Oh, yeah. Nice. I think." They both knew that her unreliable brain had let go of the information.

Charlie reached for the folder that recorded all the things her memory couldn't. "Says here, you were working on balance and strength—and that he had to tell you off for swearing."

"Dad! It does not say that," she giggled.

"It does," he teased. He loved making her laugh. "There's a list of words used. Some I haven't heard since I was last in the East End."

"Shut up! Here's your coffee. What's the therapist called? I can't quite . . ."

Charlie skipped to the end of the report. "It's, er, it's Stu." And his hand seemed to lose its grip on the handle of his mug. Coffee dripped onto the page, obliterating the name.

"That's it. Stu," she said.

Charlie held his breath and watched for a memory to flicker across her face but there was nothing. It meant nothing to her. It'd been wiped, like every detail of that night. The razor-sharp brain that had earned her a place at Oxford to study law had been catastrophically blunted in a matter of minutes. Fifteen minutes, the ambulance crew had calculated. She'd stopped breathing for the time it took him to drink a gin and tonic and her whole life had changed. When she emerged from her coma, she remembered nothing.

She was lucky. It had never left Charlie.

MRS. LYONS WAS HOVERING when he came out, brutally tweaking the flower arrangement into shape.

"Ah, here you are," she chirped as if he was a favorite guest. He wasn't.

"Now, then," she said as she seated him in her private drawing room, "we really need to get this bill settled, don't we?"

"I will be transferring the money tomorrow, Mrs. Lyons," Charlie said. "I am very grateful for your patience."

"Well, that is good news but I'm afraid that is what you said on the last occasion. And on the other occasions we have had to discuss this matter."

"As I explained last time, I have had a slight liquidity problem—I don't want to bore you with the details—but the money will be in place." He could feel the prickle of perspiration in his hairline. "You have my word."

Mrs. Lyons's mouth hardened and she stood, smoothing her dress over her jutting hip bones.

"Fine. But I cannot emphasize enough that this will be our last conversation on the subject. You are now six months in arrears and I'm afraid I cannot extend our more than generous terms any further. I feel you are taking advantage of us, Mr. Perry."

"Charlie, please."

"Perhaps you should be looking for alternative accommodation for Birdie, Mr. Perry."

HE'D YANKED A TISSUE from a fake ormolu box on Mrs. Lyons's desk as he left and was wiping at the sweat under his eyes as he walked to the main door.

"Is everything all right?" the receptionist called to him.

"Oh, yes. Bit of hay fever. All splendid, thanks."

"Birdie's such a lovely girl."

Girl. He wanted to say she was a woman—she would be thirty-eight next week—that she should have been a top-rung barrister by now. But her injuries had frozen her in time. Her vulnerability had kept her a girl in everyone's eyes.

"Yes. She is."

"She's been a popular girl today. You're not her first visitor."

"Really? She didn't say anything. And it wasn't in the folder." Charlie scrambled through possibilities in his head.

The visitor column in the weekly diary was almost exclusively confined to him and Birdie's mother—they came on different days to avoid any awkwardness. One of Birdie's old teachers came a couple of times a year but she always let him know beforehand so he could prime his daughter. Could it have been a school friend? The girls in her set had fallen away after they'd left for university but Birdie followed a couple of them on social media.

"No. Well, when I told him she was in treatment, he didn't stay." The receptionist leaned forward confidentially. "He said he'd come back one day next week, after lunch."

He. Charlie's skin prickled. "Er, did he leave a name or number? I could get in touch and organize something."

"No, he said not to mention his visit to her. He wanted to surprise her."

"Well, make sure you call me if it happens again. I don't want my daughter bothered."

When he reached the car, Charlie found his emergency packet of cigarettes, lit one with a shaking hand, and sat with his eyes closed.

THREE

Dee

W HERE THE HELL IS my tea?" Pauline is shouting when I open the door to the caravan today. And I think she means me. *I'm not your bloody servant,* I think. And then realize I am.

"Morning, Pauline," I call. "It's me. Charlie's just popped out to the garage. I passed him on the driveway."

"He's never where I need him," Pauline snaps. "He's always out doing his good deeds, chatting up the old ladies or sneaking off to see bloody Birdie."

Birdie is not Pauline's—"The product of an earlier, disastrous relationship," she tells people. "I never wanted children." Poor Charlie. Everyone says he's a saint, putting up with Pauline and driving up and down the A3 to see his disabled daughter.

He doesn't talk about her in front of me. Pauline cuts him off if he mentions her and there are no photos. The only pictures in the caravan are of Pauline pouting for the camera a hundred years ago.

She used to try to go out when I cleaned. There isn't room for us all in here and she hates to be reminded. She used to get all arsy with poor old Charlie, made him take her to the big shopping center in Southfold—"I can get artisan bread and that special wine I like"—but she doesn't do her main shop there. She may use posh carrier bags but she goes to the cheapest supermarket like the rest of us.

But I never say anything to anyone.

The mums at the school gates would love to bitch about her but I never go in for the whole "You ought to see Pauline's fridge" thing. It's a disgrace, actually. It smelled like something had died in there the other day, but when I said I'd give it a deep clean, she made a face, said she hadn't noticed a problem, said it must be a steak she'd bought for Charlie and forgotten. I don't know how I managed not to laugh. Pauline can hardly make toast, let alone a steak dinner. But people go along with her fantasy about being a domestic goddess. To her face, anyway.

There are other cleaners in Ebbing but I think people choose me because I don't gossip. I've always found it's a two-way street, gossip. I mean, you've got to be ready for people to talk about you if you're dishing it out. And I prefer to keep my stuff private. People know my husband's a plumber and we have a seven-year-old son. And that I'm not a local.

It's important here. In a big city, people wash in and out, but here, people stay for generations. And the "cradle Ebbers," born and bred—or inbred, as my Liam says—run things. They make the unspoken rules that mark you out as a newcomer. Like who can run the cake stall at the Christmas Fayre or have a child as an attendant in the Spring Princess Parade. We're allowed to buy and watch. But luckily there is a common enemy we can bond over: weekenders.

The Ebbers hate them for invading their town and buying all the best houses for a handful of days a year. The newcomers hate them because the Ebbers do and it gives them something to talk about. Actually, weekenders are some of my favorite clients but I keep it quiet—I would lose work if people knew.

It's changed so much since I was here as a kid in the mid-nineties—no one had a holiday home in Ebbing then. If you could afford one, you bought farther down the coast where there was sand and no social housing or industrial units. But the prices in those towns went crazy and so they've come here, snuffling for bargains. Ebbing is on its way up, apparently. Anyway, it's good news for me. Weekenders are usually gone by the time I put my key in the door—and they pay London rates. If I'm having a bad day, I can rearrange the cute wooden fish swimming on wires and Scent of the Sea diffusers before I get on with cleaning grit out of the showers. I could try on clothes but I don't—well, apart from shoes, obviously. Everyone does, don't they? And the occasional dress but only over my own things. They'd never know. They probably don't even know what's in the wardrobe.

Liam doesn't like me working for them—he says they're like fat leeches sucking the blood out of the town. I tell him to save it for his mates down at the Neptune. I'm sick of all his "Come the revolution, comrade" stuff.

I haven't yet worked out how you change it up. I mean, how long do you have to live here to be a local? Is there a secret waiting list? Do you have to wait for someone to actually die to take their place? I've lived here five years but I'm still totally on the sidelines. I don't mind—I don't want the attention—but it really bothers some people.

Charlie rushes up the steps while I'm wiping down the sink. "Breakfast is here, my love!" he calls to Pauline, and winks at me.

"Where have you been all this time?" Pauline shouts from her bed.

"I got caught by Dave Harman. Still ranting about the pop

festival in a couple of weeks. I said, 'It's a bit early on a Saturday for this, old man,' but he carried on, accusing weekenders of ruining the town, predicting Armageddon in Ebbing over the August bank holiday. He and his friends have been fired up like this for weeks. He'll give himself an ulcer."

"Well, he's right," Pauline said. "We don't want our town invaded by the great unwashed. There'll be drugs, anarchists, and burglars. And where will we park in town?"

"Absolutely. Anyway, I have sourced the finest croissants for you. I'll warm them and bring you a tray."

"What are you after?"

"Nothing, darling. Can't I spoil you a bit?"

"Huh, you forget I know you, Charlie."

I'm cleaning the windows when the row starts in the bedroom. "Twenty thousand? You are joking!" Pauline shouts. "That money is for my swimming pool, not a care home. I didn't sign up for this when I married you."

"Darling, you're not being fair," Charlie says as if he's talking to a child. She won't like that. "You knew from the beginning that Birdie needed to be cared for."

"But not that she was bleeding us dry. How much have you spent already? Oh, God, don't tell me. I can't bear it. But it stops now. Do you hear? Now."

She must know I can hear but she doesn't care. I rub the glass a bit harder and try not to catch Charlie's eye when he comes through. He looks terrible. I don't know how he stands it.

FOUR

Elise

DI ELISE KING WAS making herself an herbal tea—"Dust and twigs," her neighbor Ronnie called it—but, according to the box, it was supposed to be calming. Elise wondered how long it took to work.

She'd had only four hours' sleep and her eyes were gritty. The owners of the holiday home next door had arrived after midnight, conducting a symphony of slamming doors and car boots, cursing London getaway traffic and shouting at their teenage twins and incontinent Labrador. It happened a lot. Ebbing seemed to double in size every Saturday morning and Elise had learned early on that all the sourdough bread would go unless you got to the bakery first thing.

She'd lain there as the great unloading took place—"Why the hell have you brought a food mixer? Move those bloody paddle boards before I trip over them again"—with fists and teeth clenched, devising suitable retribution. *Hoovering shared walls at dawn, perhaps? Lighting a barbecue with damp wood?* But she didn't have the energy.

And they were always perfectly pleasant in that detached, passing-through way they had when they met Elise on the pavement.

"Hello there! Beautiful day!" they said when they saw her, never using her name.

She didn't know if they even knew it—or that she was a senior officer on the Major Crime Team—but she knew theirs. Kevin and Janine Scott-Pennington. She'd looked them up on the computer—on a need-to-know basis.

The only thing they really had in common was a cleaner. "The S-Ps are good clients." Dee had smiled when Elise had complained about the Friday night arrivals. "They always pay on time. Don't tell anyone, but I don't mind weekenders."

Elise had wondered for a moment if Dee ever discussed her with them. It had made her want to hide all her things. Her mum had laughed when she'd told her but Elise wasn't used to having anyone in the house. She'd never had a cleaner before. Hadn't wanted one. Didn't want a stranger rootling through her underwear drawer or reading her bank statements. But cancer had changed so many things and her surgery had meant no heavy lifting or stretching while she healed. And got back to work. Work. That was what she needed. To be back running a murder investigation, running on adrenaline and cold coffee. *Not herbal bloody tea.*

But the fighting talk had been silenced when she caught sight of herself in the mirror—sunken eyes and tufts of hair prickling her scalp. She barely recognized herself.

"How am I ever going to be me again?" she'd asked the woman in the reflection.

"Oh, shut up, Elise!" she'd answered. "Just get on with it."

She was trying. With Dee's help. Anyway, her cleaner was in the minority on weekenders. Dave Harman, landlord of the pub opposite, told anyone who'd listen that they were driving the real townspeople out, turning the town into Kensington-sur-Mer. Pronounced *Murr.*

Elise knew that Ebbing wasn't like its neighbors, Bosham or West Wittering. It didn't feature in the Bayeux Tapestry or have thousands of visitors surging in like a spring tide on a nice day. An old fish factory with a corrugated roof squatted in the armpit of the curved seawall guarding the harbor, and the ten thousand inhabitants lived mostly in prefabs, housing estate boxes, and salt-stained bungalows rather than thatched cottages, but Elise didn't mind. It felt a bit more real—and it was all she could afford on her own if she wanted to be by the sea. She'd never really considered it until recently—she was a city girl, through and through—but she'd worked up this fantasy that the sea would be company.

While she waited for the tea's magic properties to kick in, she sat at the window that looked out on the High Street like an unblinking eye. She'd hung some net curtains as soon as she'd moved in. The previous owners hadn't bothered but she hadn't wanted to be on display to strangers. It meant she could sit unobserved unless she moved suddenly—or someone put their nose to the glass.

When she'd first come home from hospital in May, Elise had sat in the other window, the one overlooking the sea. Watching the tides. It was what she'd pictured herself doing when she'd bought the place a year ago. But somehow she'd never found time, what with work and—well, work, really.

But she'd got all the time in the world now.

The shock of that first empty Monday had been like a bereavement. She hadn't got out of bed all day. The thing was, her job was the center of everything. Take that away, what was left?

And she'd felt so battered after the mastectomy, she could hardly move, but she'd staggered about, arranging cushions and preparing to be lulled. She'd lasted less than twenty minutes. The sea was supposed to be soothing but the constant movement, the endless ebb and flow, had put her on edge. It was like the free-form jazz her ex, Hugh, liked. Swirling around with no discernible purpose—like Hugh, really . . .

Elise liked an achievable aim, a time frame and an end point. And Alanis Morissette.

It'd been a mistake to hook up with Hugh—well, she knew that now. He'd been her first—only—work romance. She'd taken her time to establish herself when she'd joined the Sussex Police, refusing to go full ladette, knocking back pints and cracking dirty jokes like some of the girls. She'd socialized but never dated anyone on the force—it was number one on her list: "Don't allow anyone to discuss your tits at work."

She hadn't been a nun but she'd been careful. She'd gone out with friends of friends or had holiday flings. Until she met Hugh. She'd been thirty-three and on a joint operation with his force. He'd been a couple of years older and a bit of a heartthrob at Surrey Police HQ but she'd liked that he didn't play up to it. And he'd been as driven as her.

It'd been a slow burn. They'd e-mailed and texted for weeks, the flirting so subtle, it'd been barely visible to the naked eye. And then he'd suggested meeting up.

On the train to Woking, Elise had rung her friend Caro in a panic from the filthy toilet.

"I don't know if I'm doing the right thing."

"Oh, shut up. You'd think you were going undercover in a crack den. It's a sandwich in a pub with a bloke you fancy."

She could still see him on the platform waiting. Watching for her. But that was all in the past. Pre-Ebbing.

SHE'D MOVED HER CONVALESCENCE to the front of the house, dragging a chair carefully to avoid pulling on her stitches. She'd known it couldn't be healthy, just sitting and staring, but she couldn't take her eyes off the street outside. It was like being back on surveillance. The hours she'd spent in stuffy cars, hearing about the life and loves of colleagues while they watched for a suspect, noticing every detail, waiting for the call. She'd loved it.

Promotion had meant she'd lost that skin-to-skin contact with crime. She'd had to be all about strategy—seeing the big picture, meeting targets, doing budgets—and she'd been good at it. And she'd thought she'd loved that too. But sitting in her window, she felt like she'd come home. Eyes on the street.

And there was plenty to see. The local drama over Ebbing's first music festival was well into its second series. Battle lines had been drawn as soon as the posters went up in July. You couldn't miss them. Acid yellow, blue, green, and red blotting out the usual sun-bleached notices and burning off the dust and gloom of the High Street, where shops seemed to open and shut before she had a chance to use them.

Never mind Glasto—come to Ebbo! the posters had trumpeted. *The Diamond Music Festival is for everyone!*

"That looks like it could be fun for the kids," she'd said to the newsagent.

She'd forgotten his name as soon as she'd started speaking—it had been happening more and more since her chemo had started—and stammered, leaving it at "mister." She'd put it on her list of things to ask Ronnie.

Mister had scowled, baring a gold bridge in his mouth. "If you say so, miss. It's a scandal it's being allowed—we got turned down for a beer festival last year on health and safety grounds. But Pete Diamond's been here only five minutes and he's got permission to turn his garden into a rock arena for two nights. Something's gone on—that's what everyone's saying."

They were. And the accusations had got more extreme as a petition to have the festival canceled went unheeded by the authorities. "He's putting this on just to launder money," a young mum with a child on each hand had said in the supermarket. "Everyone knows he's using Ebbing to hide dodgy activities."

Elise had looked at the others in the queue, nodding grimly along as if they had an inside edge on organized crime. And she'd felt slightly queasy. People festered about things they saw every day: garden boundaries, blocked views, bad parking. Festival posters. It could fill their every waking moment until it became a full-blown feud. She'd once nicked an ex-mayor who'd stabbed his eighty-year-old neighbor over an unpainted fence panel.

She'd wanted to say that she'd checked their nemesis out very early on, having nothing better to do, and Mr. Diamond was as clean as a whistle. But no one would have wanted to hear that.

I hope things don't get out of hand, she'd thought.

ELISE WAS SWALLOWING THE last bitter drops of her tea when Charlie Perry entered her frame of vision, greeting passersby with a mock salute. He was what her gran would have called a bit of a dandy in his pink striped shirt, silver hair parted and slicked back. The first time she'd seen him, she'd almost been able to smell the tang of Old Spice that her grandad used to wear on Sundays.

He had a word with everyone as he strolled down the street. Making people laugh or smile warmly. He'd passed the time of day with Elise in the post office queue once, twinkling and full of self-deprecating charm, but she hadn't rushed to join the fan club. The thing was that she'd never been big on all that "Hello, dear lady" shtick. No one was like that, really. He was bound to have a dark side. *Membership of a right-wing organization or a weakness for S and*

M, she'd entertained herself with the possibilities in the privacy of her own head. But not out loud. She'd quickly learned that he'd been practically canonized by the folk of Ebbing.

Charlie suddenly changed direction and crossed the road toward the cottages. He was heading for her door. *Shit, I'm not dressed yet.*

The knock was soft but insistent.

"Good morning," Charlie said as soon as she cracked the door open. "Oh, goodness, I've disturbed your breakfast. Please forgive me."

"No, no. How can I help you, Mr. Perry?"

"Charlie, please. I called the other day but you were out. I'm on my rounds, collecting raffle prizes for a fund-raiser—it's one I do every year for a lovely little charity—and I wondered if you would like to contribute."

"Er . . . I'm not sure I've got anything suitable."

"It doesn't have to be anything grand—a bottle of wine would be lovely."

"Right. Well, I'll have a look."

"That is so kind of you." He lowered his bag to the pavement, the contents clanking. "Oof, that's heavy. I'm doing really well today."

"Which charity is it?" she asked, and stopped herself from asking for his ID.

"It's local—we support young people with brain injuries. It's something very close to my heart. My daughter, you see." His voice caught and he wiped his face with a hankie. "Sorry," he said. "It can still catch me out sometimes. Even after all this time."

It had caught Elise on the raw too and she teared up, reflexively tensing her chin to stop the wobble. She was crying way too often these days. The cancer nurse had said it was a good thing to let her emotions out but every sob felt like it weakened her, flaying off another layer of protection. How would she ever be right again?

"You can't afford to feel too much in this job," she'd been told as a new recruit, and she'd worked so hard to allow only what she could bear. And now she felt everything.

"Oh, please come in and sit down," Elise said.

She felt like a complete cow. Poor old boy. She needed to do something about her knee-jerk distrust of everyone.

"Better?"

"Much, thank you." He lowered himself into an armchair. "Look, I mustn't hold you up."

"You're fine. Stay where you are and I'll have a look for that prize."

She went into the kitchen and swept the cupboards for an unopened bottle, lighting on a liter of vodka in a box covered in snowflakes and icicles. It'd been a Secret Santa present from a colleague who hadn't known she hated spirits—and Christmas.

"Would this be okay?" She held it out in front of her. "A bit naff but you could take it out of the glittery wrapping."

"Oh, no, a bit of sparkle will help ticket sales. Anyway, how are you settling in? You've done lovely things with the house. Ebbing's a great place, isn't it? Wonderful people. Salt of the earth—or the sea, I suppose!"

"Yes. And the views," Elise said. "I'm looking forward to running the coastal path when I can."

"Ah, yes, I hear you haven't been well?"

Elise bridled but of course the town was talking about her. Gossip was currency in small communities. Her breast cancer was probably being pawed over at coffee mornings and school gates.

"I'm fine, thanks," she said. "I'm back at work next month."

"Making our streets safe, eh? Excellent. Well, I'll leave you. Thank you again for your kindness. I hope our paths cross again soon."

FIVE

Twelve days earlier

Charlie

CHARLIE HADN'T SLEPT. HE'D lain like an effigy on a tomb beside Pauline, drifting between panic and reason in the dark until the seagulls had started their dawn tap dance on the roof.

He hauled himself out of bed, stripped off and folded his pajamas, and stepped into the shower. It was what he did every morning. He'd had to until he was sixteen and could finally wash when he chose. But it was ingrained. And things had steadily improved since the slimy communal facilities of the children's home. There'd been an individual cubicle then, and when he'd really started making money, power showers with sixteen options and that fabulous waterfall-effect one in the Hampstead Heath house. Today his ablutions were taken under a dribble of warmish water but it was still his day-setting moment. Alone. While Pauline snored gently.

The sun was already heating up the caravan, beating down on the metal a foot above his head as he soaped himself. He lost his balance when he bent to do between his toes and slumped against the wall. He could hear the plastic cubicle creaking dangerously. Like his life.

In their ten years of marriage, he'd never discussed money with

Pauline—it was agreed it was his department, and as long as he never stinted on her spending, she never asked questions.

And Charlie had had it all under control; he'd quietly paid Birdie's bills and then invested a lump sum from the sale of the Hampstead house when they'd moved down to Ebbing. He'd been sure there'd be plenty to keep his daughter in her five-star nest until he died. And then? Well, his life insurance would pay out. It was worth three quarters of a million. He hadn't told Pauline but he was leaving everything to Birdie.

And he'd thought he could relax. His retirement was to be a warrior's rest: a penthouse seaside retreat, the occasional luxury Caribbean cruise, and some long boozy lunches. But Pauline had had other ideas.

"A flat? Don't be ridiculous! I'm not ready to move down the property ladder," she'd announced.

And scanning through the Sunday supplements she'd seen a picture of Tall Trees—a once-grand boutique hotel on the south coast. And then she had taken him to bed. And that had been that. Why was he so weak?

And of course, it had been a money pit—he'd known it would be the moment he set eyes on it, and what with interest rates on his investment tanking, the debts had begun to mount and he'd had to forget retiring and look for new business opportunities. And keep Pauline at bay.

But she was on his case morning, noon, and night now. Birdie was in her sights. "You've got to find her somewhere cheaper," she'd said as she removed her makeup the evening before. "She isn't forty yet—we've still got decades of paying out these ridiculous fees. We could put her in a suite at the Ritz for less. No wonder you never told me. Bottom line, Charlie, is that we can't afford any more. Surely there's a council place she could go to?"

He couldn't bear to imagine Birdie's face when he told her she would have to move out of the Manor. It was her world. He'd be letting her down again. He felt tears prickle behind his eyelids and stuck his head under the water. And hauled himself back to things he could deal with. The first task of the day was to take the Howell sisters to the big supermarket to do their weekly shop. He could go and drop off the raffle prizes he'd charmed out of his neighbors while the sisters were browsing the shelves for biscuits and Epsom salts.

And then . . . then he was going to take another trip up to Wadham Manor.

IT'LL BE ONE OF *her old crowd showing up,* he'd told himself on the drive home last week. *I'm fussing about nothing.*

But his gut, a reliable indicator over the years, had told him different. He'd decided to make the ninety-minute round trip each afternoon this week, telling Pauline he was on charity business. *Just to have a look. Put my mind at rest.*

He parked well away from his usual place when he arrived, tucking his car in beside a large delivery van, and waited.

Charlie undid the windows and fished out the last of the emergency ciggies from under the seat and inhaled it deep into his lungs. He'd been a forty-a-day man when he'd met Pauline and she hadn't seemed to mind, but as soon as she moved into his house, she'd announced her body was a temple and had to be kept smoke-free. She'd bought him nicotine patches and gum and he'd almost kicked the habit. Almost. He'd have to buy a new car deodorizer on the way home.

Half an hour had passed and he took a swig from a bottle of now-warm water. He'd give it a bit longer and then pop in and surprise Birdie. In the meantime, he'd focus on finding the money for her care. *All you have to do is keep the plates spinning for a bit longer,* he told himself. And was immediately back beside his primary-school teacher, Miss Hargreaves, the smell of her face powder and damp knickers competing with the stink of caged animals. The council had paid for its poorest kids to go to the circus and he'd sat on the hard wooden bench, watching with his mouth open as the magic unfolded. There'd been a lion, terrifying clowns, and flying acrobats but what had stayed with him was the man in a sequined suit who bounded about the ring, keeping an entire dinner service spinning on sticks while the band played.

Charlie had been ten, a quiet, tightly knotted child who'd been careful never to show enthusiasm about anything. Liking something led to misery, he'd learned. He'd seen the fraying seams of the shiny costume and the dead eyes beneath the greasepaint smile. But he'd been entranced. He hadn't been able to put a name on what he'd loved until much later but it'd been the brinkmanship: the imminent possibility of disaster as a single bowl slowed in its orbit and the audience held its breath, the lopsided wobble apparently unseen by the performer until the last moment. And then triumph as he rescued it with a flick of a wrist. The hero of the hour.

Charlie had found a stick and a cracked saucer back at the children's home and practiced for hours in the yard. Later, he'd made a career out of it—in a different sort of arena but he'd never lost that thrill of whirling the first plate.

Until now. He tried to summon up fresh energy. *If the plan doesn't work, change the plan, never the goal,* he told himself. It was something an old boss had had pinned to his office wall. Mind you, *Just bloody well get on with it* was normally enough to stiffen the sinews. But not today.

The rumble of a taxi pulling up on the gravel brought him back to the real world.

He struggled to sit up and saw the passenger get out and stand there with his back to him, staring at the main door until the cab left.

He opened his door and the sound made the visitor turn his head.

"Fuck!" he said.

"I could say the same thing," Charlie said.

NOW

SIX

Dee

LATER, WHILE I'M PULLING a clot of hair out of the drain in the shower, I hear Postie Val calling, "Hello!"

"Coming!" Pauline shouts back.

"I've got another registered letter for Charlie. I need his signature."

"He's out," Pauline snaps. "I'll do it and give it to him when he gets back."

Val chats like she always does while Pauline tries to sign with her fingertip, fishing for goss, but she isn't getting anywhere. And I watch the postie walk back to her van through the window as I hoover. Pauline comes through and slumps on the sofa with the brown envelope on her lap. A registered letter is never good news, is it?

WHEN I'M DONE, I take the full bin bag out to the dustbin and it splits as I lift it in. A bottle clatters out and I hold my breath in case it breaks but it just rolls around. It must be one of Charlie's—Pauline puts her fizz empties in the recycling box but he's hidden his brandy bottles since Pauline said it was affecting his performance in bed. Poor Charlie. She must know he's still drinking. I'm sticking it in the bin when Pauline comes out and nearly catches me.

She's talking into her mobile. "Did my husband call in last night? I've mislaid him."

"Dee, the most terrible thing has happened," she shouts when she finishes her call, and I swallow hard.

"What? What's happened to Charlie?"

"No, not him. Two teenagers overdosed on drugs at the festival last night."

"Yes, I know," I call back, and open my car door. *People who take drugs deserve everything they get. No one's forcing them to take them.*

But she puts her hands over her face. "No one's seen him," she says, and her shoulders start shuddering. But when she takes her hands away, her eyes are dry.

"I want you to drive me into town," she announces. "He must have stayed over with someone." And she goes to get dressed.

THE POLICE ARE BY the Old Vicarage gates when we arrive and there's yellow-and-black tape flapping about farther up the drive.

Pauline tells me to stop and gets out and does her walk across to them, all teeth and tits.

"I'm looking for my husband," she says in her silly, breathy Joanna Lumley voice. "He didn't come home and we have an important appointment. I thought someone might have seen him last night."

"Umm, well, there were about eight hundred people milling around for the festival," a woman police officer says. "And we're a bit busy with an ongoing incident." She sounds tough but she's got a hair slide with little hearts in her hair. *She must have kids.*

"I thought the police were supposed to look for missing people," Pauline snaps.

"We are," the officer says. "Sorry. Let's start again. I'm DS Brennan. Why don't you tell me why you are worried about your husband? How old is he? Is he in poor health?"

"Charlie's seventy-three—some years older than me," Pauline simpers, but it's clearly wasted on the officer. "And he's fit and well."

I want to say he takes blood pressure tablets—the silver blister packs sit on the bathroom shelf beside a dusty box of Viagra—but it will mean being part of this. So I stay silent.

"I see. And has he ever gone off before—"

"Well, there has been the occasional evening when he's stayed out. When he's bumped into old chums," Pauline says.

"I see. And the appointment—is it medical?"

"No, he's supposed to be taking me shopping in Brighton today."

The police officer stops making notes and sighs. "Okay. Well, I'd try the chums if I were you and we'll keep an eye out for him. Perhaps you could let us know when he gets in touch."

But she's not looking at Pauline anymore. A tight knot of people is walking fast toward us. At the center is a raw-faced man who looks like he hasn't slept for days.

"Where is he? Where is the bastard?" he bawls, pushing past me in his search.

DS Brennan reaches into the group and takes his arm, steering him to her side.

"Leave me be," the man shouts. "My daughter Tracy's lying unconscious in hospital. . . . The doctors say she might never wake up." And his voice breaks. "She's only eighteen!" he croaks. "Someone did this to her. Gave her this filthy stuff."

"Yeah," one of the others adds. "We knew this would happen, didn't we? Nobody wanted this bloody festival in Ebbing. Except

Pete Diamond, of course. He's the one making money on the bodies of our kids."

"Come on," DS Brennan says gently to the father, "you must be beside yourself with worry. But this won't help. Why don't we go and find somewhere quiet to talk?"

His face crumples and she's about to lead him away when Pete Diamond appears at the gate wearing an *Ibiza Rocks* T-shirt.

"What's going on?" he says. "I need to get my car out. You'll have to move."

And the dad breaks away from DS Brennan and screams in his face. "My little girl's dying. You've got her blood on your hands!"

"Of course I haven't," Pete shouts back. "Your little girl was popping pills. I'm not responsible for that. . . ."

Tracy's dad gets hold of him, banging his head against the railings and yelling abuse. I realize I've got my hands over my eyes. Like when I was a kid. Looking through my fingers when something scary was happening. I can still smell the sharp smell of my grubby hands as I crouched down, away from it. Looking but not looking. Hoping not to see.

Pauline starts shrieking for them to stop and DS Brennan fights her way between them. Her head gets jerked backward and the little hair slide goes flying. I pick it up for her but she's busy shoving Pete inside the gate and putting her arm round the dad. He's sobbing, and he goes down on his knees on the pavement. His mates huddle round him. But the anger is coming off them in waves.

"This isn't over," one of the men mutters as they lead him away.

SEVEN

Elise

DS CARO BRENNAN TAPPED on the window as Elise tried to take off her backpack without using the muscles in her upper body. She jolted at the sound and let out a groan.

Ronnie stood to help her. She'd appeared through the door as soon as Elise had got back from a jog on the beach—"Just doing my ward rounds," she'd said, and stayed.

"Give me that," Ronnie said. "What were you thinking of? Going for a run after all that drama last night?"

"I walked most of the way. I'm fine. Come in, Caro," Elise shouted. "Are you up at the festival site?"

"Yeah, I'm helping out. So I heard you were first to the victims." Ronnie started singing, "'I need a hero . . .'"

"Thank you, Ronnie. Yes, they were unconscious when I reached them."

"Never mind that—I've had the ambulance report, thanks. What were you doing at a pop festival?"

"Ask her! Caro, this is Ronnie, who lives next door. It was her idea. I'd rather have set fire to my feet."

"That's what you're saying now. . . . What did you wear?"

"Shut up."

"What did she wear, Ronnie?"

"Leopard-skin bodysuit like the rest of us . . ."

Elise sighed and let them enjoy the moment.

She should never have gone to that bloody festival. *Obviously.* But apparently Elise had agreed. Her neighbor Ronnie might have been forty years too old for dancing in a laser storm but she'd insisted.

"YOU NEED TO GET out, Elise," she'd said. "How old are you?"

"Er, forty-three, and what's that got to do with anything?"

"The longer you stay in, the harder it'll be to get out there again. Look, it's at the Old Vicarage in Ebbing, not a field off the M25. There'll be toilets and it'll be a laugh. I'm married to a man who whittles. Let me have some fun. . . ."

And she'd found herself queuing to have her bag searched by a bored teenager who'd confiscated a bottle of booze from the young couple in front of them. He hadn't bothered to look in hers or Ronnie's.

"Thank you, ladies." He waved them through.

"Just because we're older doesn't mean we're not smuggling in heroin or knives," Elise snapped at him.

The lad's eyes practically popped out of his head. "Er, right. Are you?"

"What do you think?" Ronnie said. "She's joking. . . ."

"This security stinks," Elise muttered. "Drugs must be flooding in."

"Hush, Detective Inspector King," Ronnie muttered back. "You're not back at work yet."

Elise took a breath and Ronnie produced drink vouchers she'd bought at the gate.

"I'll have a Cheeky Vimto," Ronnie told the barman, and Elise gave her a look.

"We don't do cocktails." The barman smirked.

He looked like one of the boys who cycled up and down the seafront, skidding up to girls, swearing self-consciously, and honking with laughter. She didn't know his name but Elise was certain he wasn't old enough to serve alcohol.

"Give us a cider each, then." Ronnie pouted.

The first glass overflowed and liquid washed over the counter onto Elise's sandals, sticking her toes together.

"I should have worn wellies," she shouted in Ronnie's ear.

Ronnie nodded but she couldn't have heard her friend. No one could hear anything. The sound system started to howl and squeal like a herd of feral cats until finally someone threw a switch and the music emerged with a heart-stopping blast.

The boom! boom! boom! made Elise's chest vibrate and she put her hand up to protect the nubble of scar tissue under her T-shirt.

Strobe lighting flashed and the crowd pulsed in slo-mo. People too old to throw their hands in the air like they just didn't care did so, the flickering lights hiding a multitude of dancing sins. Elise automatically scanned for faces—a professional tic as hardwired as breathing.

"You go and dance," she screamed into Ronnie's ear. "I'll hold your handbag and make sure no one spikes your drink. . . ."

Ronnie grinned her thanks and pushed into the crowd to lose herself in the music.

On the podium, Pete Diamond, the man who had triumphed over the locals to hold his festival, was conducting the crowd. His tee had ridden up to expose a hairy belly button embedded in an impressive roll of fat. Elise laughed out loud for the first time in ages.

Ronnie's right. I do need to get out more. She took a mouthful of warm cider and watched the surreal spectacle of a chubby marketing exec playing acid house and referencing Pete Tong and Fatboy Slim as if he were part of a triumvirate of rave gods.

Ronnie was at the front, jerking up and down like a character in a flicker book. She seemed to be dancing with a man in a baseball cap who was ricocheting off people—a ball bearing in a human pinball machine.

It was only when the pinball dancer took off his hat to wipe his face that she realized it was dear old Charlie Perry.

What the hell is he doing here?

Charlie's face looked ghoulish and distorted in the green spotlights raking the crowd, his eyes bulging and his mouth wide open. *When did he learn the words to "Praise You"?*

But the next time the spotlight froze on him, she knew he hadn't. Charlie was shouting, not singing. Was it anger? Or fear? And then he disappeared.

She scanned those around him, trying to make sense of the scene, but everyone was dancing. Or seemed to be. But as she looked, a space opened up in the middle of the crowd; a wave of people was breaking away from it, and they were screaming silently against the wall of sound.

Something bad is happening.

And she was running toward it, pushing through the crowd.

The strobe carried on and she fought against stop-start figures. Suddenly the music and lights stopped dead and the silence made her ears ring. And she was there. On the scene. *Two bodies down.* She felt for her phone to call it in, shouting for people to move back. To give them air.

They were so young—late teens. A boy and girl convulsing on

the damp grass, and she struggled to get them on their sides into the recovery position. She felt their pulses racing and their limbs were flickering as if the strobes were still playing on them.

The crowd had shuffled back but remained watching, the kids with face paint sliding down their cheeks, green neon wands hanging limply in their hands. And then Pete Diamond burst through the human cordon to join her.

"Christ!" he breathed before turning to his audience. "All right, everyone, let's not panic. They've probably had too much to drink. Give us a few minutes to get it sorted out. They're serving hot dogs and burgers in hospitality area."

"This isn't alcohol," Elise hissed at him as people started drifting off, laughing, relief making them giddy. "They've taken something. What's circulating? Your security lads must have found some drugs at the gate or heard something?"

"What? No! Oh, God, I'm going to be crucified for this, aren't I? The festival will be shut down. Christ! I'll have to give people their money back if tomorrow night doesn't go ahead."

"Let's worry about these two first, shall we?" Elise was on her knees, checking their breathing.

Pete Diamond looked at her properly for the first time. "Sorry. Who are you?"

"DI Elise King."

And his face had sagged. "Christ . . ."

"Look, I'm off duty. We need to know what they took."

"Dad." A teen in tiny shorts snaked past Elise and lodged under Pete's arm. "Will they be okay?"

"'Course, sweetheart. Help is on its way."

The sound of an ambulance filtered through, faint at first but growing louder by the second. It was as if they'd turned the music back on.

As Elise moved back to let the medical team work, she felt something under her sandal and reached down. A black leather wallet flattened by hundreds of dancing feet. When she peeled it open, there were a couple of till receipts, a folded photo of a smiling girl, and a loyalty card for Ebbing Wines. C. Perry's loyalty card. No money.

God, Charlie, you had a really crap night, Elise thought.

EIGHT

Elise

CARO'S CACKLING ABOUT HER festival outfit died down only when Elise's neighbor realized she was late for a tae kwon do taster class at the hall and scurried off.

"I'd better get off too," Caro said. "She's a real laugh, isn't she?"

"Hilarious." Elise sighed. "Look, give me a minute to change my T-shirt. I thought I'd stroll up there with you."

"Okay," Caro said carefully. "But it's all a bit ugly—the father of one of the victims has tried to punch the organizer—so you're not to do anything apart from observe."

"All right, Sergeant," she snapped, and Caro's eyes widened. "Sorry. Bit on edge this morning . . ."

If Caro had taken offense, Elise knew it wouldn't last—she knew her DS too well.

They were very different animals: Caro was brilliant at thinking on her feet but incapable of being anywhere on time, while Elise was borderline OCD. They'd never have been friends in normal life and hadn't clicked at work until a couple of old coppers had tried to date-stamp Caro's arse. It was considered a rite of passage for young female officers in some stations—the sort of Neanderthal enclaves where female constables used to be seen as dykes or bikes. But Elise had walked in on it. They'd been trying to get Caro's trousers undone and Elise had launched herself at them. She'd been on the tallest one's back with her arm round his neck and he was bellowing for her to get off. Caro had kneed the other one in the balls and date-stamped his face before the men had fought their way to the door. When it was all over, the two young women had sat there, sweating and shocked. It'd been Caro who'd said: "This stays here." And Elise had agreed. Neither of them would make the same decision today—it was assault, plain and simple—but then, nearly twenty years ago, no one would have wanted to hear it.

Anyway, as Caro said, it was the start of a beautiful friendship— and nobody had messed with either of them again. The squad called them King and Kong for a bit and Caro ignored it. "I've got thighs like barges and mad hair—it could be a lot worse. We need to pick our fights."

"HOW ARE THE VICTIMS?" Elise asked, returning the nods from a clutch of familiar faces outside the supermarket.

The women turned to watch as she and Brennan passed and she heard one hiss: "They should be locking up Pete Diamond for this."

Caro rolled her eyes. "Still unconscious," she said. "The ecstasy was a bad batch—double strength—and Tracy Cook's been put in an induced coma while they control her seizures. Her family is waiting for news."

"God, I wonder if it's the first time she'd taken it."

"The dad seems to think so—but no parent believes their kids take drugs, do they? He's in bits—he and his mates had a real go at Pete Diamond just now."

"What about the boy?"

"The doctors say he'll be all right."

"Any idea where they got them from?"

"We're talking to the Southfold team about active dealers in the area but there's nothing from the scene. Proper security would have had some intel for us but this was amateur night."

"I know. They were using schoolkids on the gate and their whole focus seemed to be confiscating alcohol so that Pete Diamond could overcharge for beer and wine."

"Yeah. The male victim's father must have been furious about that—he runs your local, the Neptune."

"It was Dave Harman's son?" Elise said. "Christ, I didn't recognize him. That's going to cause all sorts of trouble. Dave had put himself in charge of stopping the festival. He said it would bring drugs into the town."

"Well, turns out he was right. I'm talking to him later." Caro got out her notebook to jot it down. "Oh, shit, I've got to ring round the hospitals to see if Charlie Perry has been admitted."

Elise's scalp prickled. "Charlie? Why?"

"He's gone missing, according to his wife. It's not the first time, and, to be honest, I think she's more worried about her trip to the shops. I've had her up at the festival site, playing it to the hilt. It's been a busy morning. . . ."

"Really? Poor old Charlie."

"So you know him, then?"

"Sort of. He came collecting for a charity last week and we got talking about his disabled daughter. He got really emotional. Lovely old boy."

"Well, that's nice. Did you see him during your night out?"

"Actually, yes." And Elise hesitated. Should she tell her sergeant she'd thought Charlie had looked frightened? Was she sure he had been? She'd seen his face only for a second. *Just stick to the facts, Elise. Caro has got enough going on with the drugs and the local lynch mob.*

"I only got a glimpse of him in the crowd. He'd had a lot to drink, according to one of the barmen," she said. "But I found his wallet minus any money near the stage when the place emptied. I was going to drop it off at his caravan this morning. Look, he's probably sleeping it off somewhere—he knows everyone in Ebbing. And he'll turn up and get seven kinds of hell from his wife. I wouldn't want to be in his shoes when he does."

Caro laughed. They walked on and Elise put away the image of Charlie's gaping mouth shouting into the crowd.

SHE LASTED ONLY A few minutes at the scene—it was just too hard watching the team working. She felt like a spare part. And she knew she was in the way, making her DS feel she was second-guessing everything Caro was doing. She hadn't been. She was too busy second-guessing herself.

Procedure should have been burning a hole in her brain. But she had been ditsy since the treatment—chemo brain, they called it on the support group forums. She'd always prided herself on being able to master a brief in one reading but now she felt like she was groping around in a fog. She forgot words, her own ideas, what someone had told her five minutes ago, what day it was. It was the cruelest torture for a woman like her. It meant keeping a lot of lists.

How am I ever going to be me again? Some days she missed work so much—even the crap. The paperwork. The shirkers. The endless personal problems of her colleagues.

But other days, when she thought about her actual return, she felt like she was having one of those exam anxiety dreams. Where you turned the paper over and couldn't understand any of the questions. She tortured herself with the thought of standing in front of a whiteboard, the team looking at her, knowing she was no longer up to the job.

And that moment was barreling toward her. Her appointment with the consultant was in four days. She'd had the blood tests and a scan in preparation. She knew she should be worrying about the results but it was the idea that he could declare her fit that was making her stomach churn. A start date had already been penciled in by Human Resources. September eighteenth. Just three weeks away.

NINE

Elise

B Y THE TIME SHE reached the cottage, the sun was scalding the pavements. She stood in a cold shower for five minutes, sluicing off the heat and disappointment, and put her pajamas back on to do her exercises.

She started, bringing her arms up over her head and down like in the YouTube video, but she felt as though she was signaling for help. *Oh, God—not waving but drowning . . .*

Caro and the team would be plowing through witness statements and the hundreds of selfies and videos on festival-goers' phones, trying to find drugs transactions. She, on the other hand, had nothing to do but squeeze a virtual orange between her shoulder blades. She caught her movement in the mirror and she saw her face, slack and vacant. It scared her, how blank it was.

She looked out of the window at the sea to be soothed. But the tide was on its way in and the waves were thumping against the stony beach like a giant fist knocking at her back door.

———————

CARO HAD PULLED A face when Elise had told her she was buying in Ebbing. "The seaside? All those chip papers and seagulls. And the traffic . . . It's an hour's commute to headquarters and you won't be able to get in or out in the summer."

"I'm not always sitting in HQ anyway—the joy of the Major Crime Team is that I can be working on a case anywhere in Sussex. And Ebbing is central. Back off!"

She'd ignored DS Doom and bought 5 Mariner's Cottages in June 2018. The estate agent had bigged up the view. "It's breathtaking," she'd said, ignoring the fact that it was a wonky two-up two-down with a small kitchen extension, a patch of garden overlooking the sea, and a front door onto the pavement.

"Cute," Caro had said on her first visit. "If you like that kind of thing. But promise me you won't put anchors and lighthouses everywhere. And where are the cupboards? Where will you store your Christmas decorations?"

"Sod off, Brennan. I don't do Christmas, as you well know." She and Hugh had liked to go somewhere hot and all-inclusive. Before.

Caro had been round a few times since Elise had gone on sick leave. But she'd told her to stop—"You've got a kid—you can't spend your precious days off with me. I'll ring you. And I'll be back at work before you know it."

She wasn't short of company, anyway. A bit overblessed, if she was honest, what with Ronnie popping in and out.

The first time Ronnie had appeared at the door, on the day Elise had moved in, she had been knee-deep in packing cases and bad memories but Ronnie hadn't let that stop her. She was small, sixtyish, with a beaky nose and a lot of mascara, and she was wearing a T-shirt that read *Old Age Is for Sissies*. Ronnie had brought a welcome cake—a shop one ("I don't bake")—and stayed for an hour, probing like a pro. Elise had managed to keep Hugh to a footnote, where he belonged.

She pushed back against her neighbor's interrogation on that first visit and took the lead in the questioning, quickly learning that Ronnie had a daughter in Australia who didn't phone often enough, and used to work in the local library three days a week, manning the desk and taking a keen interest in other people's business.

"People have time to talk in a library," Ronnie said as she rifled uninvited through Elise's books. "It starts with 'Have you got the latest Lee Child?' and ends with them telling me about their fibroids. It was where I heard it all. . . . I love other people's stories, don't you?"

And Elise nodded. She did.

Ronnie had been beyond thrilled to discover Elise's job on the Major Crime Team. "That's the murder squad, isn't it? I'm working my way through every detective novel on the shelves," she said as if that made her a sister-in-arms. "It's fascinating, isn't it? Killing people . . ."

There was a pause before Ronnie added: "I might take it up myself."

It turned out her recently retired husband, Ted, was about to be murdered.

"He's turned into an old man. . . . He's building a model railway for God's sake!" Ronnie ranted. "And now he wants to join a bowls club. He's bought a white trilby. . . . I said to him, 'You're sixty-five, not eighty-five.' I'll put weed killer in his porridge if this carries on. I suppose I shouldn't be saying that to a detective inspector. . . . Oh, I'm so glad you've moved in. Shall I pop in tomorrow? I can give you a hand putting things away."

"That's very kind but I'm fine, Ronnie," Elise said. She didn't want to be anyone's project. *I should have had it made into a sign for the front door,* she thought. *"Elise Is Fine."*

"Well, you know where I am. Just shout—it's only single brick in the extension and I can hear you through it."

While she'd still been working, Elise had chatted to Ronnie as they'd wheeled the bins round, but they'd been neighbors, not friends, until February and the cancer diagnosis. Ronnie had somehow become part of Elise's recovery. "In charge of morale," she'd said.

ELISE HAD LET HER mind wander—*fatal*—and was back at Friday night. But not thinking about the kids she'd run to help. It was Charlie Perry. His pale, sweaty face. She'd dealt with hundreds of drunks in distress and forgotten them immediately—why couldn't she let Charlie go? Was it because he'd made her tear up that day in her sitting room? They'd shared a moment.

She suddenly wondered if he'd said anything to Ronnie while they flailed about.

Elise knocked three times on the kitchen wall and Ronnie knocked back. The signal had been her friend's idea—something to do with a hit song when she'd been young.

Five minutes later she was sitting on the other kitchen chair.

"Nice jimjams," Ronnie said. "But you were dressed when I last saw you. . . ."

"I'm doing my stretches. Look, Charlie Perry—"

"Missing. I know," Ronnie said.

Elise tried not to look disappointed. She'd been expecting to be breaking the news, but of course Ronnie already knew. She was always swapping intel with her network—from the moment she woke up most days.

"I thought he looked upset last night," Elise went on. "Did you notice that? And I found his wallet as I left, so he may have been robbed. Did he say anything to you?"

"No! Poor Charlie. He did look terrible—one of the walking dead—but doesn't everyone under those lights? However, I do know that he has money troubles," she said. "Postie Val, who delivers up there, says there've been letters from a debt agency and the bank, and I hear Pauline's been doing her dying-swan act in town. I shouldn't be unkind but she does love a spotlight. She's telling people the police aren't interested in finding him."

Pauline was probably right—Caro had been pretty dismissive when she'd told her—but Elise was immediately defensive. This was her tribe that was being bad-mouthed. "He's only been gone overnight—and they've got their hands full finding out who gave Tracy Cook and Dave Harman's kid the dodgy ecstasy and keeping the townspeople from marching on the Old Vicarage with pitchforks."

They sat in silence for a moment.

"Why don't we go and have a chat with Pauline?" Ronnie perked up. "Maybe we could help her find him?"

"But I'm on sick leave."

"We're concerned neighbors. . . ."

Elise rolled her eyes—she suspected it wasn't the first time Ronnie had adopted this role. But she felt a little flutter in her stomach.

"Come on," Ronnie urged, "what else were you going to do today?"

TEN

Elise

THEY SCREECHED UP TO the Perry residence in Ronnie's ancient Mini. Elise had left her Mazda convertible—a post-Hugh present to herself—in the car park at HQ. She hadn't been able to drive after the operation and it was more secure than leaving it sitting on the street. But somehow she hadn't had the energy to pick it up. Caro had sent her a couple of pictures of it, crusted with sand and bird shit. "Your brain will be in the same condition if you don't come back to work soon," she'd written as a caption.

Ronnie hadn't stopped talking all the way. "Pauline used to be a model—she'll tell you. She tells everyone. She's Charlie's second wife and she's been married twice before. I'm not sure why I'm still on my first."

She'd left Ted a cheese and pickle sandwich and hidden the telly controller. "So he can't go on the shopping channel—last time he bought a beard-grooming kit! I said 'Ted, you haven't got a beard,' but he said he was going to grow one. Just to annoy me. . . . Anyway, this is great—a couple of hours away from him and his model railway. Oh, God! I'm married to the Fat Controller," she said, and Elise prayed they'd get there quickly.

The door to the caravan opened as they drew up. Minis were not built for women of Elise's height and she tried not to show her knickers as she unfolded herself from the passenger seat.

"Hello, Pauline," Ronnie called, and waved. Elise raised her hand too.

"Come in, Ronnie," Pauline shouted. "You'll have to take me as you find me. . . . I look a mess. Oh, who are you? Sorry. I usually make more of an effort," she added when she spotted Elise. "I used to be a model, you know."

Elise managed to avoid Ronnie's eye.

"Elise is my next-door neighbor," Ronnie said. "She bought last year from that snooty couple with the dalmatian. We wanted to see if there's been any word from Charlie."

"No," Pauline said sharply, and slumped down on a chair.

"When did you decide he was missing?" Elise said gently.

Pauline shrugged. "When he didn't come back."

"Okay. Have you tried his friends?" Elise said.

"That's what the police officer said," Pauline muttered.

"Elise is a police officer too," Ronnie offered. "A murder detective."

"Are you?"

Pauline looked at Elise properly for the first time, and Elise wondered if she'd remembered to brush the wayward tufts growing back since the end of chemo. You got out of practice.

"Well, yes. I'm not on duty but I want to help if I can, Mrs. Perry."

"Oh, call me Pauline. Everyone does. Why?"

"I was concerned about Charlie when I saw him last night. And I found his wallet."

"Oh! It's kind of you to return it," Pauline said, reaching for it.

Elise noted she wasn't interested in why she'd been concerned about him. "Where did he drop it?"

"I found it on the ground last night." Elise handed over the battered-looking wallet.

"In the High Street?" Pauline said, and looked to see if there was any money in it.

"No, at the Old Vicarage. I was at the festival there last night," Elise said. "Anyway, I'm afraid there wasn't any cash, or bank cards, in it. I think someone must have emptied it."

"One of the weirdos who came for the festival must have dumped it after they stole it." Pauline tossed the wallet on the work top. "I said the town would be filled with them."

"Well, it was very crowded. You couldn't move on the dance floor—it's the sort of place where pickpockets operate."

"Are you saying Charlie was at this ghastly event, then? What the hell was he doing there?"

"I think he was dancing," Elise said.

"Dancing? He never dances—he hates it. That and loud music."

There were an unfinished bowl of soup and two dirty mugs sitting on the kitchen table. Ronnie started sweeping the dishes into the sink and turning on the tap. "Where's your washing-up liquid? Oh, here it is," she chatted. "Sit down, Elise. You're making the place look untidy."

"So, friends—or family? I understand Charlie has a daughter."

"No point asking her anything. And no one else has seen him."

"Okay, the thing is, Charlie looked upset last night"—Elise got them back on track—"and he'd been drinking."

"Well, he likes an occasional glass in the evening—just to be sociable," Pauline said.

Ronnie and Elise exchanged a glance. It was a lie she must have told a hundred times—to the outside world and to herself.

"Of course," Elise said. "Was he upset?"

Pauline shrugged again and got up to plug in the kettle. Elise could see the tension in her back.

"Anyway, the police are checking the hospitals—unless you've done it?" Elise said. It would've been the first thing she'd have done.

"No, I haven't." Pauline gnawed at a nail. "Will they let me know?"

"Of course."

Pauline didn't move from the counter as she waited for the water to boil. In the silence, Elise's eyes slid to a letter sitting half out of its envelope on the table. She could only see the first paragraph but that was enough.

Pauline turned and caught her looking. "I hope you haven't been reading my private correspondence," she snapped.

"Sorry," Elise said but held her eye and it was Pauline who looked away.

"I don't really know what it's about," she muttered. "It came this morning. Money is Charlie's department, not mine. I'm a bit of a featherhead when it comes to finances."

"Well, it's from a debt agency and says they're going to take legal action to seize your assets," Elise said, picking up the letter. "The house, I assume."

"I had no idea things were this bad. No idea." Pauline looked up at Elise through her lashes but her little-girl-lost act was wasted on the other woman. Elise had met real little lost girls. Pauline didn't come close.

Elise wanted to say that the postwoman and her neighbors in Ebbing knew things were this bad but there seemed little point.

"Did you and Charlie discuss it?"

"No. As I say, money was his thing. Oh, what's to become of me now?" And she picked up an emery board to saw at her nails, a fine mist powdering the tabletop.

"I think you probably need to talk to a lawyer. . . . Can I ask if Charlie is on any medication?"

"Umm, well, he sometimes takes pills for his blood pressure."

"Perhaps you could look to see if he's taken them with him?" Elise wanted to check if the disappearance had been planned—she suspected the debt might have a great deal to do with it.

But Pauline didn't move off her chair. And as a "concerned neighbor," Elise felt she couldn't push the point.

"Perhaps you could look later, then."

Ronnie joined them as she dried her hands and cut to the chase. "Why do you think he went off, Pauline? Was it the financial problems? Had you had a row? Have you been having other trouble?"

Ronnie might have been small but hers was clearly the kick-the-door-down kind of approach and Elise tried to warn her off with a look but Pauline laughed, a loud, harsh bark, and swept her cup around her world.

"You mean apart from living in this? He promised me we'd be in the big house last year but nothing's been done for months and months. And he's spent the money for my pool cabana. Bloody Charlie! Sorry, but marriage is never a picnic, is it?"

"Tell me about it." Ronnie smiled. "What is it with men? I think mine's starting to smell of wee. What's that about?"

"It'll be his prostate, dear. Charlie's got the same trouble. It's meant an end to sex."

"Well, that could be a blessing," Ronnie said.

"Not where I'm concerned. I'm a woman with needs."

"Had you argued about it?" Elise said quietly.

Pauline flicked her eyes away. "My needs or the house?"

"Either . . ."

"No," Pauline muttered, and made to stand. Show over.

"When did you buy the place?" Elise walked over to a window

to look up at the building. There was a story here and she felt more alive than she had for weeks—she was nowhere near ready to be shown the door. "I heard it used to be a hotel. It's very impressive."

She'd seen it before of course, rising above the trees like the opening shots of a costume drama. But now she could see part of it had been closed off with security fencing and there was metal shuttering on some of the lower windows. The lettering on the many trade signboards was fading but it looked like there was work for the local builders for years to come.

"Five years ago." Pauline came to stand beside Elise. She was animated, almost girlish, for the first time. "No, it must be six. Anyway, it was love at first sight. Look at it!"

Elise tried but she couldn't see beyond the decay. The house looked as if it could have been harboring an ax murderer.

"Do you want to see inside?" Pauline said, grabbing a key from its hook by the door, her missing husband apparently forgotten.

The damp was like two-day-old bruises on the walls, and when Elise touched one of the mottled green patches, plaster crumbled onto the floor.

"I remember the first time I saw it—it blew my mind," Pauline was trilling. "It'd been empty for a while but it just needed some TLC."

"It might have been kinder to put the whole place out of its misery," Ronnie murmured, but if Pauline heard, she ignored it.

Living in denial might have been the only way for her to cope, Elise supposed. The alternative was too devastating. They must have plowed all their money into it.

"It definitely needs some work," Pauline said when the silence grew. "But that was reflected in the price. It's got a resident ghost and a grand salon." She threw open double doors like a telly-makeover-show reveal and Elise tripped over a plastic bucket catching drips from the ceiling. "The pipework still needs finishing. The plumber let us down," Pauline muttered, guiding them past another three containers of varying size.

"Ted's got some old buckets in his shed you can have," Ronnie said, but Pauline was on a roll.

"Look, you can see the Isle of Wight! I love it."

"And does Charlie feel the same way?" Elise asked.

"Oh, Charlie!" she muttered. "He kept on about the roof and how long it'd been on the market. He wanted to buy a smaller place but I won him over." And she twirled a lock of dyed hair.

"How old is he?"

"What? Oh, seventy-four next month. Ninth of the ninth . . ."

"What did he do before you retired down here?"

"Goodness, this is beginning to feel like a cross-examination." Pauline laughed uncertainly. "He made his money with regeneration projects in west London, as far as I know. We had a lovely home when we got married. And we had such plans—we were going to put a cinema and sauna in the basement but first the neighbors objected—and then there was the business about the money."

"What business?" Elise said.

"I think that's enough personal questions, don't you?" Pauline snapped. "That's all ancient history. It was a silly misunderstanding that was put right."

Elise could hear the red flags unfurling and snapping in the sea breeze.

ELEVEN

Dee

LIAM CAN'T SIT STILL this lunchtime. He keeps going out to his van for something and coming back empty-handed. He's obviously secretly checking his phone.

"For goodness' sake, stop it!" I shout when he gets up again. "You're driving me mad. I thought you had work to do?"

"It's Saturday!"

"Well, some of us are still working. Who are you texting?"

"What do you mean? No one." He holds up his hands to show they're empty.

"Every time you go outside, I mean. Who is it?"

"No one."

And he goes quiet again. He can sulk for days when he feels like it and I try to move us on.

"Have you heard Charlie Perry has gone missing?" I say, and Liam looks out the window.

"Has he? When?" he mutters.

"Last night. Pauline says she didn't hear him come home."

"She must have done, the state he was in."

"He looked awful last night, didn't he?"

"Yeah. I expect she's pleased he's gone off. She's always saying he's a waste of space, isn't she?"

"I know. But she's not happy. She was furious when I was up there this morning. She's told the police he's missing."

"Seriously?" Liam snaps. "Bit of an overreaction, isn't it?"

"I suppose. But maybe she really is worried? I don't know. Did you talk to him last night? You said you were going to the other day."

"Did I?"

He knows he did. The rent is due at the end of the month and he's changed the password on his business account.

"About his unpaid bill, Liam. It's been months since you finished the work."

Liam shook his head. "No. He was too pissed. You saw what he was like."

"Right. So what are we going to do? Will we be okay?"

"What? 'Course we will. I've got some work coming up, so stop nagging," he says. "You are doing my head in."

"I was just asking."

"Well, don't."

"But we need to talk about money, love. About what we're going to do long term, if your work doesn't pick up. My cleaning money won't be nearly enough to keep us afloat."

"Leave it alone, Dee. It'll be okay. Dave wants me to do a big job at the pub—he's putting in an outside bar and renewing all the plumbing upstairs. Look, I'll talk to him today."

"You can't—he'll be at the hospital. Haven't you heard anything from him about how Ade and Tracy are?"

"No." He's still not looking at me.

"Tracy's dad and his friends will string up whoever gave them the drugs. They attacked Pete Diamond in front of the police this morning."

"Bloody hell!" he says too loudly. "Look, I'm taking the dog out."

I'm glad when he's gone. He hadn't looked me in the eye once while we were talking and it'd begun to unnerve me.

I watch him walking up the path. He nearly drops Misty's lead as he answers the phone. "Hello, Dave," I hear him say.

AT THE NEPTUNE THE door is locked and there's a sign—*Closed due to family emergency*—but the lights are on. I knock just in case. I want only to know how Ade is, I tell myself.

Dave opens up and lets me in. He stands, arms hanging at his sides.

"How is he?" I say.

"The same," he croaks.

"How can the bastards who were selling those drugs live with themselves?"

He doesn't reply. Just stands there.

"Have you come home to pick up stuff for Ade?"

"No," he says. "I couldn't face seeing him like that. There was nothing I could do there except get on Doll's nerves. I came back to get things sorted here. We could be up at the hospital for days."

"Have you had anything to eat? Shall I make you something?" I say, and stroke his arm as I squeeze past him. "You need to keep your strength up, Dave."

In the kitchen he watches while I slice cheese onto bread. I expect he'll throw the sandwich away as soon as I leave.

The pub phone rings and makes us both jump. He doesn't move, so I go and answer it for him.

"Hello, Doll," I say, and her voice gets higher as she tells me the good news.

"Do you want to talk to him?" I say. "No, okay. You go back to Ade and I'll get him on his way.

"Dave!" I shout when I put the phone down, even though he's standing next to me. "He's waking up!"

And he bursts into tears, big meaty hands over his eyes. "Sorry," he sobs.

"Don't be." I push a tissue between his fingers. "You let it out. Do you want me or Liam to take you to the hospital?"

Dave shakes his head hard. "No. Sorry—look, I'm all right to drive. Will you lock up?"

"'Course. You will let me know how he is, won't you?"

HE RINGS ME AN hour later, talking too fast. "Ade's conscious and they're starting to bring Tracy round, thank God. It's early days but the doctors are hopeful there'll be no lasting damage."

"Oh, Dave, you must be so relieved. Is Ade talking?"

"About what?" Dave snaps.

"I just meant is he well enough to talk? That's all."

"Sorry, Dee. I'm all over the place. Yes, his first words were 'Sorry, Mum.' Doll was in floods. But we've been told not to tire him with questions. I just wanted to check if everything was okay when you left the pub?"

"Yes, fine. A woman police officer came as I was locking up. She said she'd catch up with you at the hospital. Have you seen her?"

"Er, no. What time was that? Look, I need to get back to the family."

But I can't let him go. I keep thinking about Liam. How he couldn't look at me.

"Okay. But, Dave . . . can I ask you something? I know you've got a lot on your plate but I'm really worried about Liam—he's been very stressed lately. Has he talked to you about anything?"

"No, no. Nothing. I've hardly seen him."

"Oh. I thought you'd discussed some work at the pub?"

"Well, yeah, but nothing's been settled. Got to go, Dee."

"But how did he sound to you today?"

There was silence at the other end of the phone.

"Dave?"

"Liam? No idea. I haven't spoken to him for days."

TWELVE

Elise

POOR CHARLIE—NO WONDER HE went off," Ronnie said when they got back to the car. "I would too if I had the lovely Pauline and her needs to come home to."

"And that house is costing a fortune he doesn't appear to have," Elise said, buckling up her seat belt. "He owes just shy of a hundred grand in unpaid loans, according to that letter—I wonder where he's hoping to get the money to pay it off. I'd say there are plenty of reasons to disappear."

If there'd been room in her ancient car, a lightbulb would have come on above Ronnie's head. She turned to grin at Elise, her knuckles turning white on the steering wheel. "Maybe Pauline's hoping he turns up dead? She'd collect the life insurance and keep her house."

"Whoa! Let's not go overboard!" Elise said. "Eyes on the road, foot off the gas. Let's put lurid theories to one side and I'll have a quiet look at his background."

"Roger," her second-in-command chirped.

Oh, God, what have I started . . . ?

"And we need to keep what we're doing to ourselves for the time being. Okay?" Elise added.

Ronnie fiddled with the radio.

"Ronnie . . . are we clear? Or I'll have to leave you at home."

"But it was my idea. And I'm the wheels!"

"Look, I'm on sick leave and my DCI might have something to say about me nosing around."

"We could just pretend it's me doing it?" And she actually tapped her nose with her finger.

"Right." Elise tried not to smile. "Or we could just do it discreetly. Let's go home and you can check on Ted and his facial hair while I crack on."

Elise switched on an electric fan when she walked into the cottage and settled herself in front of it with a notebook and her laptop. She felt the crampy twinge of anticipation in her stomach she always got from a new investigation and took a bite of an apple before pressing "go" on the Police National Computer. But Charles Perry (DOB 09/09/1945) was not known to the authorities. She leaned back from the screen and removed a shred of peel from between her teeth. She'd been so sure there'd be something linked to the "silly misunderstanding."

Elise went back to the very beginning, looking for his birth online. But either he was an immaculate conception or she was using duff information. He wasn't there and alarm bells were ringing all over the shop. Mr. Perry didn't appear to exist. She started again, checking and rechecking each step. *Nothing. What about his marriages? Ronnie said he'd had two wives.*

But she could find none for Charles Perry. *So who is Pauline married to?*

Elise decided to chase Pauline down, getting her full name and date of birth from a speeding conviction and digging out her birth certificate. She'd been born Pauline Mary Blackwell in 1944. *That makes you seventy-five.* Elise grinned. *Charlie's your toy boy.*

Pauline had married a Perry—but it was a Henry Perry, who'd died just three years later. *This is all getting a bit surreal. Did she marry two men called Perry? Brothers?*

Elise fiddled with the search filters and finally found Pauline's marriage to Charlie. Pauline had tied the knot with a Charles Herbert Williams in 2009 at Islington Town Hall. He'd taken her name.

Elise got another apple and looked for Charlie's original birth certificate. And there he was: born September 9, 1945, in Watford. Just a week after the end of the Second World War. There was no father's name listed—just his mother, Maureen. *A single mother when getting yourself in trouble still meant being shamed. Was her lover killed in France before he could marry her? Was she raped?* Elise found herself looking for Maureen's birth before she came to, teetering on the brink of a cavernous rabbit hole. *Focus!* she told herself.

She stuck Mr. Williams into the PNC with a flourish—"Thought you could hide from me, did you?"—but the computer still said no. Elise groaned and banged her hand on the table, nearly upending a forgotten glass of water. Back to the records.

His first marriage had been to the glamorously named Lila Nightingale—and Elise put her nose to the trail, listing the property companies Charlie set up and the grander addresses on London's electoral registers until the couple moved into a house in an exclusive street in Kensington. *Very swish.*

It was there that Charlie and Lila parted company. She vanished from the register during the eighties, leaving Charles Williams on his own at the house. In 2000, he moved to east London and stayed there for a few years until he married Pauline and they settled in Hampstead.

Elise tapped her fingers on the table as she put it all together. *So when did you become Charlie Perry? And why?*

It had always fascinated Elise how people slipped their skins. She'd met only a handful over the years—her favorite was a milkman with three wives/girlfriends who kept a card index of who he was on what day while he claimed three lots of housing benefit. "Hardly worth it, to be honest," he'd said when his system failed spectacularly under the pressure of a triple-birthday celebration. Elise suspected he'd lived for the almost-being-found-out moments.

She pictured Charlie drilling himself each evening: name of first pet, mother's maiden name, place of birth, favorite film. . . .

But there must be moments when he stumbles back into his real self, she mused. *When he catches sight of himself in a mirror unexpectedly. God, that must mess with your head.*

It was certainly messing with hers. And making her mouth water.

Taking on a new identity meant there was something or someone to hide from. *Which is it, Charlie?*

BEFORE

THIRTEEN

Ten days earlier

Dee

L IAM IS ACTING UP about my overtime again. I'd had the last of the sugary dust at the bottom of the cereal box and was gathering my stuff when he finally stumbled downstairs in his boxers.

"What time is it? I could murder a bacon sandwich."

"It's eight. And do you know how much bacon costs? I've let Misty out and I'm off to work." I kiss the stubble on his cheek.

"You're never home," he says. "I had to cook tea for Cal again last night."

"Oh, poor you. And what did you give him? Frozen pizza again? Try putting a bit of broccoli on his plate next time."

Cal mimes throwing up and Liam slumps down in a chair beside him. He's not laughing this morning. It's not his fault there's no work at the moment. The developers are bringing in their own men. "Cheap labor from London," Liam says, "and I bet there's not a real tradesman among them. How can I compete?"

"Look, love, we need the money. Simple as. There was a bit of waitressing going at the Lobster Shack and Toby asked if I'd do it. I'm not turning anything down until things pick up for you. And they will. Oh, I meant to tell you—Pete Diamond's given me free tickets for the Friday night of his festival—and Jenny says she'll babysit."

He grunts and starts scrolling through his messages.

"Liam . . ." I say under my breath. Cal looks up immediately.

"Yeah, Dad—no screens at mealtimes. It's the law."

Liam slams his phone down and pinches a piece of Cal's toast.

"Who made you the sheriff of this house, anyway?" He pulls one of Cal's ears. "Where's your badge?"

"Get off! What're we doing today, Dad? I'm bored."

"Bored? It's only eight o'clock. Go and get dressed. We're going over to Brighton."

"Yay! Can we go on the arcades?"

"No—I'm not made of money. I've got to see someone."

Cal sighs heavily and puts his head on his arms.

"Who?" I say, trying to keep my voice even.

"Oh, no one you know. It's a favor for Dave. He's paying for my petrol."

I give him a look. He knows I hate him going back to Brighton. Back to old times. Old ways. But he pretends not to notice.

Cal is messing about, trying to get his toast back, so I have to leave it at a look. I'll talk to Liam later.

AT THE NEPTUNE, DAVE is quiet this morning. He sits on one of the barstools while I wash up. I'm about to ask about Liam and this favor when his son comes through from the back.

"Dad . . ."

"What?"

"Any chance of a lift to Portsmouth?" Ade says. "I thought I'd go and see Tracy."

Dave gives him a death stare.

"You're supposed to be sorting out the crates in the cellar. We agreed you'd do it and I'd pay you."

"Oh, yeah . . . I forgot."

"So no," Dave says, and turns away.

"Well, can I have an advance—for the bus fare?"

"Are you kidding me?" Dave roars. "No, you bloody can't."

"Well, I'm going. I'm already working behind the bar tonight. And you can't run my life. . . ."

I'm holding my breath, waiting for Dave to go full tonto with him. It happens at least once a week lately. But I knock over my can of spray polish with my elbow and they remember I'm here. Dave gets hold of Ade's arm and takes him outside.

He's got his hands full there. I hope Cal doesn't get like that.

My phone goes off in my pocket and I look but I don't know the number, so I don't answer. Bloody scammers are ringing all the time lately. But the caller leaves a message and I listen to Claire, a social worker from the old days, give me the bad news.

"Dee?" Claire says. "I'm so sorry but your brother has died. I know you haven't been in touch for a long time but I thought you'd want to know."

"What happened?" I say when I ring back but I don't really need to ask. My big brother, Phil, had been in a terrible state the last time I'd seen him. Four years ago—at Mum's funeral.

It'd been Claire who had rung that time too. It had taken her a while to reach me by way of addresses in Brecon and Brighton and it'd been a shock—but only because I'd assumed Mum was already dead. The last time I'd seen her, she'd had a needle in her arm and barely recognized me. She'd looked a hundred.

She'd been so pretty once. And needed to be told. We were always moving to be with her next man—that was why we came to

Ebbing. It was the best year of my life. I was five and Phil was thirteen. The social worker put us in a holiday flat with a window that looked over the sea, and me and Phil used to sit on the beach and feed chips to the seagulls. Mum's bloke that year was nice—he didn't hit Phil, anyway. I don't know why she left him but it was on to the next one. Jeff, or was it Jed? Can't remember now. He didn't last long enough to commit to memory.

Mum used to try to get us to call each new one "Dad" but even she'd given up trying to insist when we got to "Dad" number four. I remember his name. Tony. A skinny man-child ten years younger than Mum who bought her sexy underwear and heroin and felt up her boobs in front of Phil and me. He didn't want us. He was too young to want kids around. Closer to Phil's age than hers.

Phil had it much harder, being the elder, but he never took it out on me. We had different fathers and it must have been a pain having a little sister to look after but he did it anyway. He'd bring home sausage rolls for tea when Mum forgot to buy food and we'd curl up in front of the TV when she and Tony went out. Phil liked violent stuff and scary monsters. Funny when I think of it now. We had enough of those in the house.

When things got really bad, Phil moved out and took me with him. He'd got a room in a squat three streets from home and I still went to school. Phil forged Mum's signature when they sent letters home about trips and nits. The lies were easy, anyway. We were used to keeping Mum's secrets. My teacher hadn't known about the drugs or that Phil and I didn't get enough to eat. So they didn't find out we were in a squat, sleeping on a mattress against the door to our room because it had no lock. I can hardly bear to think about how dangerous it was. I was about the same age as Cal is now. How did I survive? Well, I had Phil.

He'd finished with school and was picking up work by then—

running errands and collecting rent for a local landlord. He came home upset sometimes when he'd had a hard day but he used to have a drink "to stand himself up." He was my hero. He made sure I was clean and tidy for school—brushed my hair and put it in plaits. And the boy in the next room let us boil water on his little stove for washing.

We lost touch when I was taken into care. I didn't even have time to say good-bye. I did look for him when I was old enough but he'd disappeared—into a bottle, people said. It was sixteen years before I saw him again and he'd been completely wasted. I'd been watching for him outside the crematorium—hoping so hard he'd turn up. It was the only reason I'd gone, really. And then I'd almost missed him when he walked past. He'd had to hold up his trousers with one hand, like they were someone else's, and he was scratching at his face. That face.

"Hello, Phil," I said, and he closed his eyes and reached to stroke my hair like he used to when I couldn't sleep.

And I threw my arms round him. I loved him so much. Missed him so much. But I could feel the bones of his spine and his ribs as I clung to him. I helped him sit down inside and tried to talk to him about getting help but he said he wasn't worth saving. He was crying and I thought it was for Mum but he started saying that he'd done terrible things. He kept saying he was sorry and then the music started for the service.

Tony was there too. All my ghosts gathered together again. I didn't recognize him straight off either—he was all bent and thin. It was only when he spoke that I'd realized who he was.

"Come with us," he whined after a recording of "All Things Bright and Beautiful" lurched to a halt and a bloke in a dark suit started ushering us to the exit. "We're going to the pub to drink your mum's health."

"Her health? You killed her, you prick," I'd said. And watched as he led Phil away to the nearest boozer.

I cried all the way home. Then tried to put Mum, Phil, and those days away again. I had Cal to think about. And our future.

I don't cry while Claire tells her tale. Apparently, Phil had been in recovery. "He'd been making a big effort to put his life straight," she says. "He'd been doing so well with the twelve steps but he relapsed. He was found dead in a park on Tuesday morning. There'll have to be an inquest, but I don't know how long that will take. I'll let you know when the funeral is organized. Look, Phil left a few things in his room and I'll post them to you today. I hope that's okay."

I give her the address and pretend to be upset because that's what Claire seems to expect. "I'm so sorry for your loss," she says. But I just feel numb.

FOURTEEN

Eight days earlier

Elise

S TOP THE FESTIVAL" WAS currently meeting outside the pub. Elise had noticed that the landlord conducted much of his business on the pavement outside the Neptune while he smoked. He never finished a cigarette, though. Like an old con, he pinched the tip off and stuffed it in his pocket for later. She wondered how often he set himself on fire.

Dave Harman was a solid-looking bloke with a matching wife. Elise had caught only glimpses of her. "She's called Doll," Ronnie had informed her, "although I'm not sure what sort of doll she's named after. Not Barbie, anyway."

Dave had been landlord for years and the Neptune was where the locals went. It was all brown wood and crisp packets. Not Elise's kind of place.

"The Lobster Shack is more upmarket if you like that kind of thing," Ronnie had said. "It's for people with more money than sense."

Elise had known who she'd meant. Weekenders.

"Mr. Big Bollocks and his stupid festival will bring the place to a standstill," Dave bawled.

Charlie Perry, who was quietly drinking his gin and tonic in the shade of the hanging baskets, tried to say it could be a good thing.

"Maybe people will spend money." And he lifted his glass to toast the idea.

"You're living in dreamland," Dave shouted over him. "The town is dying on its arse. We need some cash coming in, not every pothead on the south coast. They'll bring their own booze and food. Weekenders and commuters like Diamond are already killing this place, buying the houses on the front and then sodding off. There's nowhere for our kids to live. My boy's going to be living with us forever."

"Well, you may be right," Charlie said.

And Dave's gang nodded along in dumb solidarity. Talk had turned to Charlie's charity raffle when the town villain appeared, sauntering down the High Street like he owned the place—the big fish in the puddle of Ebbing. The theme song to *Peaky Blinders* was playing in Elise's head as she watched.

"Hi!" Pete Diamond was saying to some shoppers, with a slow sharky smile—all teeth, no eyes. "Good to see you. How are you doing?"

It was classic instant intimacy, according to the behavioral science book Elise had read for a course. *But what do I know? Perhaps he does actually care about their state of health. People are responding to it, anyway.* They were shaking his hand; children were high-fiving him and taking bundles of leaflets from his bag to hand out.

"Hi, Dave," Diamond shouted across. "How're you doing? Can I have a word?"

Dave looked confused. "About what?"

"Bars for the festival. There are going to be a lot of thirsty customers and money to be made. I'd like to spread the love."

A silence floated through her open window and Elise leaned forward. She didn't need to.

"You can stuff your bars where the sun don't shine!" Dave snarled, looking round to make sure he still had an audience. "No one wants this blasted festival. Why don't you get that?"

Diamond didn't even blink. "Well, that's not true, mate," he said as if explaining the situation to a child, and Dave's face went an even deeper shade of red. "I sold two hundred tickets on the first day, so someone does. Look, I know you have your doubts but it'll be an event for everyone—rock bands, Grime, some country and western. Could really bring the community together and make people notice the town. So let me know by end of play today if you change your mind. It could be a nice earner, but if you don't fancy it, I'll sort it out myself."

"Don't get too ahead of yourself, mate," Dave shouted as his nemesis turned back to his fan club. "The fat lady hasn't sung yet. . . ."

FIFTEEN

Dee

LIAM'S GONE FOR A run and I'm listening to Cal doing his spellings when Claire rings me again.

When I see her number, I realize I still haven't opened the padded envelope Claire sent.

"It's from London," Postie Val commented as she handed it to me this morning. "Is it your birthday?"

"No, Val. It's nothing important."

I shoved it in my cleaning bag to look at later. But I hadn't had the heart.

"I just wanted to let you know his friends held a vigil in the park last night," Claire says. She means well—I can see that—but it's not what I need right now.

"Okay. Did you go? Were there many people there?" I ask for something to say.

"Yes, I went, and there were a couple of blokes from the hostel where he was staying. His stepfather, Tony, came. And a friend from the old days. Oh, and Phil's sponsor from AA was there of course. He identified Phil for the police—he was in bits, actually. Said how

Phil had been doing so well. He'd been sober for six months and been for an interview for a job—"

"Who was the old friend?" I interrupt. It's the only thing I want to know.

"Umm, I didn't hear a name. He was very quiet. Pale and upset. Anyway, Phil's sponsor said Phil had started step nine."

"What? What's that?" But I'm trying to remember quiet pale men from the old days.

"It's about making amends to the people you've hurt in the past."

And I wonder where Phil started. Where I'd start if it was me.

"Okay. So did anyone know why Phil started drinking again?"

"No. No one seemed to know what triggered it—he'd been upbeat at an AA meeting the morning before he drank—but his body was just too frail to cope with a binge. It's so tragic."

"Yes. So tragic. Thanks for letting me know—I really appreciate it but I've got to go."

I send Cal upstairs to play and I get Phil's envelope out of my workbag. A cheap watch slithers out and I hold the strap to my nose in case I can still smell my brother. But there's nothing of him. I pull everything else out—official stuff about his benefits, a hand-written letter to him, and a Forever Friends notebook. I open it and see "I'm Sorry" written in Phil's childish hand on the first page. Underneath are ten names. I spot mine straightaway. I'm halfway down and he's drawn a heart by it. I wonder what Phil wanted to apologize to me about. I scan through the rest of the names and recognize two others. One of them has a line through it.

I'm sitting at the kitchen table—in another house, in my head—when Liam comes back from his run.

The front door banging makes me shout with fright and my heart is thumping so hard I think I can taste blood in my mouth, but he doesn't seem to notice anything.

"I'm all sweaty," he yells as he jogs past and up the stairs.

I don't say anything—I can't speak. I stuff the notebook back into the padded envelope and try to control my breathing.

"I feel better for that," he says when he comes down. "It cleared my head. How are you doing?"

Cleared it of what? I want to ask but don't say anything. *Never ask questions you don't know the answers to.*

Anyway, I've got my own questions to deal with. When Cal gets Liam to play goalie in the garden, I read the letter to Phil. It's dated December 11, 2018.

I'm glad you came to see me last month. I'm sorry it's taken so long to write but I've been thinking about what you said—I haven't been able to think about anything else if I'm honest. I know it must have been as tough for you as it was for me. Digging stuff up like that is hard and I think both of us found out painful things. Anyway, I want to thank you for helping me understand the things that happened. I'd like to meet again one day, mate. I'd buy you a pint but I know you're off the booze—maybe a coffee? I'll be in touch.

The signature is a scrawl but I know who it is. Now I want to know what they told each other. The painful things they dug up.

Leave it alone, Dee, I tell myself. *It's ancient history. And Phil is dead.*

But I know I won't. Can't. It's never over, is it? The past is always there, flickering like our old telly in a dark corner of my head. Most of the time, I can make myself blank it out, but little things—like a song that used to make me cry or the smell of cheap Chinese takeaway, our Friday night treat—make it fizz back into focus. I've got a lot of bad memories—my childhood was one long nightmare, really. But this is different. Unfinished business—a time bomb ticking quietly like a second heart in my chest.

I ring Claire and get a number for Phil's sponsor. And dial.

"Hi, I'm Phil Golding's sister. I wanted to thank you for helping him."

"I was happy to—he was a lovely man. And I know he was planning to get in touch with you. Before . . ."

"Thanks for saying that." I choke on the thought. "I hadn't heard from him for years but it means a lot. I wish I'd known about the vigil but I didn't find out until afterward. I hear there were some old friends who came."

"Well, one. A man he'd only recently reconnected with. Apparently they knew each other when they were in their teens. In London. Actually, he said he was back staying in the same street where they used to live."

And I'm back there too. Curled up on an old mattress. Waiting for my brother to come home.

NOW

SIXTEEN

Elise

ELISE'S POST-ITS WERE COLOR coded in eye-watering tones—the only ones available at the paper shop. Screaming pink for Charles Williams, acid yellow for Charlie Perry, and neon green for Pauline. Elise started with the pinks. He'd been Williams until he'd moved to Ebbing, according to the records. Her money was on the "misunderstanding" in London prompting his reinvention as Mr. Perry.

This isn't your first tangle with creditors, is it, Charlie? Her working theory was that Charlie had done his vanishing act to escape the looming cash crisis and she pictured him sunning himself like a lizard on a Spanish beach. And wondered what name he was using now.

Except he's got a disabled daughter. Elise had been genuinely touched when he'd mentioned the girl the other day. That emotion had been real. *Would he really abandon her? Leave without a word?*

She looked through her pink notes and found the first wife's name. Lila Nightingale. *Nice and unusual. You don't want to be looking for a Linda Smith.* And found the birth of Charlie's daughter,

Sofia. She was now living in an institution about forty minutes north of Ebbing, according to the electoral register, but Elise couldn't just ring her up. Charlie had mentioned brain damage and Pauline had said there was no point trying to talk to her.

I'll have to speak to the mother.

There were three possible addresses linked to the name. Elise rang each one, her amateur-detective script rehearsed in her head.

"Hello. I am sorry to bother you but I am trying to contact people who might know Charles Williams, who used to live in Addison Gardens in Kensington."

The first two were sorry but they'd never heard of him. The third, at an address in Surrey, went quiet on her when Elise said Charlie's name.

"Ms. Nightingale? I think you may have been married to Mr. Williams in the nineteen eighties?"

"Who is this?"

"My name's Ronnie Durrant," Elise said, pinching her leg to punish the lie. "I'm a friend of Charlie's second wife."

"Well, if she wants to give him back, she's barking up the wrong tree."

"No, no. I'm ringing because we're worried about him."

"I stopped caring about Charles a very long time ago. Sorry."

And the phone went dead.

Elise sat for a moment. "Well, that's that," she said out loud, but she knew she couldn't leave it. She'd asked the first questions now. She needed to know the answers. It was like a deep itch. But she hesitated. She knew going to knock on Lila Nightingale's door was taking the next step down a tricky road. The truth was that she shouldn't be doing any of this—it was none of Elise's business.

Oh, I'm just prodding about for a neighbor, she told herself. *Just having a look, if anyone asks.*

———

RONNIE DIDN'T KNOW WHETHER to be pleased or offended when Elise told her she'd used her name. She plumped for pleased in the end and fetched her car keys.

"So I'll be DI King," she said as she started the Mini. "You'd better brief me on where we are on the case."

I'm unleashing a monster. Elise groaned silently.

Forty-five minutes later, they pulled up outside the house. It was crammed into a terraced street with a bay window, a glossy racing green front door, and an enormous ginger cat stretched out on the sill to capture every ray of sun.

Lila Nightingale took her time to answer. Elise could see her approaching in the dimpled glass of the door, a small, dark figure shimmering toward her. When Lila opened the door, she was immaculately made-up—her face was painted a uniform creamy pink and her eyeliner looked as though it'd been applied with a laser. Elise found herself wondering if it was in someone else's honor or if she painted on her younger face every morning.

Charlie obviously likes a trophy wife on his arm, Elise thought. She touched her naked face defensively and felt the treacherous stab of a whisker on her jawline.

If the beauty queen on the threshold noticed her lack of grooming, she didn't show any sign.

"Yes?" she said.

"Er, hello. I called you earlier," Elise started. "About Charlie."

"And I told you he was none of my business. Why have you come?"

"The thing is, he's gone missing."

Charlie's first wife sighed, turned, and led the way through the house to a postage-stamp-sized garden. The giant cat followed and lay in front of them, licking its bottom as they all pretended not to notice.

"So when did he disappear?" Lila plunged straight in. "What do you think has happened to him?"

"Well, he was last seen on Friday night at a pop festival in Ebbing."

"Seriously? At his age?"

She hadn't offered tea and Elise suspected the visit was going to be short and sweet.

"As I said on the phone, we're worried. He seemed distressed on Friday night and we wondered if he had mentioned any problems to you or your daughter."

Lila smiled grimly. "I'd be the last person he'd confide in. We divorced a very long time ago and communicate only when we have to discuss our daughter. She's cared for in a residential home—I don't know if you knew. The last contact Charlie and I had was a few weeks ago. The home had contacted me about an outstanding bill and I'd forwarded it to Charlie—he handles all that—and I didn't hear back from him. But he's sorted it out—I checked."

"Did Charlie visit Sofia last week?"

"Sofia? Sorry. No one calls her that. She's been known as Birdie since she was born—she was always shouting for food like a baby bird. We only use "Sofia" for official forms. I expect Charlie went— he rarely misses. He's devoted to her. He goes on Wednesdays and I go Saturdays. You could ask the staff. They record visits in Birdie's diary."

"Okay, but would it be possible to talk to your daughter? To see if her dad has been in touch since then?"

"You could try but, honestly, it's unlikely she'll be able to help. Birdie struggles with her memory, you see."

"I'm sorry," Elise said. "Charlie told me a little bit about her but

I don't really know the extent of her disabilities. Or what happened to her. Was it a car accident?"

Lila closed her eyes tight. "No, she and her boyfriend were the victim of a brutal attack," she said as if reciting a script, "during a break-in. Adam was killed and she was tortured by a drug addict—we think to make her tell him where the valuables were. An animal called Stuart Bennett put a plastic bag over her head and she stopped breathing. It caused brain damage. She's blind and has seizures and cannot care for herself."

Ronnie and Elise looked at each other in the silence that followed.

"Oh, God, I am so sorry—I had no idea," Elise said. "When was this?"

"When she was eighteen—in 1999."

"You must have been devastated," Ronnie said.

Lila took out a small white hankie tucked in her sleeve and dabbed at her eyes, smudging her makeup. "I'm sorry for crying. She is alive and I should be grateful for that—and I am—but I still miss the girl she was."

"Of course you do," Ronnie said, and reached for Lila's hand as if it was the most natural thing in the world.

Elise shifted in her seat and pretended to look at the cat. She'd never been great at that sort of thing. And even if she had been, it didn't do to show it. As a young cop, Elise had been told it pigeon-holed you among the blokes and you ended up with all the domestic shouts.

The two older women sat holding hands until Lila tucked her hankie away.

"Shall I make you a cup of tea?" Ronnie said, and got up. "Point me in the right direction."

"How did you and Charlie meet?" Elise nudged Lila back on course.

And Lila unfurled her memories in the afternoon sun. "We were on the same table at a gala evening. I'd bought a new dress and had my hair done specially and the man I was with was too busy drinking himself stupid with his friends to notice. But Charlie noticed. He said he saw me and it was like a spotlight had been switched on."

"He was quite a charmer, then?"

Lila frowned. "He could turn it on when he wanted to. Charlie could always do that. And he was fun—and generous. He bought me lovely things, but when I think about it now, he spent money like it was an illness, really. He had to have more and more things. To prove he was a success, I suppose. But I caught him out lying a couple of times—little lies but I was beginning to have doubts. Then, of course, I got pregnant and the die was cast. It was an accident but Charlie was so happy and I thought I could be too."

Ronnie came out with a tray. She'd got a teapot and all the doings. "Hope it's okay," she said. "I helped myself to your lovely china."

"Of course." Lila smiled warmly at her.

"So you got married?" Elise said as she popped a sweetener in her cup.

"Yes. Charlie insisted. He was adamant no child of his would be without a father's name on its birth certificate. It was only afterward that I discovered why. When I found out who he really was."

SEVENTEEN

Elise

CHARLIE PERRY WASN'T HIS first reincarnation, then, according to Lila. He'd done it before.

He'd presented himself as Charles when she'd met him—"never Charlie, that was too common"—an ex–public school boy in an old-school tie who spoke posher than the Queen and had top-drawer connections.

"Then his mother turned up," Lila said, pouring a second cup for them.

"Maureen?" Elise dredged up the name from her research.

"He'd told me she was dead when I asked who was coming to the wedding," Lila said. "Told me his mother was a diplomat's daughter who'd lived in Southeast Asia for most of her life and run off with his father, an artist. Charles had been their adored only child."

"Goodness, how romantic," Ronnie said. "It's like a novel."

"Yes." Lila smiled grimly. "Exactly like one, it turned out. Pure fiction. His mother was a supermarket cashier from Barnet. A single mum—she'd had a fling with a GI toward the end of the war, apparently—and put him in a children's home when he was three and she couldn't cope on her own. But she'd come looking for him after all those years."

"Wow, what did he say?" Elise tried to picture the hideous reunion.

"Oh, he claimed she was some sort of fantasist and sent her on her way. But Maureen came back when he was at work and showed me his birth certificate and photos from his early years. And letters he'd written as a child pleading with her to come and get him. It was him. She was after money, of course."

"So did he admit it?"

"No, he carried on dismissing it as elaborate lies." Lila put her cup down. "The tragedy is that I would have understood if he'd told me the truth then—that he'd been ashamed of his start in life. That he'd been afraid people would look down on him because of his background, so he'd created this new persona. I mean, my family wasn't anything special—I wouldn't have judged him. But Charles had a lot to lose, I suppose. He was a success—buying and selling property and making lots of money. He wasn't going to risk losing all that. So he carried on pretending. He must have felt the lies he'd told were too big to be unpicked. The humiliation was too awful to contemplate."

"But what did you do?" Ronnie said.

"I stayed for a while. We had a child. She wasn't a lie. And he adored her. But in the end, I couldn't be part of it anymore. Going to those dinners and parties and hearing him winding people into his fantasy was like standing on the edge of a cliff, just waiting for him to fall. And of course he knew that I knew he was a fake. He grew to hate me for it."

"What did you tell Birdie?" Elise said.

"As little as possible. When I left him, she was very young. I told Charles I wouldn't lie to our daughter if she asked questions but I didn't volunteer anything. She was a smart girl, though, and she eventually worked it out for herself when she was thirteen. She stopped seeing him and took my name, Nightingale. He blamed me—of course he did—but it was his deceit that poisoned their relationship. We were getting on with our lives without him when it happened. And Birdie had such a wonderful future ahead of her."

Lila suddenly stood and hurried into the house. She reappeared clutching a picture of their daughter. *The before photo,* Elise realized. The same one Charlie kept in his wallet.

"She was so beautiful. And she had a place at Oxford when that monster attacked her. This was taken two weeks before."

It was a studio photo of Birdie: dark, shiny hair curling over bare shoulders and a Hollywood smile lighting up her face. So much happiness and excitement captured in that moment. And snuffed out within days.

"Carpe diem," Elise's mum used to mutter when she read stories like that in the newspaper. "Seize the day, Elise. You never know what's round the corner."

Elise put that thought away—what had been round the corner had come barreling into her already. She used to think she could smell bad news coming. But she'd missed the big ones. Hugh and breast cancer.

"You don't know what it was like . . ." Lila said quietly, shrinking down in her chair. "I was lost to antidepressants for months."

"It must have been a terrible time," Ronnie said. "How did you cope?"

"How did Charlie cope?" Elise added.

"Badly. We both struggled." Lila started to weep again. "And Adam's family, of course."

Elise zoned out as Ronnie worked her magic and tried to untangle the threads of the story.

"Had they known each other long?" Ronnie said.

"No, just a few weeks," Lila said. "I hadn't even met Adam. The poor boy was beaten with a poker and died from his injuries. The police said he and Birdie were in the wrong place at the wrong time."

"What do you mean? The wrong place? Where were they?"

"At Charles's house."

Elise felt the hairs stand up on her arms. She cleared her throat. "Charlie's? Why? I thought Birdie and her dad were estranged."

"So did I."

"So was he attacked too?"

"No, he was at a dinner in town—the police were already at the house when he got back," Lila said. "The thing is that Charles had been meeting her behind my back. He'd wormed his way back into her life and given her a key and the code to the front door. She'd never have been there if he hadn't. And we still don't know why she was, that night—Birdie doesn't remember anything about it and the boyfriend is dead."

Lila looked as though she was lost in thought but she got up abruptly and started stacking the tea things. "Look, this is all so long ago," she said. "It does no good to dig things up. I have to focus on the here and now. And Birdie is doing very well at Wadham Manor. It is a wonderful place. Charles found it. It's the one thing he did right—and he pays for it. I would never have been able to afford it."

There was a beat.

"Oh, God," she wailed, "what is going to happen to our girl if he doesn't come back?"

RONNIE HAD FALLEN SILENT as the horror story they had just heard sucked the oxygen out of the car.

"Oh, my God, how could anyone put a plastic bag over a young girl's head and destroy her life?" she said. "I can't imagine anyone being that evil."

"You'd be surprised," Elise said. *Actually, it would blow your mind if you knew what people are capable of. The cruelty. The wickedness.*

"You have to remember that monsters don't look the part, Ronnie," she said. "They're not marked out in any way. If only . . . They live among us in plain sight. In their cardigans and sensible shoes. They have library cards, buy a poppy for Remembrance Day. They're the man or woman next door who picks up a pint of milk for you, asks after your parents, or takes in parcels from deliverymen." *All the while planning their next act of depravity.*

Ronnie's eyes widened. "Oh, God . . ." she breathed, and Elise could see she was running through her neighbors, looking for signs.

"Quite. It means I can never stop looking for them," Elise added.

EIGHTEEN

Elise

ELISE USED THE MAP on her phone to direct Ronnie along tree-lined country roads until she spotted the sign for Wadham Manor.

"It looks like a stately home," Ronnie said, squinting up at the façade. "It must be costing Charlie a small fortune."

The receptionist, a willowy blonde with a French manicure, was polite but unyielding. "The family has said that people need to make an appointment through them for a visit."

"Of course, but her mother knows about it," Elise said, her fingers itching to pull out her warrant card to end the discussion. "Perhaps you could call Lila?"

"If you would just like to take a seat."

Five minutes later, they were buzzed through and standing at the cream front door of Birdie's apartment.

"Hello," she said when she opened the door. There was no mistaking her parentage. She had Lila's glossy brown hair and her father's generous mouth. "Mum has just rung to say you were here. And that Dad is missing. That's terrible. I want to help but it's difficult for me. I have problems remembering things. My memory, you see . . ."

"Please don't worry—your mum has explained," Elise said. "We're very grateful for the chance to talk to you."

They sat round the table and Elise told her about the last sighting of Charlie, watching as anxiety froze the woman's face. She was older than Elise had expected—all that talk of "our girl" and baby names had made Elise stick on the eighteen-year-old girl in the photo. But Birdie must be almost forty now. Only a few years younger than her. As she talked, Elise wondered how long Birdie would remember that her father was missing. Would she have to be told again in an hour? And go through the initial distress all over again?

Birdie reached for her phone—"Maybe it's a mistake. Maybe he's gone away for a weekend and forgotten to tell anyone. I'll try him. He always picks up when he sees it's me"—and dialed. "Hi, Dad, where are you? Can you ring me—I'm really worried I haven't heard from you." She laid the handset in her lap. "He'll call back," she said. But the phone remained silent.

"Has your dad been in touch since Friday night?" Elise said.

Birdie brushed her other hand over the tabletop and picked up a folder. "Do you mind having a look. It'll be more reliable."

Elise read back through the previous week, noting Lila's visit on Saturday and Charlie's on Wednesday.

"Here he is—but he didn't come the week before. I thought he never missed."

Birdie frowned. "He doesn't. I thought he came but . . . Well, the notes are usually accurate. He would have phoned if he couldn't make it." She lifted her mobile and listened to her call history, skipping back until she reached the list of recent calls on speakerphone back to "Dad. Incoming call. Wednesday the fourteenth. Thirteen forty-seven."

"That's probably the call," she said. "He might have spoken to someone on the staff as well, so they could tell me if I forgot."

"I'll ask," Elise said. "Can you remember how he was the last visit? It was only four days ago. What did he talk about? Did he have anything on his mind? It might help us understand his disappearance."

"There was something, I think. He was upset but . . . I'm really sorry," Birdie said, her head drooping.

"Don't worry. What about e-mails or texts? Has he messaged you since then?"

Birdie opened her laptop and they listened as she scrolled through her inbox. There was only one since his last visit. The monotone ReadAloud voice recited from Thursday, August 22:

Hello, darling. Sorry I made you cry yesterday, Birdie. I hate to see you unhappy. Please don't worry—I promise I'll find a way through this. You know you can rely on me—I just need to juggle a few things. Love you and see you soon, Dad x

"Can you remember what upset you so much?" Elise said. Birdie looked blank.

"Okay, do you mind if we keep going through his messages?" On Wednesday, August 14, the day he'd missed, he'd e-mailed:

I'm so sorry I wasn't there for our walk today but something urgent came up that I had to deal with. Nothing for you to worry about—and it is all sorted now. I'll make up for it next time. Bring you something lovely, my darling girl. Much love, Dad

What was he dealing with? Elise wondered.

There were other e-mails—short loving messages. "Dad checks

in a lot. He worries about me." Birdie smiled, clicking on an e-mail from Thursday, August 8, with the subject line Hello, Darling Girl.

Lovely to see you yesterday. You looked so well. Keep up the physio and we'll walk farther next time. We can go to smell those wonderful roses in the Sensory Garden. By the way, I've asked the staff to make sure visitors make appointments and speak to me before they see you. Nothing to worry about, darling, but I don't want you bothered. Anyway, I've got some jobs to do—the charity raffle is going great guns—but I'll ring tomorrow and see you next week. Bye-bye, Birdie. Much love, Dad

So the watch on callers started only recently.

"Did you have an unexpected visitor around that date?" Elise said, flipping over the pages in the folder. "There's nothing in the diary."

"I don't know but you could ask at the desk. They're super helpful."

"Yes, absolutely," Elise said. Ronnie could have a go at winning over the gatekeeper. "Okay, I'm leaving you my number in case you hear from your dad," Elise said, keying it into Birdie's phone.

Ronnie headed straight for reception and Elise stood back while she troweled on the charm.

"Thank you so much for letting us see Birdie. She's so lucky to live somewhere as beautiful as this. Have you got a brochure? I have a friend who might be interested."

The receptionist leaned on her counter to point out the many features of Wadham Manor as Ronnie hummed her appreciation.

"Birdie certainly loves it here," she said.

"Yes, we'll really miss her when she moves," the receptionist said.

"She's leaving?" Ronnie raised an eyebrow.

"Well, we are expensive. . . . Not everyone can afford it long term."

"How distressing for everyone—Birdie's father must be very upset. Charlie is devoted to her, isn't he?"

"Oh, yes, very attentive," the receptionist said.

"And very protective—well, you can understand that, can't you?"

"Yes. Actually, he got a bit huffy when I told him there'd been a visitor for Birdie a couple of weeks ago. Said we had to ring him if anyone just turned up."

"Oh, who was the visitor?"

"He didn't leave a name—and he didn't see Birdie. She was in treatment, so he said he'd come back the following week."

"And did he?"

"No. He must have changed his mind."

"BRILLIANT WORK, RONNIE," ELISE said when they got outside. "Charlie must have told Birdie about the move on his last visit. No wonder she cried. But he didn't tell Lila, did he? She knew he'd been late paying a bill recently but not this. Things were obviously coming to a crisis point here as well as at the bank."

"Where on earth would you find the money to pay those fees?" Ronnie said, shutting the car door and adjusting her rearview mirror. "We're talking tens of thousands a year, according to my friends."

"Also, who came to see Birdie?" Elise said. "It spooked Charlie enough that he put a layer of extra security in place."

"Do you think he knew who it was?" Ronnie said. "Someone he owed money to?"

"Why would they go to Birdie's residential care home?"

"To put the frighteners on him."

Elise looked at Ronnie and grinned. " 'The frighteners'?"

"Shut up." She grinned back. "And don't pretend you're not enjoying this as much as I am."

"Well, let's try and stay in the here and now, shall we? I don't believe he would abandon his daughter without a word. Those e-mails are so loving and caring. His disappearance was sudden. Unplanned. Something made him run."

BEFORE

NINETEEN

Dee

THE HOSTEL IN WEST London is like a big dirty hive with the residents buzzing around the entrance, sharing cigarettes, laughing, and pushing, and others sitting on the wall, dead eyed, with secret cans of Special Brew.

Everyone stops and looks at me when I push through to get to the door. I thought it would be hard to find the right place. The sort of place a quiet, pale man might stay when he came out of prison. But it stood out from the cheap hotels and flats as soon as I walked out of the tube station.

"I'm here to see Stuart Bennett," I say.

THE CHEAP CARPET ON the stairs is full of static and my hand sparks off the metal banister, making me jump.

He cracks the door open when I knock and all my confidence evaporates. We are only inches apart but he can't hold my eye, flicking nervous glances beyond me. *Looking for what's coming. That's what a lifetime inside must do.*

"Hello, Stuart." I dry-gulp over the words. "I'm Phil's sister. Can I come in?"

His eyes go all wide and I think he'll slam the door but he lets me in. He looks so old—his skin has that gray sheen from years in prison and all the dark hair I'd remembered has gone—it's shaved close to his skull now. But the serpent tattoo is still there, wrapped round his neck. I was fascinated by that snake once. I sit on the stool closest to the door while he takes the bed, pulling the duvet up over his rumpled sheets. The room is so small, I can smell his instant-coffee breath.

He keeps looking away and I know I'll have to push to get anywhere with him.

"How did you find me?" he says finally, and I shiver.

His soft lisp takes me somewhere else. And I'm standing in another room.

"The vigil," I stutter.

"I didn't see you."

"No, I spoke to people who were there. They said Phil had been in touch with you."

Stuart looks at me and I wonder what he sees. What he remembers. If he sees me as I was—a kid with plaits, in a dress two sizes too small. And I tug my fringe over my eyes.

"Yeah. He wrote to me in prison last year and came to see me. I hardly recognized him, he looked so rough."

"Why did he come? What did he want?"

"He wanted to say sorry."

"What for?" I say, and he looks away again.

"For wrecking my life. He said it was because of him that I was in prison."

"Phil? How was he responsible? He wasn't even there," I say.

And he looks at me.

"No. But he sent me," he says.

"Phil did?" I say too loudly, and he recoils.

"He gave me the address, told me there was good stuff in there. And he knew the owner would be out. Phil would sell the stuff for me. I was going to hand it over that night. But that didn't happen. Anyway, Phil told me all about why he'd done it. It took a lot for him to come and tell me," Stuart says, and stops. He grips the duvet cover as if he's about to fall. "And I told him about that night. How it all went wrong. All wrong," he whispers. "About the lad and the girl who should never have been there. Phil hadn't known. He swore he hadn't. But I told him everything—all the stuff that never came out in the trial—and he sat and cried."

I can't speak. I just sit there while he goes on, talking about how he'd like to follow Phil's example and make his peace. But all I can think of is the Phil who sent Stuart to the house in Addison Gardens. He'd only just turned seventeen and looked younger. He was working for a landlord, banging on doors for rent. Collecting cash from people like him. People who were too poor to have bank accounts. And he hated it. It was when he started drinking. "Dutch courage," he called it, and I didn't like it. It made him too loud, like Tony. Looking back now, I can see he was a frightened kid but I keep asking myself if there'd been a side to him I hadn't known. Had he been sending people to break into houses? I was only eight years old. I wouldn't have known, would I? My son, Cal, is almost the same age I was then and what does he truly know about me?

But Phil cared about people. About me. He'd never have left me on my own to go robbing. He was home with me every night. Well, nearly every night.

My head wanders further on. I know it won't lead anywhere good. I try to stop it but it keeps slipping out of my grasp. So I close my eyes.

Make it go away, Cal would say. Everything is so much simpler when you're a kid, isn't it?

"I don't believe it," I say, and Stuart stops talking and leans toward me. I think for a second that he's going to take my hand and I freeze.

"My brother wasn't like that," I say, tucking my hands under my thighs.

"No, he wasn't," Stuart says. "But there were people who were."

TWENTY

Seven days earlier

Charlie

H E WAS WORKING EVERY hour of the day to raise money—going back to former contacts and old schemes—but he was getting nowhere.

He looked round at the space that seemed to close in on him daily. And being cooped up in the caravan with the curtains drawn and the television on mute was clearly getting on Pauline's nerves too. But it had to be done.

The last time he'd been in trouble, they'd had four reception rooms and a home gym to distract her. But there were no distractions now. She'd given herself a manicure and a pedicure, plucked what remained of her eyebrows, and shaved her legs. The only thing left to do was to keep up a continuous loop of nagging and whining. Charlie wanted to scream but he gave her a foot massage as demanded, stroking the moisturizer into her cracked heels. He thought he'd managed to placate her until she suddenly realized she was about to miss her next appointment at the hairdresser's.

"My hair needs doing. Today!" Pauline screeched at him as he tried to dodge her flailing nails. "This is like being in prison. I should never have married you. You're a complete failure. In every department."

"Pauline," he ventured. "Darling . . . it's only for a few more days and then you can go to the salon hourly if you want."

"I will. But it won't be in your honor. . . . I have other friends who'll appreciate it."

His mouth soured at the thought of his wife's friends but now was not the moment. He'd deal with them all in good time.

"Of course you do, my darling. The thing is," he explained patiently, "I have to ring some people. Boring but essential. You know that."

"Well, your phone calls don't seem to be doing the trick," she snorted. "What the hell is going on?"

"Just a minor blip. You have been marvelously patient and I'll sort it out. Perhaps I should work in one of the outbuildings for a bit."

"Yes, do that. I'm getting a headache."

"Of course, there's no electricity—"

"Just go! You can come back when it gets dark to plug in your laptop and phone."

A WAVE OF EXHAUSTION washed over him when he entered the dark shed and he put his head against the rough surface of the nearest wall.

He couldn't work there. Maybe he should set up camp in the house. The bloody house. The noose round his neck.

What he needed to do was to get out of there. And find a drink.

The pub was the place to be when things were tricky at home. Drink oiled the wheels, loosening inhibitions, and striking up a conversation with a stranger was welcomed—expected, even.

Lunchtime was best. Men were more likely to be drinking on their own—no better halves to distract them or put an oar in.

He took a deep happy breath as he pushed in through the door of the Neptune.

The pub was heaving with sticky flesh. The temperature outside was rising and the bar was thrumming with thirsty customers. It was a young crowd, trade, workmen on weekly wages. Charlie slipped off the Old Harrovian tie he'd knotted expertly that morning and put it in his pocket. It was too bloody hot for neckwear.

"Hello, old man," he hallooed Dave, fluttering his last ten-pound note above heads.

"Gin and tonic, please, with plenty of ice."

The landlord smiled and nodded, reaching for a tall glass. "How are you today, Charlie? Hot enough for you?"

"It's positively Mediterranean out there, David. Good for business, though . . ."

All around him, off-duty workers from the new builds were glugging lager as if it was their last drink on earth. He swallowed half his G&T.

"What about this festival, then?" Charlie asked Dave. "Is Pete Diamond funding it himself or has he got sponsors?"

Dave's face reddened. "Mr. Big Bollocks?" he spat. "It's all his own show, apparently."

"That'll cost him. He's probably writing it off against tax."

"That's illegal, isn't it?" Dave leaned closer. "I could turn him in."

"Ah! But he's probably got an accountant to sort out a loophole. People with that sort of money do."

"Not like me, then?" Dave snorted bitterly. "Another?"

"Lovely."

He watched the landlord shoveling ice into the glass and wondered what Dave was actually worth. Did he have property? Savings? A maiden aunt about to pop her clogs? A pension?

"You work so hard," Charlie said when the fresh glass was delivered. "When are you hoping to retire?"

"Not yet! I'm not that old."

"What are you? Fifty?"

Dave smirked at the ridiculous compliment.

"Fifty-seven."

"Ah, the golden age . . ." Charlie laughed.

"Sod off, Charlie. What are you on about?"

"Financially, David. Look, you're sitting pretty, actually. You can now cash in your pension and reinvest it in something that actually pays out a decent dividend."

"Yeah, I've done that, actually. I've put it in a savings account for the time being."

"Have you? You've got to be careful, though. You need to put it to work to get a proper return."

"Absolutely," Dave said, ignoring the customer in front of him urgently asking for a refill. "Doll!" he called down the bar. "Can you take over here."

His wife gave him a look but started pulling the pint.

"Sorry, Charlie. What were you saying?" Dave moved them both down to the shallow end of the bar near the toilets.

"Well, all I'll say is that you might as well put your pension under the mattress if you don't invest it cleverly. It's what I've done."

"Oh, where have you put yours?"

Charlie took a slow mouthful of his drink.

"Come on." Dave smiled winningly. "We're mates, aren't we?"

Charlie put his glass down carefully, then nodded to himself and lowered his voice so Dave had to put his head closer. "Listen, old man, this is completely confidential but I belong to a small private investment company—I help run it with some old chums from the City. We put money in and lend to companies who can't get short-term bank loans. At a premium rate. We've done rather well, actually."

Dave listened as Charlie trotted out figures and interest rates while up the bar Doll tutted about being rushed off her feet.

When Dave was finally guilted into helping out, Charlie finished his drink and looked around.

"Excuse me." A voice at his side interrupted his flow of thought.

"Sorry. Are you trying to get through?" Charlie turned sideways to let the customer get to the bar.

"Thank you. I see we were at the same school," the good-looking stranger said.

Charlie felt for the tail end of his tie hanging out of his pocket. "Ah, the old alma mater. What house were you in?"

Two drinks later he and Kevin Scott-Pennington were thick as thieves. Charlie had told him he'd been involved in the same line of business. "Digital technology is so fascinating. I was on the periphery, of course. The financial side, not the genius brigade." He grinned.

"The problem, naturally, is money," Kevin told him. "Investors have no patience but these things take time to mature."

"'Course." Charlie nodded. "Research and development are the beating heart of any innovative industry."

"Well, mine needs a defibrillator. . . ."

"Ha!" Charlie put a warm hand on Kevin's arm. "Look, old boy—I may be able to help."

TWENTY-ONE

Dee

CAL AND HIS DAD have gone down to the beach early to watch the surfers—Cal wanted me to go too but I said I had to go to work and Liam went all moody. He's still sulking about me going to London on my own. Honestly, it's like having another child sometimes.

He was so sweet when I told him about Phil dying—he'd never met my brother but he hugged me tight and said how sorry he was. He tried to get me to talk about Phil, asking me about when we were kids, but I couldn't go there. How would I stop once I started? It would be like pulling at a thread that could unravel me.

I pushed him away and told him it was something I had to deal with myself.

"Why are you shutting me out?" he said. "I feel like you're keeping stuff from me."

"That's rich coming from you," I said, and he went all quiet.

WHEN I LET MYSELF into the Lobster Shack, the owner, Toby Greene, is standing barefoot on the cold tiles in the bar; his face is all slack and lost. I don't think he even knows I'm here. He's spooning coffee beans into the grinder but his hand is shaking and sending them skittering like black beetles across the counter.

He doesn't respond when I say hello and jumps when I open the dishwasher. "Dee! I didn't hear you arrive. I wish you wouldn't creep about like that," he mutters to himself as he walks away.

I'm rubbing up the stainless steel fittings with some baby oil when he reappears and picks up the forgotten espresso. He sits at one of the tables with his head in his hands. He's taking a lot of those homeopathic things for anxiety. I see new ones all the time in the bathroom. But they—and the empty red wine bottles in the bin—don't seem to be doing him any good.

His husband, Saul, is singing upstairs. Then comes down in a new outfit: tight trousers showing off his thighs and a shirt covered in palm trees. "What do you think? Nice for the holiday?" he says to Toby. Nothing.

"Hey! I'm talking to you," Saul snaps.

"Great," Toby says, and shuffles off upstairs.

Saul raises his eyebrows for my benefit. "He's throwing another strop today. What do you think, Dee?"

"You look great," I say. "When do you go?"

"End of the month. I'm so excited."

I know Saul and Toby's trip isn't really a holiday but I don't say anything. They're going to have a surrogate baby in America. I saw the brochures in Saul's bedside cabinet months ago and now there are sleep suits behind the towels in the airing cupboard. Six of them in different colors and patterns, still on their little padded hangers. I found Saul on the landing the other day, looking guilty and stuffing them back in. And there's a cloud mobile in its box under the spare bed. It's a shame Saul has to keep the baby things secret but I don't think Toby's ready to play daddies in front of people.

He got all snippy the other day while I was doing the kitchen sinks. He'd caught Saul looking at cots online and hissed at him, "What are you doing? It isn't going to happen overnight—it could take up to eighteen months. The agency said so."

"Not necessarily. Could be much sooner." Saul had kissed him on the cheek. "Come on, Mr. Grumpy." It normally works—Toby adores Saul—but he didn't kiss him back like usual.

"Look, they check these women out for fertility levels," Saul laughed. "This isn't ovary lotto."

"TOBES," SAUL HAS JUST called through from the storeroom.

"He's gone out," I call back. "He came down fifteen minutes ago and picked up the car keys."

"Did he say where he was going? We need to move tables together for the birthday booking tonight."

"Er, no, but I'll help you. I've finished the floors."

Saul has his phone to his ear when he appears. "Toby! Where are you? Ring me!"

He's doing it a lot lately. Disappearing without a word. And they're having rows when they never did before. I wonder if it's another man. . . . I don't think Toby's the type. Saul's another matter—he's a terrible flirt—but he's not the one doing a disappearing act.

MY BOYS ARE STILL out when I get home and I sit at the kitchen table. I just need a moment to get myself together before Liam starts asking more questions.

The only thing I have of my brother now is his notebook and I pull it out of its hiding place under the sink. I haven't shown it to

Liam. I knew as soon as I saw the list I didn't want anyone else to see it. Not even him. This was no one else's business.

I flip past the names to the pages he kept as a sort of diary. They are scrawled with his milestones—"SIX DAYS!!!! Longest without a drink for years." "Thirty days since my last drink. Feel like shit."— and flashes of his fear. "Can't do this," he wrote in tiny letters at the bottom of a page as if he was ashamed of even thinking it.

I let myself cry as I read. I can hear his voice as if he's here with me.

Toward the back, there are a few phone numbers and e-mail addresses. And I wonder if the man who sent a boy to do his dirty work is here. Stuart wouldn't tell me his name. Didn't want me getting involved. He said he would deal with it but wouldn't say what he meant. I'd told him to ring me if he changed his mind but I've been trying ever since to remember anything Phil might have said back then about his boss.

The list of names in the notebook is pathetically short. I recognize his sponsor—and Claire and Stuart—but the rest look like street names of friends. Swanky, Doc, Fat Georgie. I go to close the book, and a grimy scrap of paper floats to the floor. An old rent receipt. I pick it up—it's from December 1999, and my mouth goes dry. But I don't recognize the address. Phil had so little; why did he keep this? But then I see the company name at the bottom in small print.

TWENTY-TWO

Four days earlier

Charlie

MRS. LYONS SMILED AT him when he arrived at the Manor. "Ah, Mr. Perry. How nice to see you. Thank you for settling your account."

Charlie tried to smile back but his top lip stuck to his teeth.

"Er, good afternoon. And thank you for your patience," he croaked, and cleared his throat.

He went straight through to Birdie and took her into the garden. He had to do it quickly or he'd bottle it.

"Darling girl," he said, taking her hand.

"What is it, Dad?"

"Look, we need to talk about the future. I'm not getting any younger and I need to make sure you are secure."

"Why? What's happened? Are you ill?"

"No, no, nothing like that. It's just . . . Look, money is a bit tight at the moment. And the thing is, it might mean you moving. Somewhere closer to me so I can pop in and out every day."

Birdie didn't say anything. She sat completely still on the edge of the seat. Charlie searched her profile for what she was feeling but there was nothing.

"Darling?"

"I thought you had plenty of money to support me?" she said quietly, turning her face to him. "That's what you always tell me."

"Well, I did in the beginning. But this place costs fifteen hundred pounds a week, Birdie."

"But it's my home." And tears leaked out of the corners of her eyes.

"Darling, don't cry."

"I'll have to learn a new place and it's so hard to keep anything in my head, Dad. Please don't make me. Please."

It was breaking his heart and he didn't trust himself to speak for a minute. He watched the tears running down his daughter's face and he knew he couldn't go through with it. He'd have to dig deep and find the money somehow.

"Don't worry. Daddy will sort it out," he said before he could change his mind.

AFTERWARD, HE SAT IN his car and pulled his laptop out of the glove box. He'd have to make more calls. Twirl another plate. He still had it, didn't he?

When the screen lit up, one of the old e-mail accounts that slumbered on his desktop was winking at him. He couldn't remember the last time he'd even looked at the account, let alone opened it, but a number one had appeared beside it. *You've got mail* sounded in his head.

It'll be spam—an ad for a world cruise or a stair lift. That's all I seem to get now.

But his finger trembled as he clicked to look.

It wasn't a cruise. Addison1999@yahoo.co.uk was contacting him. Hello, it said.

Delete, he told his finger but it wasn't listening. It opened the e-mail.

I know what you did. Where are you? It's time we talked.

No name.

And he slammed down the lid of his laptop as if Addison1999 were staring out of the screen. *Who is it from? It can't be Phil Golding—he's dead. But who else knows?* Sweat prickled Charlie's top lip.

Stuart Bennett. Charlie counted up the years since his daughter's attacker had been sentenced and saliva flooded his mouth.

He could be out.

Charlie spun round in his seat, staring out of his car in case Bennett could have materialized.

Christ! Am I being hunted down? The man is a psychopath and he says he knows everything. What the hell am I going to do? Steady, he told himself, gripping the steering wheel. *He doesn't know where you are. Yet.*

Anyway, he had a much more pressing problem—finding the money to keep Birdie where she was.

He suddenly blinked twice. He knew where there was money. The appalling Bennett had it. He'd robbed Charlie all those years ago and hidden his beautiful things. He must have. He hadn't had time to sell them before he was arrested and they'd never been found. A quarter of a million pounds. Just sitting somewhere.

Charlie needed time to think. He started the car and roared out of the car park as if he'd stolen it.

———————

WHEN HE SAT AT his desk an hour later, he knew exactly what he was going to do.

He was going to meet Stuart Bennett.

Charlie had pulled up an old photo of his quarry—the one of Bennett being led to the prison van after the trial. He'd looked like a killer in a film, with his snake tattoo and wild dark eyes. Charlie wondered what he looked like now and his mouth went dry.

You've been in riskier situations before, he told himself.

You weren't seventy-four then, a voice whispered back but he flapped it away.

He was going to start with an offer—splitting the proceeds. Seventy-thirty seemed generous, as it was his property. But he would move swiftly on if Bennett didn't agree. He was going to threaten to tell the authorities that Bennett had contacted him and offered to sell him back his stolen goods. The ex con would know he'd be recalled to prison immediately. He'd do a deal.

Charlie pressed "reply" on the e-mail.

I can meet you on Sunday. I'll let you know where nearer the time.

That would keep Bennett on his toes. He'd be waiting on Charlie's instructions.

It took a couple of hours for Addison1999 to answer. The e-mail just said, Okay.

NOW

TWENTY-THREE

Dee

TOLD LIAM I had to nip to the shop but I've had to come to Pauline's on the way. I left my white jacket here yesterday with the cash she paid me in the pocket. And I need it for Cal's footie fees—we're two weeks behind as it is and Liam didn't have a penny on him when I asked this morning. He just emptied his pocket onto the table. It was all odd screws and nails and fluff. I tried to talk to him about our money situation. But he's not listening. He's off somewhere in his head. But then so am I. Phil and his wasted life won't leave me alone.

I haven't heard anything from Pauline but I suppose Charlie got back. I bet he was in a terrible state. When I saw him Friday night, he looked awful. He was lurching along the pavement with the festival crowds. It made me think of Phil, and that horrible knot retied itself in my stomach. I turned away. Didn't want to get caught up.

I tried to blot everything out and I let myself think I was a teenager again, clutching my ticket, with a fiver for drinks in my bra and already dancing on the spot to the music leaking out of the venue.

I was supposed to meet Liam by the trees near the car park field for the festival on Friday night—he and Ade Harman had got a bit of paid work helping set up the bars.

"Does Dave know? He'll do his nut," I said when Liam told me.

"Ade's an adult—and he needs the money as much as I do," Liam snapped.

I was looking for him but I kept an eye out for Charlie. I couldn't help it—he seemed so weighed down with stuff lately and I felt guilty for not talking to him earlier. I stumbled into him sitting on a tree stump and he looked even worse, like he'd been crying.

"Are you okay?" I said, and knelt down in front of him.

I was getting a tissue out to tidy him up when he suddenly grabbed at me.

It made me scream and fall backward. I got up but he was on his feet too, and for a second I didn't know what he'd do. I turned and ran until I found Liam.

"This is going to be a great night," he said, and swung me round and went on about my dress and played with my hair. I'd tied it up like I used to. "You look like a little girl with your plaits." He laughed, and I tried to laugh along with him.

We were dancing when Charlie crashed into us. He'd been clawing his way through the crowd. Liam put his hand on Charlie's shoulder to steady him and he spun round, shouting: "Why are you here?" and then stumbled off.

It upset me but Liam wouldn't let me go after Charlie. And we were still dancing when Ade and Tracy collapsed. I sent Liam to see if he could help but the police and ambulance came really quickly, so we just went home. We were both shaken—it was such a horrible end to our night out. We didn't really speak until he dropped me off at home.

THE CAR ISN'T HERE at the caravan and I curse. It didn't occur to me they wouldn't be in on a Sunday morning. Pauline says it's her day of rest. But no one is answering the door. I go and try the house in case Pauline's popped over there for something, but it's locked. I open the letter box to have a look and I hear a soft whistling noise. Like a window cracked open. Or something breathing. I let the flap go with a bang and run down the steps. I know it's stupid, but ever since someone told Pauline the house had a ghost, I've been creeped out. Of course, Pauline loves the idea. Thinks it's "so romantic." But how are dead people romantic?

I let myself into the caravan—I'll be only a minute and she won't mind. It's funny how quickly people give you keys. Some do it the first week so they don't have to bother being in. The weekenders hand them over without a thought. I'd never do that. I've got loads of keys—most I don't even need anymore—to places that have been sold, and full sets for those who are security conscious. Keys to dead bolts, mortices, and lever locks.

I was pretty sure I'd hung my jacket behind the kitchen door but it's not there. Nor is Charlie's. I look but there's no sign he's back in any of the other rooms either.

I think I see a flash of white in their unmade bed, but when I push the duvet to one side, it's a man's T-shirt. Not something Charlie would wear. He doesn't do casual—even his T-shirts have collars. Pauline's getting very careless about her "entertaining" and I can't help thinking she'd have lots of time to spend with Bram if Charlie disappeared permanently.

I finally find my jacket down by the kitchen bin but the ten-pound note has gone and I swear out loud. I bet she's "borrowed" it.

I'm dialing her phone to ask her when she'll be back when my mobile beeps—it's about to run out of battery. They have a phone charger plugged in behind the toaster and I pull the cable free. But it's got a handset attached.

She's left her bloody phone behind.

But when I look at it closer, I can see it isn't hers. This one is old and cheap and there's no screen saver. It definitely wasn't here yesterday when I cleaned. I wonder whose it is.

Pauline isn't answering her phone. I know I should just go but I'll give it another five minutes in case she comes back. Money is so tight at the moment. Tighter than it's been for a long time. I've been pretending to be on a diet to try to make the shopping go further and I open Pauline's fridge to see if there's anything I can eat. But there's nothing much except prosecco.

I can't wait any longer, so I start looking for a bit of paper to write a note for her, pulling out drawers. Most need a good clean and I'm putting it on a mental list for next week when I open the one in the kitchen table and see a passport. It's too tempting. I open it to find out Pauline's real date of birth, betting with myself she's nearly eighty, and find myself looking at Charlie's face. But it's got the wrong name on it and I can't stop staring at it. Trying to make sense of it. Telling myself not to be stupid. That Phil dying and seeing Stuart have spooked me. Made me jumpy and paranoid. But I take a photo of the passport with my phone so I can look at it again later. When I've calmed down.

When my mobile pings, I drop it in fright. It's Liam texting me to hurry up, so I shove the passport back in the drawer. As I drive away, I realize I've left my jacket. And the ten pounds Pauline owes me. I'll have to go back.

My head is spinning. There's too much going on already. I'll have to do it later.

TWENTY-FOUR

Dee

"THE POLICE RANG ME when I was watching Cal's match," Liam says as I heat up some baked beans for lunch. "They want me to go in this afternoon to have a chat about Friday night."

"Why?" I try to keep calm but my voice goes shrill.

"About Ade. It's no biggie." But I can hear the stress in his voice too. "They're talking to everyone who saw him that night. They're trying to build up a picture of what happened before he and Tracy collapsed."

I breathe out too fast and go a bit dizzy.

"And did you see him?"

"You know I did. He helped me hump some crates for Pete Diamond, remember?"

"Oh, yes, sorry. My head's all over the place. Okay, so this is nothing to worry about?"

"No," he says but he hesitates and comes to stand beside me with that look on his face. The confession face.

"What? Tell me!"

"I'm going to tell them I gave Charlie a lift home the night of the festival," he says.

And I shut my eyes.

"Charlie? What are you talking about?"

"I saw him when I went to the garage, after I dropped you home—I went to fill up the van, didn't I? He was staggering along the road—I was just trying to help."

"For Christ's sake, Liam, why didn't you say anything at the time?"

"Because it was nothing. I give people lifts all the time—everyone does round here. And then you said he'd gone missing and the police were involved and . . . well, I didn't want to be dragged into something. I thought he'd show up. Like you said. But he hasn't, has he? And I can't stop thinking about it."

"Did something happen in the van, then?"

"Like what?"

"I don't know."

Liam shakes his head. "No, Dee, nothing happened," he says, talking to the tabletop. "He was really drunk and wasn't talking any sense. He was rambling on about seeing someone at the festival."

"Who?"

"I don't know. Anyway, I shoved him out of the car door as soon as we got there. I didn't want Pauline blaming me for the state he was in."

"Right."

"But I need to tell the police, don't I? I've heard they're starting to ask questions about him. It's been two days. They'll find out about the people Charlie owes money to—the roofers, the scaffolders. And me."

"But they're big companies—their bills must be huge. The police won't be interested in you. You said ours was only a couple of hundred."

"Well, it's a bit more than that."

"How much?"

"A couple of grand," he mutters under his breath.

"How much?"

"Just under four thousand. Look, Dee"—he cuts me off before I can explode—"he was so clever about it. I did all that new pipework, but as soon as I gave him the bill, he asked me to do more, kept the job rolling on, slipping me 'interim payments' of a couple of hundred here and there for materials. But it kept mounting up. And then he started avoiding me."

"Four thousand." I can hardly speak. "How have we been paying the rent? Have you been paying it?"

Liam ignores the question, talking over me.

"The police will start sniffing about, and if I don't say something first, they might find out about the debt and me giving him a lift and say I've got something to hide."

My mind is sliding all over the place.

"But how will they find out? Did anyone see him get in the van? Have you told anyone else?"

"No. There was no one about when I stopped. That's why I picked him up."

The noise in my head is deafening. The frantic buzz of questions and fear. I try to breathe in his silence as I think. I'll need to hold him close if we're to get through this. Hold everything close.

"Okay, telling the police would be a mistake. Like you said, they'll make something of it. Turn it on you. He was only in the van for five minutes and he was all right when you left him. So it's not important, is it? I think if anyone asks, you should say you didn't see him at all, okay?"

Liam is breathing through his mouth as he takes it all in. He looks like a little boy.

"But, Dee," he says finally, "it's him in the wrong, not me. Not paying. The police can't make something out of nothing. And I've got nothing to hide."

But we've all got something to hide.

I was looking up our landlord's e-mail to ask for time to pay when my phone goes and Janine Scott-Pennington begs me to come and save her.

"I know you're not due until tomorrow," she says, "but the beds need changing and the kitchen can't wait. We've had friends staying and it looks like a bomb's hit it. I'll pay double as it's a Sunday."

Cal's gone for a sleepover with his best friend, anyway, so I say yes and meet Janine on the pavement warming up for a run. She bounces on the spot outside Elise's window and I try to see if Elise is watching—and listening to Janine spitting out her outrage.

"We're horrified, Dee!" she says as soon as she sees me. "Can you believe it? Drugs! In Ebbing! We come here to get away from all that."

I nod but I wonder if she's ever really been horrified. So horrified she couldn't breathe or move or close her eyes? So horrified she wet herself?

The bed takes only ten minutes really but I string it out, plumping pillows and repositioning cushions to up my payment before I move downstairs.

"Hi," I call softly as I open the kitchen door.

Nothing. Janine's husband, Kevin, is hunched over the kitchen table, staring at the screen of his laptop.

"I'll be as quiet as I can," I say to the back of his head, and he doesn't make any sign he's heard. But when I start filling my bucket at the sink, he spins round.

"Oh, hello. It's not Monday, is it? Sorry. Got a bit of a work thing going on."

"No, I'm a day early. Sorry to disturb you—Janine's asked me to do in here." But he's back in his trance.

I glance at his screen. It's an e-mail with the subject line: Payment Now Overdue.

I wipe down surfaces around him, scrubbing at wineglass stains and encrusted food but I keep looking at him. Wondering who he owes money to. If he's even bothered. Like Charlie. He just stares. I don't think he's even reading the e-mail. His eyes look all glassy. Suddenly they snap back to me, catching me looking.

"What?" he says, and I feel myself go red.

"Sorry, nothing. I . . . I was just thinking," I blurt. "About someone who's gone missing." I hadn't meant to say it. It'd just come out.

"Charlie Perry? Yes, I heard." He slams the lid down on the e-mail. "Where do you think he's gone?"

I've got his attention now but I don't know what to do with it.

"Er, I didn't know you knew him."

"Ebbing's a small world."

"Yes, well, I expect he'll be back." I'm just thinking aloud but his eyes are fixed on me. "One of my clients said that most missing people don't go far."

Kevin laughs, a nasty bark. "Sounds like kitchen gossip, Dee. He's probably on a plane somewhere."

"I doubt it," I say, stung by his snarky tone. "I saw his passport earlier."

"Did you?"

I don't respond. I shouldn't have said anything. I go back to shaking crumbs from the toaster into the sink.

Kevin pushes his chair back, scraping the tiles so the hairs on my arms stand up, and he walks out without another word.

TWENTY-FIVE

Elise

ELISE WAS NUMBERING HER notes before bed in case she'd forgotten something when she heard the sirens and Ronnie came knocking.

"Sorry!" she said, all breathless. "I know it's late but I saw your lights were still on. An outbuilding at Pete Diamond's is on fire. The fire engines have just gone down there."

Elise pulled on a jacket and set off in Ronnie's wake. It was a still night and the smell of smoke didn't hit the back of her throat until she turned the corner onto Beacon Lane and saw the flare from the flashing blue lights.

The Diamonds were standing by the gates, the ghostly outline of the word "Scum" spray-painted on the fence visible behind them in the festival floodlights.

"Who did that?" Elise asked Ronnie.

"A well-wisher," she said, and pushed forward through the rubberneckers.

Elise hung back. "What happened?" she asked a local police officer sitting in a squad car.

"Er, we're not sure yet. I think you need to stand back while the emergency services do their job."

"I am the emergency services," she said, and pulled her warrant card out of her pocket.

His eyes widened and she stuffed it straight back in. She'd forgotten. Just for a moment.

"I'm with the Major Crime Team but I'm off duty," she muttered.

"Sorry, ma'am," the officer said. "It's a home gym they've had built in the grounds and it looks like arson. There were rags found and it stinks of solvent down there. There's a lot of bad feeling locally about what happened at the festival."

"Yeah, I've seen the artwork on the fence."

"But we've got a bigger problem. We're looking for the daughter of the owner. She wasn't in her bedroom when the parents checked."

"Who else is here?"

"DS Brennan. She's down at the scene. I'll let her know you're here."

"Inspector King," Pete Diamond shouted across, his voice hoarse, "what the hell is going on here? First they paint obscenities on our fence. Now this."

His wife took his arm, her eyes shining with tears. "It's like a nightmare. Celeste isn't answering her phone."

"Where was she this evening?" Elise said.

"In her room," Pete Diamond said. "She's been spending a lot of time up there—we've hardly seen her since Friday."

"But we couldn't find her when we realized my fitness studio was on fire," Millie Diamond sobbed. "We don't know where she is."

Caro Brennan appeared while they were talking, wiping soot smuts from her face.

"I heard you were here," she said, and pulled Elise aside. "The Diamonds say their daughter is missing."

"Could she have been in the gym?"

"We don't think so but we don't know for sure. It'd taken hold before the alarm was raised but no one can get in until the fire's out. They're almost there."

"Okay. I'll leave you to get on," Elise said. It was the right thing to do. This was someone else's job.

Caro nodded and led the Diamonds back toward the house.

In the twenty minutes Elise had been there, Ebbing had turned out in force to witness the latest show at the Old Vicarage. Rumors were swirling and darkening.

"It's an insurance job," someone behind her said. "Just the kind of thing his sort would pull."

"The daughter's missing," another voice stated. "Maybe she was in there, burned alive."

A woman beside Elise started crying.

"This is outsiders," someone growled. "The police should be looking at those foreigners at the building site. The papers are always talking about violent criminals coming here on the run from their own countries. Who knows who we're harboring . . . ?"

Two police vehicles pulled up and officers started getting out and pulling on high-vis jackets.

"I'm going home," Elise said. "I can't be here and just watch."

Ronnie stayed, her eyes shining in the lights.

ELISE CAME DOWNSTAIRS IN the morning to find Ronnie with her nose pressed against the window, trying to see in.

"Have you been there all night?" Elise said as she unlocked the door.

"Don't be daft. The Diamond girl has turned up. I've heard she was bunked up in one of the static caravans—bit embarrassing for her dad. He's been campaigning to get the site cleared. It spoils the view from his back bedrooms."

"Come in, come in," Elise said. "Tell me what you've heard and who from."

"Just that. And I heard it from the window cleaner just now. He heard it from someone in the launderette."

"So it's thirdhand hearsay."

"Top information, if you don't mind. You could always ring your sergeant and confirm it."

Elise should have told her to get lost but Ronnie's excitement was infectious. And Elise hadn't had anything to get excited about for too long.

Caro picked up and hissed: "Bit busy at the moment. Can it wait?"

"Quick one. Did you find Celeste Diamond?"

"Yes, she walked back in about six a.m. Wouldn't say where she'd been."

"Right. I've heard she was up at the workers' village."

"Really? Well, have you heard we've arrested Ade Harman?"

"No! What for?"

"Hold on. . . ."

Caro put her hand over the phone and Elise could hear a muffled exchange before she came back at full volume.

"For supplying ecstasy at the festival. He woke up over the weekend and I went to talk to him first thing this morning. He was in pieces about how ill Tracy had been. I sat holding his hand while he cried and he just came out with it. He confessed to giving her the drugs."

"Wow! Where did he get them? Who else was involved?"

"We don't know yet. He won't say. You should have seen his dad's face when he walked in with the coffees."

"I bet. Poor old Dave Harman—it was his son, not outsiders, who brought drugs to Ebbing."

"Got to get on. Wish me luck."

Ronnie was leaning so far forward in her chair, she was practically falling on her face.

"Go on, then! Don't make me suffer!"

"You were right. Top information, Ronnie, but there's more."

TWENTY-SIX

Dee

M UM!" CAL SHOUTS. "WHERE'S my sandwiches? Mikey's mum is waiting to take us to camp."

I've got the knife in my hand. I've buttered the bread. But I can't think what goes on it next. I'm trying, trying hard, to keep it together, getting Cal's packed lunch ready for summer camp, making him laugh with a silly joke I'd heard. But I can hear how false I sound.

"Come on, Mum," Cal says, patting me on the back and hopping up and down on the spot. "Hey, how did you hurt your face?"

I put my hand to the tender spot under my cheek. The bruise is coming out and my finger catches on the small scab at the center and I don't want to think about what happened. Can't think about it. "It's nothing. I'm fine." And I stroke my boy's head.

I stuff some ham from the back of the fridge in the bread—it's the last slice and I shred it so it goes further and get the cling film out.

"Here, here you are," I say, and pull him into me so tightly, he struggles out of my arms. "Sorry, Liz," I shout through. "All over the place today. Thanks so much for having him last night—hope he was good?"

"He's always good," Liz shouts back. "I'd have done his lunch but he didn't want peanut butter. Anyway, he can come for a sleepover anytime."

"See you at teatime, Cal."

In all that time, Liam has sat at the table, staring into space. On his own planet.

"Have you been smoking?" I say as I pass and catch a whiff of smoke in his hair.

"No. I was up at the Old Vicarage, wasn't I? The fire . . ."

"Oh, yes."

He's moody about me making him sleep in the spare room.

"Why?" he said, all hurt last night when I came back from my walk. He hates sleeping alone. "I've said I'm sorry for going off on one about you going to London."

"Look, I've got a terrible headache, that's all. I'll only keep you awake."

It felt weird when we met on the landing this morning like we were guests in a hotel, but Liam just said: "How did you sleep through all that noise last night?"

"What noise?"

"The fire engines, Dee. The arson at the Old Vicarage."

"Arson? What are you on about?"

"The gym that the illegals built on the sly has burned to the ground. I looked in on you when I left, told you where I was going, but you were dead to the world. I didn't get back until the early hours."

"Poor Millie."

I FEEL LIKE I'M on automatic pilot this morning when I get to Elise's. She's sitting in the window. As usual. I can't imagine what she finds to look at all day.

"Hi, Dee," she says. "I wasn't sure you'd be working on a bank holiday Monday."

"Oh, I work every day."

Ronnie Durrant suddenly comes out of the kitchen with cups. She always seems to be here.

I get on with the kitchen floor so it can dry while I do the rest of the house and they sit together talking. Elise has left the radio on in the kitchen and I can't hear what they're saying properly. The fire, I think. But then I hear Charlie's name. *Is there news? Elise is a police officer. What's she heard?* I turn the music down a bit. Just enough so they don't notice.

I keep swishing my mop but I'm cleaning the same tile by the door over and over.

"What do you think has happened?" Ronnie says. "If you were in charge, where would you be looking?"

They haven't found him.

"The festival site initially—it was the last known sighting. I'd be fanning out the search, looking at footage from security cameras in the town. He didn't have a car with him—it's still parked on the drive—and you've checked with the local taxi firm. They didn't pick him up, so he must have been on foot. Someone must have seen him. Or maybe taken him somewhere . . ."

I start coughing and they stop talking. I've made myself visible, so I come in and start wiping down the shelving unit. At least I'll be able to hear properly.

"You clean for the Perrys, don't you, Dee?" Ronnie says.

"Er, yes," I say, and carry on.

"What do you think has happened to him?"

"No idea," I snap, and Elise's eyes narrow. "Sorry," I say. "I'm just worried about him. He's had a lot to cope with lately."

"Like what?"

I take a deep breath and try to control the telltale squeak in my voice.

"Well, like that huge house they can't afford. Pauline won't let it alone. Nagging him all the time about the repairs and the cost of keeping his daughter in a home. And then there's Bram. . . ."

"The man at the garden center," Ronnie pipes up. "Always taking his shirt off unnecessarily."

"Look, I never gossip about clients," I carry on. "Ask anyone. But I'm worried about Charlie. All I'm saying is that people are saying Bram calls round to the caravan when Charlie's out and the grass isn't being cut."

Elise looks at me hard. "Does Charlie know?"

"I don't know. But he and Pauline row about sex a lot. She says terrible things to him."

"In front of you?"

"People forget I'm there."

"Right."

And her eyes narrow and I expect she's wondering what I know about her. That she takes antidepressants. That she's got a vibrator in her bedside table drawer.

"How do you think Pauline is coping with his disappearance?"

"Well, she doesn't seem that upset to me. She's always saying she'd be better off without him. Poor man. Everyone says he's a sweetheart except her. I just hope he's okay."

"We all do. . . ."

She's looking too closely at me and I try to stop my hand shaking as I dust.

TWENTY-SEVEN

Elise

WOW!" RONNIE SAID AS soon as Dee left. "It must have been very tense in that caravan."

"I know. There's a lot to unpick," Elise said, already reexamining Pauline's earlier answers. "She said she was a woman with needs. What is this Bram like? Would I have seen him?"

"Probably. You'll definitely have heard him—he drives one of those monster four-by-fours that shake windows. How much do you think Pauline knows about Charlie's past life?"

"No idea but I think I ought to be talking to Caro about this."

Elise picked up the phone and dialed. Engaged. "I'll try again later," she said.

"Well, I'm going to see Pauline," Ronnie announced. "I said I'd take her my old buckets, didn't I? Do you want to come? We could ask her who does her garden."

When they got to the caravan, they were startled by Pauline throwing open the front door of the big house as they walked past. She was carrying a blue washing-up bowl and looked as surprised as they did. She whooshed the contents over a clump of weeds at the side of the steps.

"Just emptying the water from the leaks," she said, slamming the door behind her. An overpoweringly rank smell made Elise put her hand to her nose.

"Sorry. My treatment makes me oversensitive."

"It's been standing for a while," Pauline said. "Why are you back?" She didn't sound friendly anymore.

"I've brought those buckets," Ronnie said. "They're in the car."

"Oh, just leave them on the steps."

"Has there been any word from Charlie?" Elise said as Ronnie wrestled the Mini's boot open. "It's been more than two days. . . ."

"I am well aware, but there's no need for you to concern yourselves in my business any further," Pauline snapped. "I've heard from him."

Both women stared at her.

"Well, that's good. When?" Elise said.

"This morning. He's fine," Pauline said, not looking anyone in the eye.

Elise could see how jangly she was, her mouth pouting and stretching and her hands plucking at her clothes.

"That's great news!" Ronnie said. "You must be so pleased."

"But where did he go?" Elise asked, and Pauline's mouth tightened.

"As I said, it's really not your concern."

"For goodness' sake, Pauline," Ronnie said. "We've been so worried—we've been running round trying to find him."

"I didn't ask you to. Look, it was just a quick call," Pauline muttered. "He didn't say where he was."

"Have you told the police? They'll still be looking for him," Elise said.

"They've never looked for him."

"That's not true," Elise said. "They've rung the hospitals and . . . well, it would be good to call them. Do you want me to do it?"

"No, thank you," Pauline said. "I am quite capable of making my own calls. So I'll say good-bye now."

Elise and Ronnie stood and watched her retreat into the caravan.

"Right," Elise said. "Well, I don't envy Charlie his homecoming. I thought Pauline would be hugely relieved that he's resurfaced. But she clearly isn't."

Nor was Elise if she was honest. She felt completely deflated. She hadn't realized how much she'd been looking forward to probing further. She had no excuse now.

"I'm going to walk back," Elise said. "I need the exercise. It's only a couple of miles."

She should have gone back up the drive to the road and through the little car park next door to get on the public footpath but she could see the shapes of people walking past the back of Tall Trees. All she had to do was push her way through some overgrown shrubs. But she quickly realized she'd need a machete to reach it as she tried treading the branches down. She was getting scratched to bits.

She was admitting defeat and turning back when the hairs on her arms suddenly rose. She turned her head slowly from left to right and closed her eyes to focus. It was a smell. A smell once experienced never forgotten—it lingered in your nostrils, clinging to the tiny hairs, embedding itself in the tissues of your throat, and lodging in your brain. Putrescine and cadaverine. Death.

Elise stumbled forward toward the source, pulling her sleeves down over her hands for protection against the brambles. Following her nose. And almost falling down a gaping cellar hatch. She stopped to steady herself but had to pull her T-shirt up over her nose and mouth when she knelt to look down into the darkness.

It'll be a fox or a badger, she told herself. But it wasn't. He was there, as she'd known he would be. Lying on his side, his face blackened and the air filled with the frantic buzz of blowflies.

TWENTY-EIGHT

Elise

WHEN THE SCENES OF Crime Officers arrived to start collecting evidence, Caro took Elise aside. "What were you doing here, Elise?"

Elise noted she wasn't calling her "boss." She was a civilian here as far as Caro and the team were concerned.

"Look, I tried to ring you earlier to talk about the case but you didn't answer. I just came to see if Charlie had come back, that's all. I was worried."

"He was on my list too," Caro said.

"Don't be defensive—of course he was. But you were busy with Ebbing turning into a crime capital. I've only been asking a few questions around the place because I saw him on Friday."

Elise caught a glimpse of someone in the caravan. Pauline was standing motionless in the window. Watching.

"Look, his wife was in a very strange mood when we got here," she said. "Definitely hostile—and nervous. She said she'd had a call from Charlie this morning, saying he was fine. It didn't ring true when she said it, and, judging by the state of the body, I'd say it was highly unlikely."

"Why would she lie? Was she hiding his death?"

"I don't know. But that's what I'd be asking her about."

"Okay, I'm on it. So did you find out anything else of interest before I speak to her?"

Elise took a deep breath. "Yes, Caro, I did. That's why I rang you. Charlie was born Charles Williams. He took Pauline's name when they moved down here—and they are about to have their house repossessed."

"Right . . ."

"And not necessarily relevant but . . . his daughter from his first marriage was left with life-changing injuries in a botched burglary at Charlie's home twenty years ago. Really nasty case."

Elise was doing so well today. Brain clicking into gear. And Caro scribbled it down, trying not to look too impressed.

"Right, thanks. Have you got the daughter's name?"

It vanished as Caro asked. "Begins with an S—or is it a B? I'll have to look at my notes. Sorry . . ." *Shit. It's in here somewhere.*

"Text me when you've remembered. I'll start looking at his finances—and his real identity."

"Well, actually, I can give you a steer." This was starting to get embarrassing but Caro needed to know everything. "I visited his ex-wife and daughter yesterday. I'll text you the contacts."

"Are you joking? What were you playing at?"

"Nothing. I went round to see Pauline as a concerned neighbor and it sort of developed from there . . . and I was going to tell you when we found him."

"Were you?" There was an angry flush rising above Caro's neckline.

"Look, I'm sorry," Elise said, "but I've only done a bit of legwork. It'll save you the bother. And I've got to do something with my time."

"Anything else?"

"Charlie was nervous about an unexpected visitor at his daughter's residential home a couple of weeks ago. The visitor said he'd come back but never showed up." Oh, and there was something about a shirt she needed to say. "Oh, yes, there's gossip that Pauline is having an affair with a man who takes his shirt off a lot."

Caro tried not to laugh but failed. "Bloody hell," she snorted, "it's a whole season of a soap opera. Look, we're jumping through all the hoops at the moment, gathering evidence at the scene, but the Senior Investigating Officer isn't ruling out accidental death—that the old boy stumbled into the cellar. You said you almost did and it must have been pitch-black when he got back after the festival. The hatch doors have rotted away completely—they should have been boarded over—and he's got a nasty head injury."

"Really? Who is the SIO?"

Caro looked at her feet. Her tell.

"Who?"

"Look, don't go off on one but it's Hugh. He's just finished his secondment with City of London and come back to Major Crime. I thought maybe you'd heard."

"No." Elise looked round, heart thumping. "Is he here?"

"No, he's on his way from HQ."

A car pulled into the drive and Elise felt her knees go.

Caro steadied her, cupping her elbow. "Hey! It's only the pathologist. We've got Aoife Mortimer, thank God. I've got to go and talk to the widow Perry. Will you be okay?"

Elise nodded. And then caught her sergeant's arm as she turned away. "You probably shouldn't tell Hugh that I got this info. He might not like it."

Caro nodded back. "Got it. I'll make sure he gets all the details for himself when we talk to Mrs. Perry. I'll give you a call after."

She knew Caro meant she should go but she couldn't face the walk now. She loathed being dependent on anyone but she rang Ronnie. "Can you come and get me?"

"I told you it was too far. Where are you?"

"I'm still at Pauline's."

"On my way."

Elise sat on the grass by the entrance to the drive and waited. Hugh's accident scenario played in her head even as the questions crowded in: How did Charlie get home? It was more than two miles from the festival site. He was completely wasted yet he managed to get through the security fence and right round the back to the cellar. *It's a nightmare to get to.* And she looked at her arms, scored red by the vicious suckers. *I wonder if there's another way in from the rear.*

When Ronnie skidded up, Elise opened the door without speaking and practically fell into her seat.

"Is everything all right?" Ronnie said.

"Not exactly. I've found Charlie."

Ronnie stalled the car, jerking them both forward in their seats.

"You're joking? What? After I left? Where?"

"In the cellar under the house. He's dead, I'm afraid."

There was silence.

"Ronnie?"

"Poor Charlie," she said, his name choking her. "Who did that to him?"

"We don't know that anyone did it. There were no doors on the outside hatch and the team is keeping an open mind. They think it might be an accident. . . ."

"But you don't."

"No. I don't."

TWENTY-NINE

Dee

THEY'RE SAYING CHARLIE'S DEATH is unexplained—the police are, anyway. It's all over the local radio. But they're calling it murder in every shop. Chewing over their theories like they know something.

"I heard his head was bashed in," someone says in the supermarket, and it stops me in my tracks.

Bashed in? Really? I edge closer to hear.

"No!" another woman says. "I was told he was found in the coal cellar."

And I stare at her. *The coal cellar?* And I'm trying to picture what could have happened to him.

"I wonder how Pauline's taking it," the first woman says.

"Well, she won't be lonely for long, will she? I expect someone will be along to comfort her. Bram, I hear. He's a good-looking lad. . . ."

I'm so busy listening that Karen the hairdresser makes me jump.

"Dee! Isn't it terrible! Who would do that to Charlie?" she says.

"I don't know any more than you." I turn away and look for floor wax. "Ah, this is it. Sorry. I'm due at the Neptune."

There's a knot of people outside and I don't recognize some of them. Must be weekenders or tourists. I bet they've never even met Charlie but they're lining up to give their expert opinion to a woman journalist videoing them with her phone. I expect she was at the Old Vicarage with the other press on Saturday, asking people about the concert and the drugs. The Cooks spoke to them about their little girl and gave them photos of her looking young and innocent. Like the drugs were forced on her.

But the media has moved on to the next tragedy, like they do.

"Charlie was a lovely old boy," Brian, who owns the Golden Plaice chip shop, is telling the reporter. She's got her sunglasses perched on her head and holds her mobile a little closer to his face. "He'd do anyone a good turn. And he had some great stories about his life. He was well-connected, you know?"

"Really? Anyone I'd have heard of?" I hear the reporter ask as I walk off to the Neptune.

Doll is standing behind the bar with her back to me when I let myself in. "Hello," I say. "It's really humid out there. Feels like we might get some rain." And I go through the back to get started.

Doll doesn't say anything. It must be awful, with everyone knowing that your son was responsible for nearly killing Tracy Cook.

I do the sinks and then make her a coffee and put it on the counter behind her. Keeping everything normal.

"I thought you might need this," I say quietly.

She turns round and looks at me. "This is a terrible mess, isn't it?" she says.

"Don't worry. I'll do in here next," I say.

"No, Dee," she says. "I'm not talking about the bar."

She looks as though she got ready in the dark this morning. Her hair hasn't been brushed at the back and she's missing an earring. But I can't take my eyes off her mouth. Normally Doll outlines it in pencil, then fills it in with lippie—rose for summer, plum for winter—but today she hasn't bothered. She looks like a stranger.

"What happened at the festival. That terrible mess," the naked mouth says. "We've got to sort it out."

"We?"

"You must know as well as me, this drugs thing wasn't down to Ade. He hasn't got two brain cells to rub together—or money to buy pills. He has to borrow bus fare. Someone must have given them to him. Who would do that? Your Liam might know?"

"Liam? What are you talking about?"

"He used to take them, didn't he? Maybe he still does? He's always boasting about his wild days," she sneers.

I just stare at her. *Bloody Liam and his big mouth.* "Of course, it's nothing to do with him. That's just talk—you know what Liam's like. Gets a bit carried away with his stories. Anyway, Ade has confessed."

Doll's mouth hardens into a line and her lips disappear completely.

"My son didn't know what he was saying—he was in a state of shock and should never have been interviewed," she snaps. "He's made a new statement."

"What's he said?" I clutch my hands together to stop them from trembling.

"That he was still affected by the ecstasy. And that he can't remember what happened. Now we'll see where the police look next, shall we? Be in no doubt, Dee, the truth will out. And in the meantime I'd like you to go—and leave your keys, please."

"But, Doll—"

"On your way! And tell your husband I know he's in it up to his neck."

I sit in the car outside the pub looking at my phone. I should ring Liam and warn him but I don't want to talk to him. The look on his face when he heard the radio this morning.

"They've found Charlie," he whispered.

"Yes, but remember what we said? This is nothing to do with us. Let's just get on with our lives. . . ."

And I thought we could. But now I'm not sure Doll is going to let us.

THIRTY

Elise

CARO BRENNAN WAS AT the postmortem in Southfold, and for the first time in days, Elise didn't want to be in her shoes. Or the white wellington boots she'd be slipping over them.

There wasn't much Elise disliked about the job, but a trip to the mortuary was top of the list. It could make her gag just thinking about it.

Caro loved all that. "It can be beautiful to watch a pathologist at work," she'd said once—she'd had a few drinks, to be fair. "Stripping back the layers to find the tiniest piece of evidence. Solving the puzzle."

Elise preferred to read the report afterward. Nice dry words laying it all out in tabulated form. And scent free.

RONNIE CALLED OVER THE courtyard wall when she heard Elise at the bin. "Come round to me—Ted's gone to a railway reunion. He needs to be with his own kind for a bit. He's gone very quiet again."

Ronnie had a wall chart in her kitchen, stuck up over her

bucket-list pictures. Instead of white sand and palm trees, she'd printed out a street map of Ebbing and plastered it with bits of paper bearing people's names. And there were pins with colored wool wound round them to show possible links.

"I see you've been busy," Elise said, following the wool trails with her finger.

"It's flip chart paper I got in Poundland and knitting remnants from the charity shop," Ronnie said proudly. "I used Blu Tack so Ted didn't have a go about it marking his walls. I put the pins in after he left for his saddos' reunion."

Elise's own version of the story so far fitted on two A4 pages folded into her notebook, but Ronnie was never going to give up the chance of a full-on incident room chart.

"Now, what do we know?" she said, and Elise wondered for a second if she'd got a pointer.

"Well—"

"I thought I'd collate the investigation so far and current lines of inquiry. I'll be good at that."

"And you've got the stationery," Elise muttered. *It's harmless and it'll keep her occupied.*

"So," Ronnie said, and produced one of Ted's garden canes and tapped the chart, "shall we start with Charlie on Friday night?"

CARO RANG ELISE'S MOBILE as soon as the PM finished. "I'm on my way over to Ebbing. Can I call in? This is a tricky one."

"I've got to go back to mine," Elise told Ronnie—she definitely didn't want Caro to see Ronnie's charts.

"Can we ask if I can sit in?" her neighbor said as she opened her front door.

Elise didn't have time to ask the question. Caro was sharing the headlines as she walked in.

"We're waiting on Aoife's full report but this wasn't an accident. He's got a head injury but it wasn't caused by a fall."

She suddenly noticed Ronnie and stopped.

"It's fine, Caro. Ronnie is like the grave," Elise said, and looked at her friend, who nodded furiously and pretended to zip her mouth closed.

Caro looked doubtful but Elise pushed on. "He was murdered, then?"

"We don't know. Aoife says the head injury would probably have killed him but it isn't clear yet if it was sustained before he died."

"Really? So what's the cause of death, then?"

"The certificate says, 'Cardiac arrhythmia, unspecified due to coronary artery atherosclerosis.'"

"Right . . . so she's saying that someone may have bashed him over the head after he had a fatal heart attack?"

"She's sending the brain to the neuropathology unit for further tests. What we do know is that the body was moved—there's hypostasis to show he was on his side for some time before being moved."

"So at least one person was involved?"

"Yes . . . 'Unexplained' is as far as the boss will go in the press release. But something horrible happened in that cellar whichever way you look at it."

" 'Something wicked this way comes,' " Ronnie breathed.

"What?" Caro said.

"It's Agatha Christie—*By the Pricking of My Thumbs*. The one in the old folks' home."

"Anyway," Caro said, "when you've finished your book club meeting . . . Charlie's clothes are being examined for DNA and fibers to find who'd had contact with him, and the boss . . ." She had the grace to look embarrassed. "Sorry, Elise, but Hugh is the boss on this one. He's meeting me at the Perry caravan in half an hour— Oh, God, twenty minutes. I've got to get a wiggle on."

"Well, good luck," Elise said. "Pauline's a piece of work. She can turn the charm on and off like a light switch."

"Oh, I know. She was all over Hugh yesterday—'course she was. The boyish good looks, the dark brown voice. Her false eyelashes almost fluttered off. Do you think she sleeps in them?"

Elise could hear that voice in her ear. Smell the sweet musk of his sweat as they lay tangled up in the duvet. *Stop!* she screamed at herself. *Not going there.*

"She might not be so friendly now," she snapped. "The PM results might stop the fluttering. Have you asked her about Charlie's previous identity—and the boyfriend?"

"Mellors," Ronnie added.

"I thought you said his name was Bram?" Caro said.

"It is," Elise said. "Ronnie is referencing *Lady Chatterley's Lover*—she used to be a librarian. She can't help herself. . . ."

"Sorry," Ronnie muttered. "I'll shut up."

"So Bram O'Dowd. Yes. We asked if he was with her on Friday night and she denied it but forensics is on it and the boss has gone to talk to Mr. O'Dowd. Oh, and Pauline says Charlie decided to use her name when he retired—to start down here without 'any baggage,' apparently."

"What baggage? And we need to push them on the relationship." Elise caught herself slipping into senior officer mode. She looked to see if Caro had clocked it but she was reading something on her phone.

The trouble was, she was there, walking up to the door, watching for the initial reaction on the doorstep, listening to the voice, spotting the lies, the guilt. But it was wasted adrenaline. Her place was on the sidelines. A spectator with the rest of them.

"What about the visitor at the residential home? Any joy?"

"The receptionist has given us a pretty ropey description—tallish, thinnish, might have had dark hair—but insists he didn't come back."

"It's worth having a look at the security cameras at the entrance to the home. Birdie got very few visitors."

"Yes, yes, but I need to get going," Caro said. "Actually," she interrupted herself, "another thing on my list is that we need you to make a statement about finding the body. Should have done that yesterday, but with you being the Job, I forgot. Can you come into Southfold this afternoon? I can send a car."

"I'll take you," Ronnie jumped in. "What time?"

THIRTY-ONE

Kevin

KEVIN SCOTT-PENNINGTON WAS PACKING the BMW when Janine came running out.

"You won't believe what I've just heard!" she announced. "They've found a body. The police have found a body. In Ebbing! It's just been on the local radio."

Kevin carried on jamming slimy flip-flops into every crevice of the boot.

"Kevin! Did you hear me? God, do you think it's connected with that poor girl nearly dying at the festival?"

"What?"

"They haven't said who it is but I'm going up to the supermarket now. They'll know in there."

"Janine!"

"What? I'm just taking an interest. I want to buy some bottles of water for the journey anyway. Have you nearly finished?"

"Almost. We don't need water. We need to get on the road."

But she power walked off, arms pumping with excitement. He sat on the pavement and put his head against the hot black metal of the car.

"Are you all right?" a voice asked, jolting him back.

"Er, yes, just checking a scratch I saw earlier." He squinted into the sun.

"Oh," Saul said.

There was nothing else he could say. Kevin Scott-Pennington was clearly not looking at a scratch. His face had been resting on the passenger door.

"So how are things?" Kevin said wearily.

"Er, okay, thanks. Toby's a bit stressed—he's not sleeping well but it's been so hot, hasn't it? And super busy in the restaurant. Did you enjoy your meal the other night?"

"Yeah, excellent, thanks. And it looked like business is good."

"That's what I keep telling Toby but . . . Never mind that—have you heard about the body?"

Kevin put his hand up to shield his eyes. "Yes, Janine just told me," he said. "She's gone scurrying off to find out who it is. Awful thing to happen."

"Oh, everyone knows who it is," Saul said, his strangely angular face lighting up with the knowledge. "It's Charlie Perry. He went missing on Friday night. Did you ever meet him? Lovely old bloke with a nightmare wife and a big house."

"Er, I'm not sure. Might have done but we don't really mix with the locals much—we're only here at weekends usually and then we often have visitors staying."

"He used to come into the restaurant bar a lot at one time. But he hasn't been in for a while."

"Right."

"Yes, well . . . when are you off?"

"Imminently," Kevin said, standing and slamming the boot shut. "We should've been back in London yesterday but there were things I had to sort out."

"THAT KEVIN SCOTT-PENNINGTON IS weird," Saul said as he unpacked the shopping. "I think he was kissing his car. Mechanophilia, it's called. I googled it on the way home. What are you doing?"

Toby slammed his phone down on the table. "Nothing. Just looking up an e-mail from the meat supplier."

"Why? Is there a problem?"

"No. Everything's absolutely fine. Stop fussing!"

But it obviously wasn't. Toby's face looked waxy and there was a burst blood vessel in his right eye.

"Did you not sleep?" Saul said. "I heard you walking about downstairs in the early hours again. You look terrible."

"Thanks. That's made me feel so much better. I'm a bit tired, that's all. Lots going on."

"Look, I've got everything under control. I'm already packed. I've bought you a new shirt—did I show you? And Barry is all sorted for running the restaurant—he's arriving Friday. He's looking forward to his fortnight by the sea and I'm so excited— Oh, I should have told Kevin about our trip to LA. I told him about Charlie Perry, though."

Toby whirled round and almost fell off his seat.

"What? What did you tell him?"

"Look out." Saul steadied the back of the chair. "That he's the body they found."

Toby's face went blank. "Right," he said. "Awful thing to happen."

"That's exactly what Kevin said."

THIRTY-TWO

Elise

E LISE WAS REHEARSING WHAT she needed to say in her statement about finding Charlie when the text reminder of her appointment with the oncology consultant pinged on her phone.

She pushed her lunch away and sat staring at the tabletop.

A ring at the door made her jump up. *Ronnie's early,* she thought, grateful for the distraction. "Finally found my bell, then?" She smiled as she opened the door.

But it was a woman with sunglasses on her head.

"Er, hello," Elise said. "Can I help you?"

"Oh, I hope so." She smiled warmly. "I'm not having much luck."

"Right. So . . . ?"

"I'm Kiki Nunn—from the Sussex Today website."

"Ah . . . not sure I have anything to say to a reporter."

"But, Ms. King"—and Elise noted she hadn't mentioned her rank. *Does she know I'm a cop?*—"I'm told you might have known Mr. Perry. And I understand you're a police officer. . . ."

Right.

"I am but I'm on sick leave."

"Yes, I heard that. Sorry, but I promise not to take more than five minutes of your time. There's a lot of mad gossip and speculation circulating and I just want to tell the readers a few facts."

"What sort of speculation?"

"That Mr. Perry was beaten to death. And 'immigrants'"—she raked the air with quote marks—"are responsible. Horrible stuff."

"Why are people saying that? Do they have any evidence?"

"'Course not. People just do. This sort of garbage always fills an information void. You only have to look at social media—people with an ax to grind or a conspiracy theory just stick it out there often enough, and suddenly it's true. That's why I'm trying to put some of it to bed. I'd love some real info to put up on the website."

It made sense but Elise hesitated.

"I don't know anything about Sussex Today," she said, fumbling with her phone to look it up.

When the site popped up, Ebbing was all over it. There was a photo of Tracy Cook and another of her weeping mother with the headline "Teen Comes Out of Coma After Festival Ecstasy OD." A small picture of fire engines at the Old Vicarage and a big blurry one of Charlie Perry, under "Pensioner Dead in Cellar." But no celeb-shaming photos.

"Goodness you've been busy. Has the website been going long?"

"Not really—but I have." Kiki sighed. "I've been a reporter for years but this is my first online job and it's incredibly stressful. I've got a twelve-year-old news editor and he wants me to upload content. Content! That's what they call news now. Sorry. I'm venting," she said with a laugh.

And Elise let her in.

Journalists were known by some of her lot as an unnecessary evil. Elise had never seen it that way, though; her view was that they could help one another and she never said no to help. Most of them were fine, especially the crime reporters she met over and over again. They were mainly blokes—young ones who bounced around a story like Tigger, and old boys—the Eeyores who'd seen and done everything. But she kept boundaries: She didn't go out and get drunk with them like some or go to their houses for Sunday barbecues. It was a working relationship.

"I assume you're talking to the press office?" she said. "They're the official source."

"Yes, but they've been giving out the same line since the body was found. That's no good for rolling news or the rumor mill. And I can't get near DI Ward."

"He'll hold a press conference, I'm sure."

Elise would. Would've already done it. To get the word out, get people remembering where they had last seen Charlie. What they had seen. Instead, they were letting the hate chat and lurid rumors ramp up. And if she didn't say anything, Ms. Nunn would probably knock next door and get Ronnie. . . .

"All right, tell me what you know and I'll try to guide you in the right direction," she said, and pointed to the other chair.

Kiki smiled again and sat. "Thanks."

"Okay. And on the condition that everything is off the record. You can't quote me."

"'Course not."

"So you can turn off the recorder on your phone."

Elise watched as Kiki did so and let Kiki tell the story she was writing. Elise interrupted occasionally to put her straight on small details but she seemed to have most of it.

"So Charlie Perry was seen on Friday at the festival? And then near the static caravans where the laborers are living," Kiki added.

"Really? Who said that?"

"A bloke in the Neptune." The reporter consulted her notebook. "He didn't want to give me his name."

"It's the first time I've heard that," Elise said. "Just an observation but the statics are on the Brighton road and Charlie's body was found at his home—in the opposite direction."

"Okay, I'll check it. I've heard a dog led the police to the body."

Elise laughed. "It was me, actually. I was near the footpath at the back of his property and—"

"And?"

"I smelled something."

"God! How awful for you."

"It's not my first time—"

"No, 'course not. Sorry. I was just thinking what I'd feel like if it'd been me. Finding someone I knew."

"Well, I hadn't known him long, really," Elise said. "I'm sure there will be others who knew him much better. I'd met him a couple of times and chatted in the shops. Nice man."

"That's what everyone says. No one has a bad word about him. They've been telling me about all his charity work—and his great stories."

Elise wondered how quickly the press would dig out Charlie's real past.

"It's a funny place, Ebbing, isn't it?" Kiki said as she put her notebook away. "Seems quite quiet at first glance. A bit down-at-heel, really. But it's all going on, isn't it? Drugs, arson, and now the unexplained death. It's like *Midsomer Murders*. . . ."

ELISE RANG CARO AS soon as Kiki left. "I know I'm seeing you later but I've had a reporter here."

"Poor you. Hope you shut the door in his face." Caro belonged to the other school of thought on the media.

"It was a her, actually. Kiki Nunn—do you know her? And no, I let her in because I thought it would be useful to hear what the locals are saying about Charlie."

"Okay. Go on, then?"

"Murdered by Eastern European laborers, apparently . . ."

"Good grief. I'll make a note. Look, I've got to get on, Elise—we're still reviewing all the mobile phone footage from the festival to try to spot Charlie and anyone he spoke to there. There's hours of it. Mostly people off their faces and bashing into one another."

"Okay, but the reporter also said that Charlie was seen late on Friday night up by the workers' village—those tatty old static caravans the builders are using. On the Brighton road."

"Really? Well, why didn't you say that first? That's a new sighting! Who told her that?"

"A bloke in the Neptune who wouldn't give his name. Dave Harman might be able to help."

"Unlikely—the drugs case has gone tits up. His son has withdrawn his statement. He's got a new solicitor who says he wasn't in a fit state to be interviewed."

"Oh, dear."

"He's as guilty as sin but we'll have to start again to build a case. He was helping set up the bars that night and we're reinterviewing the others working with him—one of them is of interest, actually. Liam Eastwood. Do you know him?"

"Eastwood? Sadly, I think he might be married to my cleaning lady. Is he a plumber?"

"That's him."

"Shit! I'm going to end up looking for a new cleaner, aren't I?

Just when I've got used to Dee. Actually, Liam Eastwood's been working for the Perrys. I saw one of his trade boards up at the crime scene."

"Yes, I clocked that too, thank you. But it's the conspiracy to supply MDMA that brought him to our attention."

"Go on."

"His name was on the Brighton boys' radar. A user but he hung around with some of the dealers. We had him in for questioning on day one of the inquiry but he said he hadn't had any contact with his Brighton mates for years. Not since leaving the town. Said he was stupid when he was younger, experimenting. But we're hearing different from people in Ebbing. He's boasted about more recent drug taking in the pub, apparently. We're having a closer look. I'll pass the sighting of Charlie on to the boss. Got to go. See you later."

"Okay, but when are we having a press conference? It's twenty-four hours since the body was found and these rumors are building while we're saying nothing."

"We? Don't worry. The boss is doing one in the next half hour, so it'll be on the local news."

"I'll be watching."

THIRTY-THREE

Elise

THE LIGHT BOUNCED OFF the whiteboard like an aura behind Hugh when he sat behind his desk.

There was a buzz in the room where the press conference was being held when he walked in and the cameras started clicking. It always made Elise smile when that happened to her. Why were they bothering? A hundred shots of police officers taking their seats. Was it just for their bosses watching in the newsrooms? To prove they were working?

It's like those idiots who shout pointless questions at politicians as they walk past, she thought.

"Are you going to resign, Prime Minister?"

"Did you lie to the select committee?"

Just noise.

Hugh cleared his throat like he always did when he was nervous. He looked up at the cameras and she was suddenly looking into his eyes. She prickled with embarrassment for a second.

It was all textbook stuff. Hugh appealed for witnesses to Charlie Perry's last movements—"How and when did Mr. Perry get home? Did anyone give him a lift the night of the festival? Or at any time over the weekend? Or see him walking?"

Kiki Nunn was in the second row of chairs. She had her back to the cameras but Elise recognized the glasses perched like a cat's ears on her head. She waited while the local TV and papers asked their questions, then piped up: "Hi, I'm from Sussex Today. DI Ward, do you know how Charles Perry died? Was he murdered?"

"Er, we are still investigating the exact circumstances of this unexplained death."

"Okay, do you know when he died?"

Hugh looked blank for a moment. *What is going on with you?* Elise said to herself. *You're sharp as a tack normally.*

"Erm, no, not precisely," he stuttered. "Our last confirmed sighting is Friday night at around nine thirty, at the festival, but the deceased's wife said she had a brief phone call from a man she believed was her husband early Monday morning," Hugh got back into his stride. "The caller said he was okay but gave no details of his whereabouts."

"So just a couple of hours before his body was found?" Kiki was like a terrier with a bone but Elise knew she was asking all the right questions.

"As I say"—Hugh tried to wrench the bone off her—"the Home Office pathologist is continuing to work on time of death but it's a complex calculation because of the temperatures we've been experiencing—it was quite hot on Saturday and Sunday—and the circumstances in which we found the body."

"Yes, I imagine it must have been much cooler in the cellar. So Mr. Perry could have died at any time between the last witness seeing him on Friday night and Monday morning?"

"That is why we are appealing for witnesses—as I've said, we have no further sightings after he left the festival at the Old Vicarage."

"What about the witness who said he was up by the workers' village later on Friday night?"

All press heads turned to look at her.

Her twelve-year-old news editor must be pumping the air with his fist.

"We are still in the process of confirming that sighting," Hugh said, but some of the reporters were getting out of their seats.

The hare would be running now—all the laborers would be pounced on by the media before Elise's lot had got their car keys out. They were so fast—and potentially damaging. Like a plague of locusts, Caro said. Stripping whole communities of information. But people talked to the press when they didn't always talk to the police. Sometimes, they just had too much to lose.

I bet some of the laborers don't have visas. They'll prefer to talk anonymously to Kiki. Let's see what she and the pack get.

Elise turned the telly off and sat for a bit, thinking about the last time she'd seen Charlie. His blackened face. And the blowflies. She flicked her laptop on to remind herself of their life cycle with seasonal and ambient temperature variations. It was all there online for the amateur entomologist. First eggs are laid by flies on a corpse, especially on wounds or around openings like eyes, ears, and noses within minutes of death. Then the maggots hatch—within twenty-four to forty-eight hours—and start feeding.

The team had a sixty-hour window from the last sighting alive. So if Charlie had died on Friday night, the pathologist should have found second-stage maggots of about one centimeter in length.

If he died in the twenty-four hours before Elise found him, there should have been no maggots, just eggs.

THIRTY-FOUR

Elise

AT TWO THIRTY, ELISE was standing outside Southfold police station with Ronnie in close attendance.

"Are you sure you want to stay? You'll have to sit in the waiting room. I can get them to drop me back at home."

"No, I'm happy to mingle with the criminals."

Caro came and fetched Elise, walking her down the tiled corridor to the interview suite. Elise breathed it in—the rough-edged disinfectant, the dark hint of meat stewed to shreds in the canteen. It was like opening an Egyptian tomb and smelling the air that had been shut in millennia ago. Another life.

"I see you've brought your new partner." Caro grinned. "It's all getting a bit cozy, isn't it? What does her hubby think? Is it developing into a bizarre ménage à trois?"

"Shut up." Elise punched her arm. "She's been a good friend."

"Right," Caro snapped. *Not like me* unsaid but loud and clear. "Oh, and DI Ward wants to sit in on this," she added, and pushed the interview room door open.

Elise didn't have time to protest—or steel herself. He was walking in behind her.

"Hello, Elise," Hugh said, his voice sending unwanted signals all over her broken body. "How are you?"

"Fine, thanks," she said, and had to clear her throat.

He looked completely unfazed—a bit blank if she was honest—and she was furious that she was the nervous one. She'd fantasized for so long about what she'd say the first time they met at work. She was going to be cool and distant, then be gracious. The bigger person. Instead, she was stuttering and blushing like a fourteen-year-old shoplifter.

She looked at him as he sorted through his papers and wondered if she'd ever really known him. She'd thought she had—thought they'd been completely honest with each other. Elise had told him early on that she didn't want children. That she wanted to focus on her career. And Hugh had gone along with it. He'd loved the job too.

"And we've got nephews and nieces if we want trips to the zoo," he'd said.

They'd moved in together but had never bothered getting married. Hugh had said it was a waste of money. "Can't see the point—we're happy as we are, El." And she'd gone along with it. *We are, aren't we?*

They'd spent their money on nice wine and expensive holidays and their days off going to the gym, watching dark-drama box sets, and following his beloved Crystal Palace FC. A tight couple, not needing other people to make them happy.

And for nine years, everything on her list had been ticked. Until it wasn't.

He'd chosen their favorite restaurant, where the staff knew

them. She'd thought it was a midweek treat. But afterward, as she unpicked it all, she realized he must have hoped she wouldn't have a full-scale row in front of the maître d'. He'd been a bit quiet in the weeks before, blaming his moods on work, so Elise had put up her hair, squeezed into her little black dress, and put on lipstick. She could see herself now. Thinking she looked sexy.

Sitting across from her, Hugh had folded his napkin over his lap and looked back up.

"El," he said, and stopped.

He looked so flustered, she thought he was going to propose and she flushed with unexpected pleasure. She'd told herself so many times that she wasn't bothered. Every time a relative had asked her when she was getting wed. But clearly, she had been.

She leaned forward and smiled into his eyes. "Yes, the answer is yes."

The shock on his face stopped her hand as it reached for his.

"No, wait," he said too loudly, and a man at the next table glanced round. "Look, I need to talk to you about something that has happened to me. Something completely out of the blue."

"What? Is it work?"

"No. No, er . . ."

Hugh had never been indecisive and she felt her skin prickle.

"Come on! My calamari is going cold." And she thought she'd turned the awkwardness into a joke. But he hadn't picked up his fork.

"Elise, I've met someone else."

She sat there, her back rigid and aching from the tension as he spat it out. His apologies, his guilt, his struggle to do the right thing.

"Who is she?" Elise said when he ran out of words.

"You don't know her. I met her running in the park. On my breaks."

She wanted to stand and wail but her legs felt as if they belonged to someone else.

"Why?"

"I don't know. I thought I was happy. That we were happy. But we are all about the job. Maybe I needed something that wasn't."

It was her fault, then. She'd failed him. Afterward, she wasn't able to remember the journey home. They must have taken a taxi but they were suddenly standing on the doorstep, outside their block of luxury flats, and Hugh was saying good-bye.

"I think it's best I go now," he said, like some romantic hero from a black-and-white film.

"Don't try to be noble, Hugh," Elise said. "You are shitting all over me and our life."

He stepped back and stumbled off the step.

"Let's not get nasty, El," he said. "We can do this like grown-ups, can't we?"

"Fuck off," she said, and slammed the door behind her.

In the flat, she put the safety chain on to make her situation secure. Then she smashed his favorite Crystal Palace mug—the one he'd had since he was a boy—and left the shards in the sink.

"I'd have cut the crotch out of all his trousers," Caro had said when Elise finally told her.

She'd waited a month to see if Hugh would have second thoughts but he hadn't. He'd come back to collect his things, silently selecting paperbacks from the bookshelf and wrapping photos in newspaper. Elise had hovered. Not giving any ground. Not letting him think he'd got away with anything.

"Where's my mug?" he asked.

She just looked at him. "Broken, like our relationship," she said.

It was the first time he looked the least bit upset.

She'd kept her grief close, pushing it back when it threatened to break through. Of course she'd dreaded bumping into him, but she'd been careful and they'd been working different cases. And then he'd been seconded to another force for a project. So no more tiptoeing round corners.

She'd thought she was over it, but six months later, when she'd heard he'd got engaged, she'd taken a week off and wept and slept and then started looking for a house to buy by the sea.

"So," Caro said, flashing a "Sorry. What could I do?" look as she turned on the recording equipment and rattled out the official script, "DI King, please could you start by telling us how you knew the victim, Charlie Perry."

It felt so strange being on that side of the table—Elise could hear the questions she'd be asking in her head and had to stop herself from prompting Caro. She kept using police jargon as she tried to make it sound as if she was keeping a professional eye on her neighbor but she knew it was a pathetic tale of a sick woman spying on the folk of Ebbing.

"When did you last see Mr. Perry?" Hugh said quietly, and they looked each other in the eye.

He looked away first and Elise felt she'd taken back a millimeter of control.

"Alive? At the festival on Friday." She glanced at the bullet points she'd made on a piece of paper just in case her brain clouded over. "In the arena at the back of the Old Vicarage. I got there around nine, just before Pete Diamond's acid house set began, and I saw Charlie Perry in the crowd at the front of the stage."

"Are you sure it was him?" Hugh asked his notebook.

"Yes. I'd talked to him a few times in the local shops and he called at my house a couple of weeks ago. He looked like he'd been drinking heavily on Friday night—he was flailing around on the dance floor. And I thought he looked distressed but it was hard to tell under those lights. He appeared to be shouting. Then he disappeared from sight. I didn't see him again until I found his body yesterday."

"Right, talk us through that, please," Caro said. "For the tape."

Hugh asked a few more questions but nothing Elise would have bothered with.

"How are you getting on with Mrs. Perry?" She couldn't help herself.

He half smiled to himself and it tore a hole in her heart. She'd loved that secret smile—and the shared joke or thought that prompted it.

"Interesting woman," he said. "Do you think she made up the phone call?"

"It'll be easy to check, won't it, on her mobile?" *Well, it would.*

"It would but she can't find it."

"No way. How convenient. Still, you can get her phone records."

"Yes, we're doing that now, thanks." And the smile faded.

"Have you got Charlie Perry's phone? Was there DNA on his body?"

"I think you can leave that with us."

Hugh stood and went to shake her hand—it was muscle memory from the hundreds of witness interviews he'd done—and his arm froze midpoint and dropped awkwardly by his side.

"Thanks for that, Elise," he said, pretending to tidy his papers. "It's been really helpful. Our good luck to have a senior murder detective on the scene. Have you got transport home?"

And she wondered for a moment if he was offering to drive her. *Of course he isn't,* she snapped at herself. *He's conducting a murder investigation, not running round after his ex-girlfriend.*

"Yes, all sorted, thanks."

As he left, he turned as if he'd forgotten something. "It's been good to see you," he said, blinking with the effort.

"And you, Hugh," she said. It was the first time she'd used his name since she'd walked in and it sat in her throat.

"Hope to see you back at work soon," he said, and hurried out of the door.

"I'm sorry, Elise," Caro said as she walked her out. "He insisted."

"Did he?"

And as she walked off, she found herself smiling.

"What are you so cheerful about?" Ronnie said as she fell in step.

"Nothing." Elise grinned. "Can I ask a huge favor? Do you mind driving me to HQ to collect my car? No problem if you've got other stuff on."

"What stuff? I'm having a great time. I've been talking to a woman who's been burgled for the third time. Emptied her freezer this time."

"Right. Well, shall we get going? I shouldn't have left it for so long."

"Okay. Are you sure you're ready?"

"Yep, thanks. I need to get back in the driving seat."

THIRTY-FIVE

Dee

IT STILL STINKS OF smoke in Millie Diamond's garden—like a hundred bonfires—and the atmosphere is almost as poisonous in the house. Her stepdaughter, Celeste, is coming out of her room only to get food, according to Millie.

"Still, at least she isn't up at the statics, shagging the workforce. Pete can't even look at her at the moment. Did you hear, it was the father of the girl who overdosed who set fire to my gym? They arrested him last night. Apparently he said he hadn't meant to burn it down. He just wanted to scare us. God I hate it here . . . living with these lowlifes. . . ."

She must know the "lowlifes" hate her and her husband even more.

"We're talking seriously about putting the house on the market and moving back to London," Millie carries on, but I don't react.

I need to tune her out and focus on my stuff. On what's coming next.

The thing is, I know the only way to avoid trouble is to stay out of sight. And clear up any messes quickly. And I'm trying. Shutting

Liam up about Charlie. Nudging the police toward Pauline and Bram.

But Liam just keeps making new problems for me to deal with. Dragging us back into the spotlight every time I think we're safe.

We had another row this morning, over Doll sacking me.

"What a bitch," Liam said. "I'll have a word with Dave. Get him to set his wife straight."

"Oh, great idea, Liam! This is all your fault—sounding off about your druggy past! She thinks you were responsible. What were you thinking? Leave them alone or you'll make it worse. Just keep your head down."

I'm on my knees polishing the floors at the Old Vicarage like a penitent on chapel posters when my phone rings. It's on silent—Millie says it's unprofessional to take calls at work—but there have been too many buzzes to ignore it anymore. I rummage it out of my pocket and sit back on my heels.

"Mrs. Eastwood? I'm with your husband at the police station. I've been appointed his lawyer and I've been trying to reach you for more than an hour to tell you he has been arrested."

My lips stick to my teeth as I try to speak.

"But he didn't see him. . . ."

"Sorry? Mr. Eastwood has already admitted seeing Adrian Harman at the festival—that's not at issue. He is being questioned in relation to supplying a Category A drug."

Doll must have phoned them about Liam as soon as I left the pub. "But it was Ade," I say. "Liam hasn't touched drugs for years. Not since Cal was born." But I find my fingers crossing on their own.

The solicitor isn't listening. "I'm trying to organize bail but you should know that the police are getting a warrant to search your house for evidence."

I sat heavily on the floor. "Evidence?"

"For possession of MDMA, Mrs. Eastwood. As I just explained."

"Sorry, yes."

My mind is racing to catch up with what I'm being told. I was prepared for a different story. Charlie's story. I knew what I was going to say. But I've got the wrong lines ready.

"I understand this must be very difficult for you. Your husband will call you as soon as he can. I've got to get back."

And I'm alone in Millie's hall again.

What has Liam left in the house? He's stupid enough to have hidden something. I grab my handbag as I run to the front door.

"Have you finished already?" Millie shouts from the kitchen.

"Sorry. Got an emergency at home. I'll make up my hours next time."

I drive like a maniac, speeding through town, the information banging its fists on my brain. I screech up outside the house. There's a police car already parked and faces at the windows opposite. I run up the path—I want to get inside first—but the officers are right behind me.

"Hello, Mrs. Eastwood," one of them says. "We need to come in. We have a warrant."

LATER, I HEAR SIRENS as I'm sitting on the front step. And I startle—then remember the police are already here inside, going through Cal's Minecraft collection at the moment. The wail fades away. Someone else in trouble. I can hear the officers in the bedroom above me.

I'd like to bundle Cal in the car and leave. And in my head, I'm going to. But I can't. People will notice. Ask questions. And I can't have that.

"Stay and face things," my social worker used to say each time they brought me back to my foster home in Wales. "You're only making things worse by running away."

So I stay and watch the washing flapping in the breeze until the police officers nearly knock me off the step as they leave.

"We're done here," one calls over her shoulder. *They can't have found anything.* And they're gone.

I get up and go into my house, following their trail. They've made an attempt to put things back but I can see they've been everywhere. I close cupboard doors and push chairs back into place. Then walk slowly upstairs and stop at our bedroom door. The bed's been stripped, so I make it again, folding the duvet to air the bottom sheet and plumping up the pillows as if everything's normal.

I suddenly feel so tired, I sit where I am, on the carpet, and try to make sense of the last few weeks. How my world has fallen apart since my brother died. I'd managed to keep ahead of the past for so long but it's catching up, nipping at my heels, tearing at my skin, exposing me.

I learned to tell lies as a child—I had to to survive—but I'm getting too old to be doing it now. I'm suffocating in them.

I told Doll there was no way Liam could be involved but I know he probably was.

He did some drugs when he was younger. Well, quite a lot, but he never touched any of the nasty stuff. I'd have known. I'd had practice with Mum.

I was living in Brighton by the time we met. I'd been in foster care in Wales until I was seventeen and I couldn't wait to leave but I didn't want to go back to London. I'd always wanted to come back to Ebbing. It was such a brilliant place—I was only little but we were outside all the time. Out of Mum's hair.

We were outside all the time in London too, but there was

trouble round every corner. Street kids don't play nice. They're always out for what they can get. What they can get you to do. I was too young to matter to them but Phil was older. More visible.

But Ebbing is small and I thought someone might remember Mum. Might imagine I was like her. "The apple doesn't fall far from the tree," my foster mum used to say. So I went to Brighton, where I could be someone else but still feed seagulls. Liam thinks I'm mad—he hates them. Says they're criminals with wings.

He sat next to me on a bus and smiled at me and said sorry for the plaster dust coming off him in clouds. Got me talking, found out which pub I worked in, made me laugh. Made me give him my phone number.

I tried to ignore him but Liam didn't give up. Then he told me he loved me one night as he walked me home to my little flat. And I cried. Proper crying for the first time in years. The thing is, I hadn't realized that I'd needed to hear that from someone. I was nineteen and alone. I'd forgotten what it was like to be wanted. Liam wanted to be my family and I was so tempted. But I made him promise there'd be no more getting high with his mates. And I trusted him.

I loved looking after him in our little flat high above the seafront—cooking vegetables in my only saucepan to go with the shop pies and washing his T-shirts in the sink, like a proper wifey. I knew he struggled with moving on from being one of the lads some days but Cal was the turning point. Liam's face when I told him I was pregnant and then when he held his son for the first time. I'll never forget it. You could see the change in him instantly.

But nothing is forever, is it?

"It was only a bit of weed, Dee," he said when I smelled it on him. "I just needed something to make me feel better with the baby waking every five minutes."

I put him on the sofa so he could get some sleep at night and sniffed the air around him like a police dog every time he came home. But the mania to keep him on the straight and narrow exhausted me. I decided to let him be.

Until the night he fell asleep on the sofa with the baby on his knee and Cal rolled himself over. I lurched forward and caught our son—and the smell of Liam's last joint on the baby's hair. That was the finish of it.

"I'll never do it again, Dee." Liam wept as I packed. "Please don't leave me."

"Don't put this on me! You're the one putting our child's life at risk."

He went down on his knees and begged me. And I remembered one of the dads doing the same with my mum but she'd gone anyway. She'd always left, dragging us with her. I sat and wept. I didn't want to be her. I didn't want Cal to be me.

"I will never let you down again, Dee," Liam whispered.

And I agreed I'd stay if we could move away.

We found a house to rent in Ebbing. I suppose it was where I'd always been heading: like a homing pigeon circling back to a place where I'd felt safe—happy, even.

I GO BACK DOWNSTAIRS and start putting washing into the machine. One of my bras has got caught round Liam's shorts, and when I finally pull them apart, a crumpled paper comes out of a pocket. *Bloody tissues—I tell him every day to empty his pockets.* It's a serviette from McDonald's. *When did you go there?* I think. There's something written on it—a number that has smudged on the thin paper. And a name.

THIRTY-SIX

Dee

CAL IS DELIVERED HOME an hour after the police leave. Mikey's mum, Liz, can't meet my eye and I wonder if she's heard about Liam being arrested. But she doesn't say anything.

"Here he is," she says. "He's been good as gold. We're always happy to have him. Anytime. You know that, Dee."

I give Cal a drink of juice when we get indoors. "Goodness, you look hot!" I say as I pull him close. "What have you been up to?"

"Football. It was great, Mum. Mikey's got a proper goal in the garden."

"Brilliant! Why don't you go and have a quick wash and I'll make lunch."

He disappears upstairs and suddenly shouts: "Mum! Why is my stuff all over the floor?"

I'd forgotten about his room. I run up. "Sorry, love. I lost something and had to turn the place upside down to find it. I was going to tidy up before you got home." I help him sort out his toys, sitting on the floor beside him.

"Where's Dad?" he asks, his voice muffled as he leans his face against his bent knee. And I wonder if Liz has said something.

"Work, lovey. He'll be back soon. Perhaps he'll have a kick about with you at the park. Did you have a good time in Brighton with him the other day?"

"It was all right. Bit boring, really. We had a McDonald's, though." And he glances sideways at me. He knows my views on Big Macs.

"Well, the odd one can't hurt. Did you see anyone you knew?"

"Only one of Dad's friends. He just had a coffee."

"Oh, that was nice," I say quietly, making a tower of the Legos. "Pass me some yellow bricks, will you? Who was that, then?"

"Spike. He was nice. He had green hair and amazing tattoos, Mum. There was one of a dragon flying up his arm."

Spike. I clench my fists to stop myself from shouting.

"Wow! And what did Spike have to say?"

"Boring stuff about money. Oh!" And his seven-year-old face crumples.

"What?"

"It was supposed to be a secret. Dad said he wanted to surprise you. Will he be cross?"

"No, lovey. You know I don't like surprises, anyway."

LIAM LOOKS DONE IN when he finally comes home from the police station and sits at the table.

"They've released me while they continue their inquiries," he says. "Did they make much mess?"

"What do you think?"

"I'm really sorry, Dee."

"Never mind that. They'll be back."

"I haven't done anything."

"Oh, shut up. I don't want to hear any more of your crap."

His head goes down again.

"Look, this isn't my fault," he mutters. "Someone wanted to teach Pete Big Bollocks a lesson and decided to plant drugs on him so he'd be arrested and the festival canceled."

"Are you joking? Did you tell the police that?"

"'Course not. I'm not stupid."

"No, that's right. You're really smart. Getting involved in a criminal scheme that could put you in prison was a brilliant idea."

"It wasn't my idea," he says. *The big boys made me do it,* rings in my head.

"But you were part of it."

"No, not really. I just mentioned someone who might be able to help. That's all. I swear. I heard they wanted to buy a hundred ecstasy tablets and hide them in Diamond's jacket or something. But it all went wrong."

"No shit. The girl was in a coma for nearly forty-eight hours, for God's sake."

"That idiot Ade must have nicked some and given them to her, showing off. No one was supposed to take them—the police were meant to find the drugs and close the festival down."

"You seem to know a lot for someone who wasn't really involved."

Liam gets up and pulls a packet of biscuits out of the cupboard.

"Liam!"

"I'm starving. Look, they talked about it a bit in the pub, that's all. When it was in the planning stages."

"Why didn't you talk them out of it, then?"

"I tried. . . ." And he crams a pink wafer in his mouth. "Look, don't blame me. This is all Ade's fault."

"Will they trace the drugs back to you?" I whisper.

"Me? No. I told you—I just gave them a name."

"Spike's name. You went to see him, didn't you? And took our son." I forget to whisper and the name echoes round the room.

Cal put his head round the door. "Sorry, Dad. I forgot it was a secret."

"Not to worry, mate. Why don't you get back to your game? We'll be in in a minute."

I sit and watch him. Thinking, thinking. *The police won't go away now, will they? They'll push and push until something gives.*

"You swore you'd stay away from him, Liam." I force myself to speak quietly so Cal can't hear but the strain hurts my throat. "He's toxic, for Christ's sake."

"I was only trying to help Dave," he says even quieter than me so I have to lean forward. He looks up at me. "Okay, I can see it was stupid now but I was desperate, Dee. I haven't had a decent job for weeks and Dave was promising me work. I just wanted to get him onside."

"Desperate? We'll both be bloody desperate now," I hiss at him. "People will find out you've been nicked—it's a small town—and they won't wait to see if your name's cleared. Who's going to employ you—or me—now?"

Liam comes and puts his arm round me. "It'll be all right. You'll see."

"Of course it won't." I shove him away, harder than I mean to, and he bangs into the doorframe. "But I've already lost one job, remember?" I say through gritted teeth as he rubs his elbow. "Doll fired me yesterday—and dobbed you in with the police—so you can kiss good-bye your work at the pub. We'll have to move."

"Look, love, I know you're angry but this is going to be okay. Dave owes me big-time now, so let's not panic. And I'm talking to my solicitor again in the morning. She'll get it sorted."

I go to the fridge and pull out a stray cold beer.

"Can I have one?" he says.

I walk away, back into the sitting room. I can't bear to speak to him.

THIRTY-SEVEN

Elise

ANXIETY WAS GNAWING AT her brain and Ronnie's driving wasn't helping.

"The lights are changing," Elise shrieked as they sped through on amber.

"God, you sound like Ted," Ronnie laughed. "We'll be there in a mo."

But in one piece? And without a conviction? I'll drive myself next time.

Ronnie fidgeted beside her in the waiting room, where couples sat, heads together, whispering, their fear echoing off the walls.

"Oh, I meant to say Karen's doing a cut and highlights half price at the moment," Ronnie chirped up.

Elise ran her fingers over her still-unfamiliar scalp. She'd gone to Karen's Hair and Beauty salon to get her post-chemo wisps shaved in May. Karen had talked about wigs, getting out a well-thumbed catalog of synthetic styles, but Elise had decided she wasn't going down that route.

"I don't want to look like my mum," she'd tried to joke. "I'll stick to scarves and hats until it grows back."

Karen had clearly shared the conversation, no doubt with a "Bless her!" thrown in, and the sympathetic smiles in the High Street had started. Elise hadn't been back since.

"I don't need a haircut." Elise tried to laugh. "Look at it!"

"It's growing," Ronnie said.

It was but it was coming back a different color. Gray, thick, and coarse instead of dirty blond. Elise tried not to care but some mornings she found herself sitting in front of the mirror searching for her old self. It was never a good idea. The stranger staring back at her had dark smudges under sunken eyes and her nose and mouth looked too big for her face. Mrs. Potato Head.

"Anyway, it suits you short," Ronnie added. "It brings out your eyes—you look gorgeous."

"Enough!" Elise said, a lump in her throat. "I'm fine."

"You look low today," Ronnie replied.

"I'll do some yoga later—that'll help."

"If you say so, but I'm not sure how doing a downward-facing dog is a comfort to anyone."

Ronnie rummaged in her bag for a tissue, offering to get coffee, a paper, a sandwich, a muffin, until Elise took a deep breath and said: "Okay, a cup of tea, please." She didn't want it—the only thing she wanted was five minutes' peace to get her head together.

"Right, then," Ronnie said. "Back in a jiffy."

Elise closed her eyes and breathed deeply until she heard her footsteps fade away. *It's going to be fine,* she repeated in her head. But she didn't know.

She'd found the lump when she caught the pucker of skin near her left nipple in the mirror. She'd stared for a couple of seconds, thinking it was a trick of the light, then reached to touch it. Beneath was a thickening of her flesh.

Her doctor had sent Elise straight to have a mammogram at the specialist clinic. She'd sat cold and numb behind the thin curtain of a cubicle before submitting her poor diseased breast to be squashed between two sheets of glass until she'd yelped.

It'd meant making a new file in her head.

1. Mammogram
2. Needle biopsy
3. CT scan
4. Hormone therapy?
5. Drugs?
6. Chemo?
7. Surgery?

She'd put off telling anyone in case it was all a hoax. A cyst with a wicked sense of humor. But in the end, she'd had to. She'd taken the train home to Norwich in the sleety rain back in February and told her mum and dad. Her dad had left the room to make them a cup of tea while she and her mum had cried. She'd felt terrible telling them—Mum had so much to cope with already; Elise's brother's messy divorce and his childcare crises and her washing machine on permanently to keep up with Grandad's "little accidents."

"I'm going to be fine, Mum," she'd said when her mother started talking about coming down to Ebbing to hold her hand during the treatment. "You're needed up here. And you'll be on the end of a phone."

At work, Elise had gone for black humor—the policeman's friend—and tried not to see the pity in colleagues' eyes as they laughed along.

They think I'm going to die, rang like a bell in her head.

"It's not metastasized," she told her boss in his office, blindsiding him with the new vocab she was mastering. "Spread, I mean. It's treatable but I'll need chemo and surgery."

DCI McBride had tried not to look at her breasts but his gaze kept slipping to the guilty parties.

"Take as much time off as you need, Elise," he'd said, his arm round her shoulders as he walked her to the door of his office. "But no malingering . . ."

And they both laughed too loudly and leaned together for support.

Elise had suddenly wanted to tell him not to write her off. But that would have been admitting it was a possibility. But she needed to say it.

"I'll hurry back, Graham. Don't worry," she said at the door. "Don't write me off."

"As if." He'd smiled back. "Ring me when you're ready."

She hadn't made the call yet. Maybe tomorrow.

THE ONCOLOGY REGISTRAR LEANED against his desk while he was speaking to her as though he were chatting her up in a bar. Elise wanted someone older, with serious glasses and a white coat. But the consultant was elsewhere giving someone bad news. Elise's results were all good, so she got the one with a holiday tan and a braided bracelet. Elise tried to concentrate on what he was saying but her mind kept slipping away.

I should have brought Ronnie in with me, she told herself. *She'd have been able to tell me all the important points after.*

"Do you have any questions, Miss King?" he was saying.

"Er . . ." She wanted to ask the risk of it coming back and if she still might die but she'd pushed the words down too far to retrieve now.

"Good. Well, we'll carry on with the hormone therapy and send you an appointment letter for your next blood test. But you are good to go back to work in a managed return."

And she was back in the waiting room.

"How did you get on?" Ronnie said.

"I don't know. I can't remember a single thing he said." *Apart from being ready to go back to work.*

"Was it bad news, then?" And Ronnie moved closer to her so their bare arms touched and Elise shivered.

"No. I'm sure I'd have paid more attention if it had been. It was sort of mood music. Good-so-far sort of thing. Keep calm and carry on."

"Are you ready to go home?"

"No. Actually, there's someone else I want to see while I'm here."

"On the wards?"

"No, the mortuary."

THIRTY-EIGHT

Elise

HI, AOIFE. HOW ARE you?"

"Elise! What are you doing here?" the pathologist said, slipping up her Perspex mask. "I thought it had to be a direct order before you set foot in here."

The autopsy tables were scrubbed and empty, so Elise slid round the door and sat on a stool as far from the working surfaces as possible. She was usually up in the gallery, watching Dr. Aoife Mortimer at work from a professional distance, but she needed to get up close and personal today.

"I've just been upstairs in Oncology and I thought I'd come and see you," she said.

"And?" Aoife said, taking another stool. "How did you get on?"

"All good, thanks. Got to keep taking the tablets but the doctor says I can go back to work as planned."

"That's great news."

"Yep," she said quickly, panic rising in her gorge. Her return-to-work interview with Human Resources was scheduled for Friday and she felt sick at the thought.

"I can't wait," she added.

It was what she'd trained herself to say when asked. No one need know what she really felt. That the excitement of taking back control of her life was being eclipsed by the terror of standing in front of her team again and not being up to it. Of dropping the ball.

"Going foggy," her consultant had called it when she'd told him. He'd recommended mindfulness. "It's normal to be worried but I expect you'll only be going back eight hours a week at first to ease back in," he'd told her as if she should be grateful, but she couldn't see how she could get any traction with a handful of hours.

How will I ever get back to full power? To DI King?

"Actually, I thought you were already back when I heard it was you who found the Ebbing body on Monday."

"Ha! No, I was actually on a walk when I smelled the smell."

"Poor you. Not a particularly pleasant corpse."

"No, well . . ."

"Look, don't do too much at first," Aoife said as if she'd been inside Elise's head. "It's going to be tough to begin with and you need to be kind to yourself."

"I know," Elise snapped. "Sorry, but I feel so unfit—the treatment's really knocked me back."

"It will. But you'll rebuild your strength quickly. Are you doing the exercises?"

"Yes, Doctor . . ."

"It'll be so important in the long run."

"I know. I'm desperate to be back to normal."

"Of course. Caro misses you terribly. We all do."

Elise felt her eyes prickle and clenched her fists against her thighs. "Thanks," she managed. "Look, I've been thinking about the Charlie Perry case."

"Not just a social call, then!" Aoife laughed softly.

"Well, I need the stimulus so I'm not thinking about cancer every moment of the day."

"Go on, then—I've got five minutes." Aoife took another stool. "What were you thinking about?"

"I wondered if you found maggots or eggs on the body."

The pathologist's eyebrows disappeared under her scrub hat. "I see."

"I'm just exploring ideas. And wondering when he died. Have you identified the weapon used to hit him, by the way?"

The pathologist crossed her legs to get comfortable. "Well, the impact injury looks as though it was caused by a heavy object. Traces of engine oil were found around the wound site, so maybe a car tool. The team is still searching for it. Look, this is all getting a bit detailed—"

"Sorry. It's just an intellectual exercise while I climb the walls at home—just trying to stretch my brain back into shape before I'm back in the incident room. So maggots or eggs?"

Aoife smiled. "Okay. I'll just say the initial observations show eggs. But, Elise, you know how complex time of death is. We've been here so many times. Nothing is black and white. It was very hot over the weekend and significantly cooler on the earth floor in the cellar, so decomposition could have been speeded up or slowed down, depending on where he died and when he was moved. Did you know he didn't die in situ and was moved later? Anyway, these are very early days—we need the labs to do their stuff. I'm being pushed by Caro—you all need to be patient."

"Of course. But are there any indications who might have moved the body? Were there any fingerprints or DNA?"

"We're still examining the samples from the scene. Look, I'd better get back to work—and, Elise, tread carefully. Your colleagues might not appreciate you conducting an alternative investigation."

"I'm not. Don't worry."

SHE WROTE UP HER notes while she waited for Ronnie to bring the car round, in case she forgot anything. But she lost her train of thought and, when she looked down at her pad, found she'd been doodling maggots in the margins. They looked cute and cuddly on the page but they were anything but. And their absence could mean Charlie hadn't died until Sunday. So where was he until then?

"Hello. How did it go?" Caro answered on the first ring.

"No maggots."

"Maggots? What are you on about?"

"On Charlie Perry's body. No maggots. Only eggs. So he definitely wasn't dead on Friday night."

"Seriously, Elise! This is not your case! Who have you spoken to—as if I don't know?"

"Not saying. Look, I did find the body."

"So you're a witness, not SIO. Hugh'll go mad if he finds out you've been talking to the pathologist."

"So don't tell him. How are you getting on with him?"

"Okay. He's a bit distracted, to be honest. But we're on it. The forensics team is processing material from Charlie's clothing—we should have some results tomorrow. Fingers crossed Bram O'Dowd left his mark. We're plowing on with the witnesses and CCTV— we've been lucky with cameras. They're outside the supermarket, newsagent, and Shell garage—plus the little parking area for walkers near Tall Trees—so we're trying to trace Charlie's journey. And anyone he might have been with."

"What are the witnesses saying?"

"We've got a few sightings at the festival. He was being a nuisance in the queue, barging into people, and we've got a young lad who was standing next to him near the entrance. He said Charlie was pissed, very unsteady on his feet—and quite nervous. He was looking around a lot, apparently, but he doesn't seem to have spoken to anyone else."

"Who was he looking for in the queue?"

"Well, most of Ebbing was there! We're taking statements—and listening to a hundred different theories. Everyone wants to help— everyone loved Charlie, apparently. He did a lot in the community, helping people out. He was ferrying old ladies to the shops regularly— his wife wasn't happy to be sharing him, I've heard."

Elise parked that for later. "What about the sighting at the workers' village?"

"We're up there but we've found no one who saw him. Nor did the media. And he's not on the security camera footage from the building site either. I think someone is yanking our chain."

"Trying to be part of it, do you think?" There was a glory seeker or two in every case, hanging around pretending they knew stuff so they could feel important. "Or maybe he's distracting you from something else? You need to find him."

"Right, if the basic detection lesson is over . . ."

"Come on, Caro—I only want to help."

"Well, come back to work! We need you here. So what did the oncologist say?"

FINALLY HOME AND ON her own, Elise sat back in the window with Hugh's get-well card in her hands. She got it out only when she was at her lowest ebb.

She just liked seeing his handwriting—big looping letters as familiar as her own. They used to leave notes for each other on the kitchen table when they were working different shifts. "Need milk,"

"Back at 10," "Takeaway tonight?" Never "I love you" but Elise had thought it'd gone without saying. . . .

Hugh sent the card when word reached him about her diagnosis. But the runner must have chosen it because it was nothing he'd have picked. A teddy bear with a bandage on its head. "Get Well Soon. Love, Hugh x."

She'd put it under her pillow when it arrived. And was holding it against her scar today as she sat quietly doing her breathing exercises to drive the dread out of her lungs.

The card was back on her bedside table when her boss rang. She knocked it flying as she grappled for the phone in the dark.

"Hello, Elise," DCI McBride said. "Sorry to ring so late. How are you doing?"

"Er, good, thanks." She fumbled with the light. "How about you?"

"Been better. I don't know if you've heard but we're in a hole with this unexplained death. Hugh Ward has gone off sick. He's got trouble at home—anyway, he's been signed off for a month and I need someone to step in."

"Right."

"And I'm told you've been busy with your own lines of inquiry on Mr. Perry's death."

Bloody Caro has blabbed.

"Well, just having a dabble online, that sort of thing. It's in the blood, isn't it?"

DCI McBride laughed. "And interviewing the wife? Talking to Aoife Mortimer? Still just dabbling?"

"Well . . ."

"Look, the important thing for me is that you're up to speed. I've talked to Occupational Health and I've swung it so you can come back. It's only a couple of weeks earlier than planned and the Major Crime Team is working out of Southfold police station, so it's practically on your doorstep. Caro Brennan can do all the heavy lifting while you find your feet. You'd just have to direct."

A fizz of anxiety filled her ears. "Well, I . . . um, well . . ."

"Elise?"

"Sorry, boss. It's just . . . just a bit unexpected."

She heard him sigh on the other end of the line. "You told me not to write you off, Elise. I'm not. I need you."

THIRTY-NINE

Elise

ELISE HAD HAD LITTLE sleep after the late-night call.

Especially after Caro filled in the gaps in McBride's cagey explanation of his SIO's absence.

"Is Hugh ill?' Elise had asked immediately.

"Not exactly. Look, Elise, the wedding's off," Caro said. "The jogger has jogged on. . . ."

Elise wasn't able to speak for a moment. She was back in the restaurant, her thighs cramping with the effort of holding it together.

"Elise? Are you okay? Look, I only heard tonight. Honest."

"Don't worry. I'm fine." Her voice was scratchy but she thought she'd got away with it.

She stayed up talking to Caro about the case, reading the files, and making notes until the early hours and then tossed and turned until the alarm went off. It was the first time in months she'd heard its shriek and she startled, then lay looking up at the ceiling, counting the seconds until it went off again.

When she arrived early for work at Southfold police station, she stood outside the redbrick building for ten minutes, tugging her jacket down, steeling herself, until Caro appeared and propelled her up the stairs. She had to sit in the end cubicle in the ladies' to catch her breath when she reached her floor. Put on a bit of lipstick she found at the bottom of her workbag, watching her trembling hand in the mirror and practicing what she'd say to them all until she wasn't able to put it off any longer.

The incident room went quiet when she walked in.

"Here she is," one of her old team sang out, "riding to the rescue. How are you doing, boss?"

"Good, thanks," she said, and perched on a desk to disguise her shaking legs. "How about you? Missed me?"

Everybody laughed but they were looking at her weird hair, her clothes hanging off her thin shoulders, taking it all in. Like they'd been taught.

"Right, where are we?" she said.

"Shall we start with the pathologist's preliminary report?" Caro took up the baton. "Charlie Perry died from a heart attack. He had severe narrowing of his coronary arteries, which is hardly surprising—he was mid-seventies, had been a heavy smoker until ten years ago, and apparently drank like a fish. If he hadn't been hit with a heavy metal weapon after death, we'd probably just be reading his obit in the local paper. But he was viciously attacked and his body was moved."

"So two questions we need answers to," Elise addressed the room, trying to keep her voice level. "First, given what happened afterwards, did he just drop dead from natural causes? Or was he put under extreme pressure—literally, frightened to death? And if so, who by? As Caro says, something horrible happened in that cellar."

There was silence. Had she gone in too heavy? She was still an unknown quantity to the local officers. "And the second," she went on, "who hits a corpse?"

"Someone who didn't know he was already dead?" a voice called from her far left. She turned gratefully but couldn't put a name to the face. Was it someone new or someone she'd forgotten? *Just keep going.*

"Yes . . . or maybe someone frustrated that he'd died?" Elise could hear the tremor in her voice. "The blow was so violent, it shattered his skull—perhaps it was delivered by someone who'd wanted Charlie Perry alive? Or wanted to kill him themselves? Who had a motive? Was it lust, loathing, love, or loot?"

"Could be loot," another of the Southfold officers said. "He owed a lot of money—his overdraft at the bank was in the thousands."

Young, female, heavy eyebrows. Elise tried to memorize her face. She should have asked Caro for a list of names.

"Banks don't usually bash heads in," Caro said, rolling her eyes.

"How about locally? Are there debts?" Elise asked.

"Tradesmen mainly," DC Eyebrows held her ground. "For work on the house. I've spoken to three or four firms but they're not owed huge amounts. I haven't found anyone going under because of him."

"Okay, keep looking. What else?" Elise said.

"My money's on lust. The wife and/or her lover," Caro said, pointing to the photos on the whiteboard. There was a good one of Pauline Perry. One from her modeling portfolio, no doubt. "We're told Pauline was regularly having sex with Bram O'Dowd in the caravan a few meters from where Charlie was found."

"Told? Who by? Do we have any evidence?"

"We're examining clothing and bedding from the caravan," Caro said. "There was a man's T-shirt found tucked down behind the headboard—not one of Charlie's, I'd say."

"And what do Pauline and Mr. O'Dowd say about their relationship?"

"They're both denying it but they would, wouldn't they?"

"Right, Pauline and O'Dowd are top of my list too," Elise said. "There was a lot going on in that caravan—a possible affair, threatened repossession of their dream house, debts piling up. It must have been like a powder keg. I want to reinterview them today. Okay, what does the pathologist say about time of death?"

Caro gave her a look. "Well, you know what Aoife's like . . . but she's as certain as she's prepared to be that it wasn't Friday night. She puts it closer to the discovery of the body—probably in the twenty-four hours preceding."

"So Sunday," Elise said. "Then why were there no more sightings of him after the concert? Where was Charlie Perry for the rest of the weekend? Did we get anywhere with the witness who saw him up at the workers' village?"

"DS Susie Atkins from this station is following it up—she's nailed the reporter's source as Liam Eastwood."

"Seriously?" Elise muttered. "Isn't he still in the frame for the drugs case?"

"We're working on that," Caro said. "But he told Susie he'd just overheard someone saying it. Anyway, she's gone back to see Mr. Eastwood this morning. She's got some CCTV footage to discuss with him." Her phone rang and she put it to her ear.

Elise went to look at the information on the board, aware that eyes were following her.

"Who is this?" She pointed at a screen grab from CCTV of a skinny middle-aged man with haunted eyes.

"It's the bloke who tried to see Charlie Perry's daughter in her residential home," DC Eyebrows piped up, and came to stand with her. "I'm DC Lucy Chevening, ma'am. The home has a security camera by the front door."

"Good. Do we know who he is yet?"

"No, but we're on it."

"Have you got the techies to use live-facial-recognition software to see if he's on our radar already?"

Elise was explaining the process when her sergeant interrupted.

"Well . . ." Caro grinned. "Shaking down the workers wasn't a complete waste of time. Perhaps we should be grateful to Mr. Eastwood. A laborer has come in with a bag he found at the Harbor Row building site. He told the desk officer that he spotted a corner of it in a skip as he barrowed rubble up a ramp on Monday and pulled it free. And took it home. He said people chucked things they didn't want in the skips all the time—there was an old washing machine the other day. But when he opened it, there was a laptop. To be honest, I think he'd have kept it and kept quiet, but underneath the clothes and stuff, there was a passport and a phone."

"Bloody hell. Whose?"

"Not sure about the phone but the passport is in the name Charles Williams. Looks like our Mr. Perry was planning to return to his old identity."

FORTY

Dee

'VE LOST ANOTHER TWO clients by text—one of them Liz, and she was my first friend in Ebbing. We met when the boys started school—the school gate was a bit lonely at first and some of the local mums were a bit up themselves but Liz chatted with me and we started playdates for the boys. I wouldn't say we were close close or in and out of each other's houses all the time—we both work, for a start, her in the estate agent's and me cleaning—but it was nice. 'Course, when I started cleaning for her, things changed a bit.

She tried to pretend they hadn't—that I was doing her a huge favor and bringing me drinks and chatting like I'd just popped round—but I think it got embarrassing: her standing over me while I cleaned under her sofas. And I suppose she must have started seeing her house through my eyes.

The place looks like she's been burgled every time I go but she refuses to pay for more than one hour a week. What can you do in an hour? She said, "I just need you to give it a quick once-over," when I started, so I gave the carpets a Brazilian with the Hoover down the middle of each room and sprayed furniture polish about but didn't dust anywhere that wasn't immediately visible. I hate cutting corners—it's like only shaving the front of your legs—and I never did the bedrooms. She said she'd do those but I looked. She didn't. I suppose she thought no one else could see it.

But she knows I could. Maybe it got too much. And this thing with Liam has given her a let-out.

"Dee! Are you listening to me?" Liam says, suddenly standing beside me.

"What? Yes, yes."

"I'm trying to tell you my lawyer says the police have got nothing on me," he mutters. "She's just rung me. And she's right. Ade is claiming he doesn't remember where he got the pills and Spike isn't going to say anything, is he? The cops will lose interest."

"You've had a lucky escape, then."

Liam looks away.

"They're busy with Charlie's death, anyway," he says. "I hear Pauline's being questioned again—people are saying she could have got someone to do it for her. The body was moved, you know?"

"I heard," I say. "Let's hope your lawyer is right and the police leave us alone."

FAT CHANCE. DS SUSIE Atkins arrives half an hour later. Looking into our hall, taking it all in as soon as I open the door. Liam hovers near the kitchen door. Ready to disappear.

"Is Mr. Eastwood in? Oh, hello, Liam," she says. "I'd like to talk to you again about Friday night. Have you remembered any more about the man you say saw Charlie Perry at the workers' village?"

I want to scream but I've got to keep quiet. *What has he done now? Why is he making stuff up like this?*

"Er, no. Like I said, there were a load of people in the pub. I don't know everyone who goes in there. You should be talking to the workers at Harbor Row. . . . Most of them don't even have permits to be here. Loads of illegals. That's what everyone's saying."

"I see. But you definitely didn't see Charlie Perry that night?"

"No, I didn't," he says too loudly.

I'm not sure I'd believe him but I'm praying the officer does.

"And, Mrs. Eastwood"—she turns to look at me—"did you see Mr. Perry?"

"Er, no. Well, it was so crowded—and I was busy dancing and we left early to get back for the babysitter, didn't we?"

Liam nods.

"Well, I've had another look at the CCTV from the High Street and seen your van with two people in the front seats."

Liam nods but doesn't manage to speak.

"That would be right," I say. "We drove home from the festival, didn't we, love?"

"Right," DS Atkins says, "but twenty-five minutes later it's at the Shell garage out on the Portsmouth road."

"We went to get some diesel on the way home," I say too quickly. "We were getting low."

"Right. How far is the garage from the Old Vicarage? A couple of miles?"

"Yeah, about that," Liam says.

"So it took you twenty-five minutes to drive a couple of miles?"

Liam goes all red and I know he's going to say something stupid.

"We stopped for a cuddle," I blurt.

DS Atkins looks at me and I hold her eye. "Where exactly?" she says.

"Down by the sea," I say straight back, and try to giggle. "We were reliving our youth—what with the festival and everything."

"Right, well, luckily there are cameras on the front, so we'll be able to pinpoint when this kiss and cuddle took place."

"We weren't on the front," I shoot back. "Just parked up on one of the side roads. Then we got the fuel and went back to let the babysitter go to the festival."

"I see. So can I have the name of your babysitter?"

She's not letting this go. I shrug as if I don't care. But my heart is pounding.

"Er, it's Jenny—she lives at number thirteen."

I WATCH THE OFFICER march up the path and wonder what Jenny will say? What she saw?

Liam comes to stand by me at the window. "A cuddle?" he says. "What made you say that? You haven't let me near you for a week."

"Dunno. It was the first thing that came into my head. I didn't hear you come up with anything better."

"Why don't we just tell the truth? Say I took him home?" he hisses.

"It'll be fine," I say.

"No, it won't! We're making this worse. When she comes back, I'm telling her."

"Don't you dare. . . ."

But I've lost him. He's going to do it. I put the kettle on and wait for the police to come back.

DS Atkins looks very pleased with herself when we open the door. "So," she says, "Jenny says you came home at ten fifteen—that would be ten minutes after your van drove past the first camera. So that must have been a very quick snog. Jenny is sure about the time because she was looking at the clock and out of the window because she was worried about meeting her friend. She says you got out of the van, Mrs. Eastwood. But Mr. Eastwood didn't come in. He drove off alone. But the garage camera shows there was someone in the passenger seat."

"That would be Charlie," Liam says. "You'd better come in."

FORTY-ONE

Elise

HER BOTTOM HAD BARELY made contact with the chair when the phone rang.

"I know Charlie Perry made it home on Friday," DS Atkins said, and Elise could hear the growl of adrenaline in her voice as she gave the details. "I'm bringing in Liam and Dee Eastwood."

"Great work," Elise said, scribbling a note to herself.

Trying to keep up. She'd only just got back in the driving seat and it was all going a hundred miles an hour. Her heart was racing as she sat and tried to untangle the knot of questions in her head until Caro cleared her throat beside her.

"Susie and I can do both of them?" Caro said.

"No, you're all right. I'll take Liam. I don't want anyone thinking I'm a lightweight."

"Boss," Caro hissed in her ear, "we've got Bram and Pauline to question as well. Don't overdo it on your first day. You'll make yourself ill."

"I'm not. And I'm fine."

"WHY DIDN'T YOU TELL us straightaway?" Elise said as soon as Caro had done the formalities. No point in beating about the bush.

"I don't know." The man sitting opposite looked as though his life was on fire, his eyes darting round the room as if looking for an escape route. "Look, Charlie was fine. A bit drunk—well, a lot drunk, if you know what I mean—when I left him. And we thought he'd turn up. We didn't want to get dragged into anything."

" 'We'?"

"Me and Dee."

"So whose idea was it to keep quiet?"

The eyes went to his lawyer, who tapped her legal pad with her pen. Elise wondered if it was an agreed signal. One tap for "Shut up"? Two for "No comment"?

"I dunno. No one gets involved with the police if they can help it, do they?"

"I see. I understand Charlie Perry owed you money."

"Well, me and every builder who worked on his house. I was renewing the pipework—the whole house needed doing—but he never paid the final bill. I chased it but he said he had a cash flow problem. Look, it happens in my business."

"How much did he owe you?"

"Not that much."

"Exactly?"

Liam Eastwood swallowed hard. "Four grand, give or take."

Elise leaned back. "That's quite a big sum for a one-man business. Did it cause you financial problems?"

Eastwood's head went down. The lawyer's pencil tapped twice. But perhaps he hadn't heard it.

"Yeah," he said quietly. "It's not right, is it? It's like he was robbing me. Screwing me over. We've got a bit behind with bills and might get chucked out of the house. Dee is trying to sort it out with the landlord."

"You must have been very angry about being screwed over."

Two taps.

"No comment," he said sulkily. And the lawyer made a note on her pad.

"But look," he suddenly added, "I might have had a word but I'd never have hurt him. He was an old man. Charlie was okay when I left him."

"But why should we believe you?" Elise leaned farther forward. "You've already lied to us about that night, haven't you? You said Charlie had been seen up by the workers' caravans but you knew for a fact that he hadn't. Because he was sitting beside you in your van."

Eastwood's feet started doing a soft shoe shuffle under the table. "I only said that after he was found dead because I thought one of them might've had something to do with it. There's all sorts up there. Have you checked?"

"We're talking to everyone, Mr. Eastwood. Did you talk to Charlie about the debt when he was in your van?"

Liam looked up wearily. "No. I couldn't get a word of sense out of him. I got him out of the van and pointed him at the caravan. Then home. End of. Ask Dee."

"We will. Did you go back to have that chat later?"

"What? No!"

"Where were you for the rest of the weekend?"

"I was working on Saturday and around the house. And Sunday? Er, football training with my boy and at home. That was the night of the fire, wasn't it? I was up there. Look, I need to use the toilet."

THE TEAM WAS CHECKING Liam Eastwood's alibis while Caro and Atkins moved on to Dee.

When Elise slipped into a chair behind the one-way glass down the corridor, her cleaner was tensed up in her chair with her hands clasped in her lap. She watched as Caro shuffled her notes and DS Atkins set up the recording equipment, taking their time, letting the pressure build.

"Look," Dee said eventually, "Liam told me he gave Charlie a lift last week. Before his body was found. I know we should have said something but he said Charlie was fine when he left him and we thought Charlie would show up. And he didn't die until later, did he?"

"How do you know that?" Caro said, and stopped flicking through the paper trail.

"What? Well, it's what people are saying. And Liam and I had other things to worry about at the time."

"Yes, those ecstasy tablets," Caro said.

Dee looked at her hands. "Liam had nothing to do with that. Ade's family is trying to find someone else to blame. They don't want it to be their son."

"That matter is still under investigation." Caro closed her down. "You know the Perrys well, don't you?"

"I wouldn't say that," Dee muttered. "I clean for them once a week. Do a bit of ironing. But I clean for lots of people."

"But you know all about their personal lives, don't you? You told DI King that they talked openly about their problems in front of you and rowed frequently about their sex life. And that Mrs. Perry was having an affair with their gardener."

"I was worried about Charlie," Dee said quietly. "I thought the police should know that it wasn't all hearts and flowers in the caravan."

"Do you think Pauline Perry had something to do with Charlie's death?"

Dee's head went up, eyes wide. "I don't know. But she was horrible to him. Cruel. Said she wished she could get rid of him. That's all I'm saying."

"You sound very protective of Charlie. What was your relationship with him?"

Dee's spine straightened and her feet curled around the chair legs as if bracing for a crash. Elise wondered if the officers were seeing the same body language. Were they touching a nerve?

"Relationship? What are you going on about? I worked for him."

"But you told DI King he was a sweetheart and a lovely man," her sergeant plowed on. "It sounds like you were very fond of him. Did he ever confide in you? Or meet you away from the caravan?"

"'Course not!" Dee snapped. "Look, we weren't friends—or anything else. I said that because that's what everyone said about him."

She paused. "But I didn't really know him."

FORTY-TWO

Elise

B RAM O'DOWD HAD BEEN sitting in the interview room for more than an hour by the time the detectives finally walked in.

The Eastwoods had taken longer than Elise had expected. Then there'd been the Lithuanian laborer with the suitcase to deal with. They'd pushed him as hard as they could but he had a cast-iron alibi for the weekend—in the cells at Bournemouth police station from the early hours of Saturday to first thing Monday morning after a fight at a nightclub. An officer was doing background checks with Interpol just in case he had form but the focus was on the contents of the suitcase and what forensics could make of them.

"It's a bizarre haul," Caro said. "He wasn't packing for a fortnight on the beach. There's a screwdriver tucked into the underpants!"

"It looks like Charlie was getting ready to leave but he never made it out of the door," Elise said. "So who took his bag and hid it in a skip? The person who moved his body?"

"Come on, let the lab boys work their magic. The lover's waiting," Caro said, and handed her a list of the CCTV sightings for O'Dowd's pickup truck near Tall Trees over the bank holiday weekend.

"He's been a busy boy . . ." Elise murmured as she scanned it.

O'DOWD HAD SLIPPED HIS flip-flops off and one leg was stretched languorously under the table so that his grubby foot was under Elise's chair. She made sure to catch it when she pulled the seat out.

He pulled a face as he reached down to rub his ankle and then sat back, his porn star tan displayed to full effect in a tight white T-shirt.

At least he's got it on.

"I understand you do not want a lawyer present?"

"No, I'm fine without," O'Dowd said. "Is this going to take much longer? I've already told DI Ward everything—and I've got a job waiting."

"Sorry about that. Anyway . . . how long have you known Pauline Perry?" Elise opened the proceedings.

The gardener appeared to consider the question carefully. "A year? About that, anyway. I started doing work at Tall Trees when I moved to Ebbing."

"You're not a local, then?"

"No, I came to do seasonal work at the garden center and liked it, so I stayed."

"How did you come to work for the Perrys?"

"Like I've already said, Pauline came into the center and we got chatting. About plants. And she asked if I'd help her with some new beds. . . ."

Caro flicked a "Seriously!" look at Elise.

"I see. And when did you start a sexual relationship with her?"

"This is ridiculous." O'Dowd sat up straight in his chair. "I was working on her property, nothing else. They're a load of gossips round here—women with nothing to do but bitch to one another. I told DI Ward. He understood."

Elise tightened her grip on her pen. "Well, I don't want to be rude, but I've seen what passes for the garden at the property. It doesn't look like it's been touched for months. Hardly an advert for your skills—"

"I only go occasionally." He sulked. "They couldn't really afford me—"

"You were there Friday night, though, weren't you? Your vehicle was recorded arriving."

"Who by?"

"There's a camera at the entrance to the parking area just before the Perry property. And it's positioned so that it catches vehicles slowing down and indicating to turn into Tall Trees."

He frowned. *He didn't know.* Elise smiled to herself.

"I'm a big walker," he muttered. "Pauline lets me park round there when I fancy stretching my legs on the footpath."

"Right. In the dark?"

He shrugged. "I go stargazing sometimes."

"Do you? Well, we found a man's T-shirt tucked down the back of Pauline Perry's bed during our search of the caravan."

O'Dowd's head went down.

"It's being examined in the lab for DNA. As are the sheets."

There was a long pause but Elise was happy to wait.

"Look," he said finally, lifting his eyes to hers. "It was only supposed to be a one-off. A pity shag. But she wouldn't let it go."

Poor Pauline, Elise found herself thinking, despite herself.

"No one needs to know, do they?" he pleaded. "I mean, she's old enough to be my mother."

"Grandmother," Caro murmured.

"If it was so embarrassing, why did you sleep with her?" Elise said. "Was she paying you?"

"No!" The gardener's voice went up an octave. "Well, she bought me a few presents."

"Like what?"

"Clothes, mainly. Look, I suppose I felt sorry for her. Living in that awful caravan with her boring old fart of a husband. And she still looks good. She used to be a model, you know?"

"We do. What about Charlie? Did he know about the two of you?"

Bram shrugged. "It was nothing. We had sex occasionally. End of."

"You weren't planning to set up together? Pauline wasn't going to dump Charlie and move you into the caravan?"

"No way! It wasn't anything like that."

"Not for you, but perhaps Pauline had other ideas?" Elise said. "Did Charlie catch you that night? He'd had a lot to drink and it could easily have turned nasty. It's just I notice you've got marks on your upper arms and neck."

The gardener's hand went straight to his throat.

"Pauline gets a bit physical," he muttered. "She's broken a nail before now. Anyway, I didn't see Charlie Friday night. Not at the caravan or on the road when I drove home."

"What time was that?" She knew because his departure at twenty-one fifty-five had been recorded on the camera but she wanted to see if he'd lie.

"Ten, I think. The news headlines were playing on my car radio."

"What about when you came back Sunday lunchtime?" she said, running her finger down to the date beside the reference number.

"I . . . well . . . I want a lawyer if you are going to carry on like this," Bram said.

Elise slipped back into the ladies' quickly to splash some cold water on her face while the duty lawyer was called in. She'd sent a team to go over O'Dowd's place and bring in his pickup for examination. Pauline would be on her way in. Elise stared at the woman in the mirror. She was there. DI Elise King was back.

FORTY-THREE

Pauline

PAULINE STOOD AND SWISHED the curtains across the window when yet another car pulled up. She wasn't answering the door anymore. Bloody press.

She counted to ten after the knock at the door and then watched as the reporter—a young man with rather a sweet face—walked away backward, filming the caravan and house before getting in his car. She cursed the day she'd met Charlie.

She'd played with the thought of asking Bram to take her away from it all many times over recent months. When the warning signs had started. The letters from the bank that Charlie tucked into his pocket as soon as they arrived. But she'd known it wasn't sensible. *Gorgeous bottom but he's got no money, Pauline,* she'd told herself. And now, of course, it was out of the question.

She should be okay financially, though. When all the fuss over Charlie's death died down. There was a very generous insurance policy. She'd seen it in his desk drawer years ago and made a note of the policy number just in case—but she hadn't found a will yet. That was a bit of a worry. Their old solicitor in London said he hadn't got it. Where else would it be? Had Charlie hidden it? Why? The specter of bloody Birdie making off with all the money haunted her when she was at her lowest.

But for now she had to concentrate on sticking to her story that she knew nothing about his debts. "Money was Charlie's department," she practiced as she applied some lipstick.

It was an approach Pauline had decided on long ago with regard to Charlie's business life. She never asked questions because if you don't know, everything is deniable. Her second husband had taught her that—it was pretty much Henry's only legacy.

Henry had died on his ride-on mower just three years after they'd married. One of the neighbors had actually said he'd died in the saddle. And being a widow instead of a divorcée had been quite nice at first. She'd enjoyed the attention. And black was so slimming. But the sympathy suppers had petered out after she'd flirted with one of the husbands and the women in the book group had stopped appearing at her door with cakes and casseroles. She'd been cast adrift. She'd faced her first winter alone in the converted farmhouse in Morpeth, most of it in the three-foot circle around her wood burner, the cold creeping around her back and her heart.

But even that thin comfort had been snatched away from her. Henry's money had gone with him. He'd left it to his bratty children and they'd insisted on selling the farmhouse from under her. They'd never liked her.

"He hadn't got round to changing his will," she'd told friends. "Neither of us expected him to die so young. But I'll be fine."

And Pauline had been sure she would. She was nothing if not a survivor. She'd had Charlie bubbling away on a back burner for a while. Her plan B. They'd been introduced at a business do in London she'd attended with Henry. He and Charlie had got on like a house on fire and he'd been very attentive to her while Henry chatted up the waitresses. There'd been the occasional runner-up's lunch for Charlie when she came down to town, letting him pat her knee under the table and giving him a peck on the cheek outside the restaurant. All very aboveboard but she'd fed his hope that he might reach the winner's podium one day.

He'd traveled all the way to Northumberland for Henry's memorial service and held her round the waist for a second too long as he kissed her cheek. "A woman like you shouldn't be on her own, Pauline," he'd said in her ear. "I'll look after you."

And he had. Of course, it hadn't all been plain sailing. There'd been the daughter in the home. Pauline had gone with Charlie to visit Birdie during their courtship, but once they were married, she'd declared it "too depressing" and sent him alone. And then that business with some investors turning nasty and coming knocking at the door. It'd all been settled. But it'd left him short and he'd borrowed some company money to pay for work on their home. Not entirely by the book but Charlie had always intended paying it back. They'd had to sell the house but they'd made a profit and she'd always wanted to live next to the sea. And she'd found Tall Trees.

"A fresh start," she'd told Charlie when he'd tried to talk her out of it. But she'd found herself starting more and more sentences lately with the words, "Do you remember . . . ?" The carefully edited anecdotes she'd told over a hundred Hampstead dining tables came tumbling out to the cleaner now—a washing line of rinsed-out big moments, disasters, loves, bereavements, and triumphs—each slightly overused.

Today she sat at the kitchen table in her old slippers, their froufrou limp with age and wear, and cried. Here she was, a woman on the outer edge of middle age and still desired, but all this business with Charlie and the police was taking its toll. The handsome DI

Ward had been very kind but there had still been questions to bat away.

She had no idea what Bram might say. He hadn't been near her since the police arrived. No one had. She felt alone and vulnerable. Even when she slipped on her Louboutins, she didn't feel fabulous anymore. She felt fake.

She sat staring at the skin forming on her frigid cup of tea, thinking about her next move. She couldn't go it alone at her age. She'd need someone to cherish her. She loved the word "cherish," rolling it round her mouth and through her pouting lips. She just needed to find the will and sort out the insurance money.

The doorbell rang—three short rings. Bram? And she rose, straightening her spine and tugging her neckline down an inch farther.

"Mrs. Perry," the police officer on her doorstep said, "we need you to come with us to the station."

FORTY-FOUR

Elise

PAULINE PERRY SASHAYED IN on high heels. Elise had seen the word written down somewhere—never heard it—but she hadn't really understood the movement until that moment. The widow Perry had come prepared. At her elbow was a local solicitor—Mr. Grimes, a pink-faced individual in a linen suit with an office over a charity shop. He looked more nervous than his client and Elise wondered how long he'd been qualified. He looked completely in awe of Pauline and her hypnotic hips, and he held her handbag while she took off her jacket.

"Good morning," Pauline said as she entered the room.

"Oh," she said when she spotted Elise, "what are you doing here?"

"I'm now leading the investigation into your husband's death," Elise said, holding her eye, and Pauline put on her sad face again.

"What's happened to the lovely DI Ward?" she said.

"I'm afraid he's off sick."

"Goodness, you're an unhealthy lot, aren't you?" Pauline patted Mr. Grimes's knee.

"Shall we concentrate on the matter in hand?" Elise carried on.

"Well, I can't help you," Pauline said, tapping her nails on the table. "The story keeps changing, doesn't it? First, I'm told Charlie went to a pop festival, got drunk, and fell down the cellar hatch, then that he had a heart attack and someone hit him over the head. Then his body was moved. It's making my head spin."

Elise doubted it. "Well, let's start again, shall we? When first interviewed, you said you last saw your husband at six o'clock on Friday night. You watched some television on your own and then went to bed with a sleeping pill."

Pauline looked down at her hands.

"Then you reported your husband missing to me on Saturday morning," Caro said. "At nine fifty-nine, according to my notes. Yes?"

"And on Monday at about eleven thirty, you told me that you'd had a phone call from him earlier that day," Elise pushed on, "telling you he was fine."

Pauline looked at Elise defiantly, her jaw working.

"But that call came when he was already dead. In the cellar of your house. So he wasn't fine, was he?"

"Look, I've been over this with Hugh," Pauline mumbled. "I told him that it sounded like his voice. But it was a bad line. . . ."

"I see. Well, DI Ward isn't here and I'd like to hear what was said," Elise pressed. "Your husband had been missing for more than forty-eight hours by then. You were concerned enough after twelve hours to report his disappearance to the police. You must have asked him where he was, where he'd been, what he'd been doing? Why he'd gone off? When he was coming home? Any concerned spouse would."

"I didn't get a chance," Pauline snapped. "I told you he just said he was fine and not to worry and rang off."

"I see. I understand you managed to lose your phone on Monday."

"I don't know where I can have left it."

"Did you actually receive a call?" Elise leaned in. "Think very hard about your answer, Pauline. We're looking at your call history for Charlie's number. Will it be there? Or did you make it up to stop us looking for your husband?"

"Someone rang," Pauline barked, and tensed her shoulder, making her bra strap fall down her arm. "Maybe it was a prank call. People can be very cruel."

"Yes," Elise said, "they can. Why did you think your husband had gone off?"

"No idea."

"Really? Charlie was in serious financial trouble, wasn't he?"

"How would I know? That was his—"

"Department? Yes, you said. When we discussed the letter from a debt agency threatening to repossess your house."

Pauline looked at Elise in the silence that followed.

She's trying to remember exactly what she said that day in the caravan.

"It was just a liquidity problem. Charlie was sorting it out."

"I see. Did Charlie have life insurance?"

"Everyone does, don't they?"

"Not everyone. But that's good news for you."

"What are you suggesting?"

"That your financial difficulties may soon be over, I suppose."

Mr. Grimes cleared his throat and Elise let the implications rest there.

"Where were you on Friday night, Pauline?"

"Not again! This must be the hundredth time I've been through this," Pauline said quickly, back on firmer ground. "I was in bed."

"With your lover."

"Really!" Pauline rolled her eyes at Mr. Grimes. "This is such nonsense."

"We spoke to Bram O'Dowd this morning." Elise held Pauline's gaze. "He's been very candid."

"Well, a lady doesn't tell." She giggled nervously and glanced at the even pinker Mr. Grimes.

"She does if the police are asking," Caro said. "Or a lady could be accused of obstructing an investigation."

"Oh, for goodness' sake! Charlie and I have an understanding. My husband can't have sex anymore, so he looks the other way."

"Looked," Elise said.

"Yes, yes."

"So he was happy with the arrangement? It would take a special sort of man to turn a blind eye to regular adultery under his nose. Were there rows?"

Pauline's lips tightened. "No, it was all very civilized. We didn't talk about it. Charlie used to take himself out when I was entertaining."

"Is that what he did on Friday? But did he come home too early?"

Pauline's eyes flickered.

"I want to ask you again: When did you last see your husband?"

"On Monday, when I had to identify his body." She shuddered theatrically.

"Where had Charlie been until his death?"

"I have no idea." Pauline recrossed her legs, banging a knee on the underside of the table.

"Could he have been in your house all that time?"

Pauline's face hardened. "Well, if he was there, I didn't know.

It's a very big property—it's got nine bedrooms—but I never go upstairs. It's too dangerous."

"Upstairs? Was he upstairs?"

She flushed. "I don't know. You're trying to trip me up."

"And you didn't see or hear anything out of the ordinary? It's only yards from your caravan."

"Park home. And no."

"You were perhaps too busy entertaining Mr. O'Dowd. He was back on Sunday, wasn't he? When did you arrange that?"

"When he left on Friday night. Charlie had said he was going to see his daughter on Sunday," Pauline said, avoiding Elise's eyes.

"What did you and Mr. O'Dowd do on Sunday?"

"Er, we went to bed."

"And afterward?"

"Nothing. We didn't do anything." A red blush crept up from Pauline's cleavage to her throat and her hand flew up to cover it. "I had nothing to do with Charlie's death. I'm almost seventy. . . ."

"Oh, I have you as seventy-five."

Pauline flapped the uncomfortable truth away with her hand. "Look at me—how could you even think I was capable of violence? Of moving his body?"

"But you have a younger, fitter boyfriend, Pauline," Elise pressed. "And you were tired of Charlie. Don't shake your head—you'd told neighbors and your cleaning lady. The debts were mounting up, weren't they? And perhaps he'd stopped looking the other way while you and Mr. O'Dowd carried on your affair?"

Pauline gaped at Elise.

"Inspector!" Mr. Grimes interrupted. "This is all hearsay and supposition—do you have any actual evidence that my client was involved in any way in the death or disposal of her husband? If not, I think she has answered enough of these questions."

Elise ignored him. She was on a roll. "We'll need to take away all of your clothes and shoes for examination, Pauline."

And the fight seemed to go out of Pauline. She drooped in her chair, hands to her face.

"You need to be looking at what he's been doing," she said quietly. "It'll be on his laptop. He's been up to his old tricks again."

FORTY-FIVE

Elise

PAULINE CLAIMED SHE KNEW nothing more about Charlie's business practices except there'd been knocks at the door at night.

"Charlie said not to answer them—said it was kids but I knew it wasn't. We'd been here before. I thought we'd left all that behind in London," she offered before weeping mascara stains into Mr. Grimes's white shirt.

They had to let Pauline go while further inquiries were carried out and she left with her chin up. But she wasn't sashaying anymore.

Elise watched as she walked away, clinging onto Mr. Grimes's arm, and was secretly relieved. She was exhausted too.

"How are we getting on with Charlie's laptop?" she said to Caro. "Have we got access to his e-mails yet?"

"I'll find out. But it's time-out for you, boss," Caro said. "Do not speak for twenty minutes—and close the blinds so you can shut your eyes."

"Bloody hell, this isn't a nursery. . . ." Elise tried to laugh it off. But she felt her eyelids droop as she reread the pathologist's report, and when the words began to swim, she rang Aoife Mortimer.

"Hello!" the pathologist said. "What's today's intellectual exercise?"

"Ha! Actually, I'm back at work—I got the call after I got home from the hospital."

"Wow! And how do you feel about that?"

"Fine, fine. I'm feeling good," Elise lied. "But I'm having to hit the ground running. Can you talk me through a couple of things? I think Charlie Perry may have been in his house the whole weekend. We know now that he was dropped off there Friday night and there are zero sightings of him until his body turned up. I need to know what he was doing in there. Was he hiding or could he have been held prisoner?"

"Well, his wrists and ankles were unmarked—no rope or plastic tie marks on the skin, no bruises or abrasions."

"Was he drugged?"

"There's nothing obvious but we're analyzing fluids, his hair and fingernails," Aoife said. "There was nothing in his stomach. The only thing I found was sweet corn and tiny shreds of plastic in the bowel."

"Sweet corn and plastic? Right." Elise tried to sound like she was keeping up.

"We found the remains of a tuna and sweet corn sandwich in the Perrys' kitchen bin with Charlie's saliva on it. He must have wolfed it down in a hurry—it appears he ate some of the shrink-wrap covering."

"Really?"

"Plastic lurks around the gut if you swallow it. You should see a drug mule's stomach contents."

"That's a treat I'll pass on. So situation normal—it's a waiting game for results. But whoever attacked or manhandled the body must have left some trace? There should be sweat and fibers transferred in the process unless they were wearing a hazmat suit. They haven't found any matches to anyone of interest yet but the lab is working on it. When do you think you'll hear?"

"Ha! You haven't been away that long—your guess is as good as mine."

"Still here, Elise?" DCI McBride stuck his head round the door as she started rereading her notes from Pauline's interview.

"Yes, sir, just bringing myself up to speed."

"Well, you shouldn't be in the building after midday today, according to Occupational Health. Don't overdo it on your first day or they'll crucify me."

"I won't," Elise said.

"I'll give you a lift home," Caro said, appearing at McBride's side. "Leave it to me, sir."

Elise waited until her boss had disappeared down the corridor before picking up the folders and her bag.

"Okay," she said, "let's go to the scene. I need to fix the layout in my head."

"Hang on! Didn't you hear McBride?"

"He said I shouldn't be in the building and I won't be."

THE DOOR TO TALL Trees had been wedged open to allow the parade of white-suited Scenes of Crime Officers easy access. Elise put on her own suit, pulling the hood over her head and zipping it up to her throat, and looked round. She realized she looked the same as everyone else for the first time in months, and smiled.

It was way too hot for extra layers and she felt a bit heady. Inside the house, years of damp cooled her core like an ice challenge and she shivered.

Caro rustled in behind her. "Come on, boss, let's get down there while the lights are still up."

Caro led them into the cellar and Elise looked up through the hatch to where she'd stood with her shirt over her nose three days earlier. There were numbered evidence markers on the floor show-ing where Charlie's body had lain and a deep black stain from body fluids seeping into the dirt floor.

"He was on his left side, knees drawn up and arms by his side. The open injury to his head was on the right side, two inches be-hind his ear. The ear and scalp were badly torn during the assault. We're looking for some sort of heavy tool."

"Did Charlie die here?" Elise looked into the shadows cast by the police lights.

"Not yet confirmed but we're pretty sure this is where he was hit with the weapon—we've found bone fragments from his skull and a small amount of blood. He'd also been in another room. Come through."

Caro led her back down the corridor to a tiled room lit with more arc lights. "It used to be the scullery. And there's been an attempt to clean it—we've found bleach and scouring powder on some of the sur-faces but it wasn't a very thorough job. No blood has been found in here but the SOCOs detected traces of bodily fluids—possibly urine—in the grouting between the tiles in that corner. Money on it being Charlie's."

"Fingerprints?"

"Only his. Whoever was down here with him must have been wearing gloves."

I can't see Pauline Perry wielding the bleach and Marigolds, Elise thought, and had a sudden memory of Pauline throwing away the bowl of foul-smelling water. Had she been cleaning up?

"Pauline was in the house with a blue plastic washing-up bowl on Monday when I got here," she said.

"Was it one of these?" Caro said as she consulted photographs on her phone.

Elise looked at the screen. There was a blue bowl lined up with several buckets outside the caravan.

"That could be it."

While Caro went off to retrieve and bag it, Elise looked round the scullery. It made her heart sink to think of anyone spending their last moments in here with just a stinking hole in the floor.

"What was he doing down here," she said as Caro reappeared, "if Charlie had been in the house since Friday? It's freezing and damp, got no phone signal, and there's no furniture. He can't have slept in here. He had dozens of rooms to choose from—if I was hiding, this would be the last place I'd pick."

"Yeah, it's like a cell," Caro said.

"It is." Elise had been turning the idea over and over in her mind since walking into the room. "But Aoife says he wasn't tied up."

"And the door doesn't have a lock. We searched the house on day one but didn't find anything significant. DI Ward was convinced Charlie was hiding in here, ran into the cellar, had his heart attack, and was hit in frustration by the pursuer."

Elise looked round the room again. "Maybe. Do you remember Pauline said she never went upstairs in the big house when she was being questioned—and then got all defensive. I think we should search the house again. Top to bottom."

"Right."

Elise could hear the edge in her sergeant's voice as she organized the new search and wondered how she would cope with changing horses midway through a case.

"Boss, up here." Caro's voice echoed down through the floors above. Elise was panting by the time she reached the top of the house.

"Okay, we've found a door we missed first time," Caro said, cutting her off at the landing. "It's at the end of the attic. No handle—so that explains the screwdriver—the door's wallpapered to match the walls and there was a bookcase in front of it. Not making excuses, just saying. I'll have whoever cocked up."

Two young officers stopped talking as soon as Elise walked in. The only window was broken and choked with vegetation invading from the roof but she could see a stained sun lounger, a sleeping bag, a bucket, and a table spread with letters and bills.

"Never mind bollocking people. That can wait. Let's get going up here. This was where Charlie was hiding. But who from? And what made him leave? It doesn't look like he was coming back, does it?"

"No. He had his laptop and passport in his bag."

"He was going on the run. But he didn't make it out of the house."

"Look, there's lots to get on with here, boss. I'm taking you home. We'll have more in the morning."

Elise suddenly didn't have the energy to argue. She trudged back down, stepping over broken treads and clinging to the banisters as the many faces of Charlie Perry danced in her head: devoted father, local saint, frightened victim, fake. . . .

BEFORE

FORTY-SIX

Five days earlier

Charlie

THE SUN LOUNGER CREAKED ominously as he turned over and tried to sit up the first time. His watch said two twenty-five. And it was definitely daylight. So Saturday afternoon. Charlie touched his head to check it was still there. He felt like death. His mouth tasted of death. He hadn't drunk himself to a standstill like that for a while and his bladder felt like it was about to explode. He tried to swing his legs over the side of his makeshift bed and realized he was too late. It already had. He felt the sticky dampness of his trousers against his legs. Smelled it. *God, has it really come to this?* He needed to get himself together. Get ready. He found the brandy bottle and finished the last of it, slumped backward, and went back to sleep.

When he woke again, the sun was shining on his face and his watch said eight ten and it took him a moment to figure out it must be Sunday. *Christ!*

He made as if to leap into action but it took him another five minutes to inch and then heave himself upright. He shuffled over to a bucket he'd put under a leak in the roof, peed slowly and inter-mittently into it, and then rubbed his face to get the blood going.

"Come on, Charlie," he croaked. "Think."

He reached for an open bottle of water and glugged it down as he tried to track the lost hours since Friday night. They came back to him in flashes. Lots of flashes. Bright lights. Brandy. A great deal of brandy. And people. Hundreds of people crushing him. Grass. It had smelled so good when he'd lain down on it. And a van. Some-one putting him in a van. And falling down on the drive. And the stairs. So many bloody stairs to the attic. No wonder his legs hurt.

And Stuart Bennett.

Oh, God, he'd been there.

Charlie sat back down and swung round on the lounger, staring into the corners of the room as the dread surged through him. He automatically reached for the brandy. An inch would do it. But the bottle had been wrung dry. He closed his eyes and tried to take deep breaths.

But he could still see Bennett, scanning the crowd. Charlie hadn't recognized him straightaway. But when Bennett had turned his way, he'd seen the snake tattoo on his neck and thought he was going to be sick.

Bennett hadn't stuck to the plan. Charlie's plan. He'd hunted him down to Ebbing.

Charlie had ducked down immediately and disappeared into the trees on the edge of the arena and waited. He didn't know how long he'd sat there, paralyzed by fear, waiting for retribution to ar-rive out of the shadows. It played like a recurring nightmare in his head but he'd managed to get away from Bennett. Get home. That was the main thing. Now Charlie had to get things back on track.

He looked round the dump he called his satellite office. The door had been papered over at some point and he'd almost missed it on his hunt for work space. He'd been intrigued enough to trudge downstairs to fetch a screwdriver to force it open. But if he'd been expecting a comfortable sanctuary, he'd been disappointed—it'd been as empty and decrepit as he felt.

Flaps of ancient wallpaper hung down indecently and ropes of vegetation were growing in the window, where glass used to be. There was no power—the electricity board had cut them off. But still, it was the perfect hiding place: out of sight and range of Pauline's voice—and anyone else who was looking for him. He'd kept quiet about it—telling Pauline he was working in the shed—and discreetly lugged garden furniture up there: a picnic table for a desk, a folding chair, and the faded orange lounger for siestas. She'd never been interested enough to seek him out. *Out of sight, out of mind.*

He sighed. Pauline had disappointed him like every woman in his life. Apart from Birdie.

He pushed aside stems and leaves to peer out of the window. He could spit on the caravan roof from here. So he did. Just to see. It was all quiet on the home front and his stomach rumbled but he wasn't going down there until he was sure the coast was clear. He let his mind wander back to the festival. And shut it down again. He needed to focus on how he was going to bring things to a close.

He groaned loudly as he bent to retrieve his phone from the floor.

"Christ!" he growled. "It's dead."

He lumbered across the room to his desk and rummaged for the other one. The scuffed and scratched one he'd found in his car. That was dead too.

The crunch of gravel brought him back to the window. Bram O'Dowd was parking his truck in front of the caravan, as bold as brass. *Here for a second show, are we?* Well, it would keep Pauline busy for a bit.

He tiptoed down the stairs and scurried across the drive.

O'Dowd had left the key in the ignition. *Bad things happen to careless people,* Charlie told himself as he levered a screw out of an old scaffolding plank and stuck it in a front tire.

By the time he got inside the caravan, it was already creaking rhythmically on its axle and he tried not to listen to the moans coming from his bedroom as he plugged in the scratched phone behind the toaster. The other charger was in the living room and he connected his own handset and shoved it behind a sofa cushion.

Silently, he made himself a cup of coffee from the hot tap—the kettle was so old, it sounded like a plane taking off. He was starving, but the fridge contained only a half bottle of prosecco that made him dry-heave at the thought and a probiotic drink that Pauline imagined would hold back the years.

He tried to remember the last thing he'd eaten. Things were hazy but it had probably been the disgusting sandwich Pauline had left out on Friday. He'd known right away it hadn't been for him—when was the last time she'd bought him anything?—or her. She didn't eat white bread. It was for Bram. And he'd taken a territorial bite, planning the torture he'd inflict one day on his usurper's superior genitals, and looked for something to wash his rage down. Nothing. He'd had to go on a drink hunt. Find an off-license where he didn't owe money. It'd been the beginning of his lost night.

Charlie opened the tumble dryer and pulled out a change of clothes, pushing them into a holdall. He was about to make another coffee to take with him when he heard the creak of springs. *Shit! That was quick.* And he was out of the door and crouched behind the security fence before Pauline emerged, pulling on her stupid peignoir.

Bram followed her in his boxers, He hadn't even bothered to put his trousers on. They were flung carelessly over his shoulder while he kissed Pauline good-bye and hopped into the driving seat.

Charlie shoved his fist in his mouth as Bram drove off. It would take a couple of hundred yards before his tire went flat and the truck listed over. He wished he could see Bram leaping out and swearing but he had to get on. He was still grinning at the thought as he crept round to the back door of his house. Until he realized he'd left the phones in the caravan.

He knelt just inside the front door of the house, watching through the letter box and praying for Pauline to leave before she saw them. It appeared God had been listening when Charlie saw her drive off in the Jag twenty minutes later. But as he opened the door of the house to go and retrieve the mobiles, Dee's car pulled up and he quickly ducked back in.

Charlie watched her from the hall window as she walked to the door of the caravan. Her dark hair was swinging. *Just like Birdie's.* And he was back at the festival. And the face that loomed out of the darkness and he'd felt icy fingers clutching at his heart. Everything from that night was slick with terror. He sat down on the floor and tried to breathe deeply.

Pull yourself together, for Christ's sake.

But the icy fingers twitched again when he heard the letter box flap open. Dee was at the door of the house. He tried to hold his breath but the panicked wheeze from deep in his lungs threatened to explode into a coughing fit. The flap clattered down before he was exposed and he heard Dee go back to the caravan.

Ten minutes later, the door slammed and he heard his cleaner roar off in her car without locking up. *Bloody hell, what is going on?* He crept across the drive and inched the door open. Nothing.

She's probably just late for her next job, he told himself. This whole situation was making him paranoid. He needed to calm down.

And his breathing was slowing after he collected his phone

from behind the cushions and picked up the other one in the kitchen. But when he turned it on, there was an old message waiting there. **Hello, mate. Why aren't you picking up?**

He turned the phone off, stuffed it in the holdall, and searched for his passport in the drawer. He needed to keep his options open. Charlie had originally planned to meet Bennett in London to keep his new life in Ebbing secret but there was no point now. Bennett was already here. And if things didn't work out as he hoped, he might have to disappear properly for a bit. He would stash the bag in the shed just in case he had to leave fast. He just had to hold his nerve.

Charlie went back up to his office and sat at his laptop. He e-mailed Addison1999 first: "Meet me at six fifteen tonight in the car park for the coastal footpath a mile out of Ebbing on the Portsmouth road. I'll wait half an hour."

The second e-mail was to Birdie, in case it all went wrong, begging her forgiveness for letting her down. He hoped he wouldn't have to send it as he saved it to Drafts and packed his computer.

At six o'clock, when the crowds of day-trippers and weekenders started heading back to London, he picked up his bag and walked slowly down the stairs. He had an appointment to keep.

FORTY-SEVEN

Kevin

KEVIN HAD BEEN CROUCHING behind a tree, watching for what felt like an age. He'd been asking himself what the hell he was doing when he heard a click, like a door closing somewhere. He waited, trying to control his breath, an angry pulse beating in his temple. But all he could hear were the tiny sounds of something moving through undergrowth. A rat suddenly emerged into the sunshine. *Fucking vermin.* He punched the tree. But behind the rat came a shambling figure, glancing from side to side, stooping low and moving fast.

The adrenaline pumped Kevin upright like an inflatable doll. "I think we need a word, Charlie," he hissed when he'd closed the gap between them.

Charlie looked like he might die on the spot but quickly recovered himself. "My dear man." Charlie tried the shtick he must have been using successfully for years.

Kevin laughed and Charlie looked even closer to death.

"You can cut that out now. You're as fake as that accent. You never went to Harrow, did you? You're a con man. Now, where's the money?"

"There's a slight hiccup on that front," Charlie said, his eyes darting about, and Kevin wondered if he was going to make a run for it. He'd probably done it before but that must have been when he'd been young and fit. He wouldn't even make the caravan now.

"I bet there is," Kevin said, and strong-armed him into the nearest shed. "What have you done with it, Charlie?"

Kevin stood blocking the door and the light so Charlie couldn't see his face. "How much is in the company account?"

"Well, I'm not sure. I'm waiting for a client repayment as we speak. If you'll just be patient for another couple of days—"

"No, that won't be happening. You need to show me the account now."

"My dear . . . Kevin. How can I do that? We're standing in a shed in the dark."

"Give me your phone! And where is your laptop?"

"Laptop?"

Kevin slapped Charlie's face. It shocked both of them. And breached the last pretense that this was going to end in a handshake.

"There's no need for that," Charlie said, handing over his phone and feeling his cheek.

"There's every need. You need to understand that we're not going to be scammed. We know who you really are."

" 'We'?"

"Toby Greene and I discovered our mutual interest this afternoon."

KEVIN HAD BEEN WALKING along the harbor arm, his head buzzing. An hour earlier, he'd been ready to throw in the towel—Charlie and the money were long gone. Abroad, no doubt, and Kevin would lose everything he owned. He'd been in despair until his cleaner—

that mousy little woman who crept around like a burglar—had spoken up. Good old Dee had seen Charlie's passport in his caravan. He hadn't left the country. And he could be back to collect it.

But how to catch him? Kevin had been planning his next move when Toby caught up with him. Kevin gritted his teeth—he didn't want to talk to anyone—but Toby didn't pick up the signals.

"Hi!" Toby said. "How are you?"

Kevin knew Toby didn't really want to know but schoolboy manners ensnared him as efficiently as a fisherman's net. He put on the brakes and fell in step.

"Good, good," he said. "You? Business going well?"

It was what blokes of a certain class and age said to one another when there was nothing to say. Younger men would talk about football or sex. Older men: knee joints or dogs fouling the pavements.

"Yeah, all good, thanks. You?"

Kevin suddenly felt exhausted with the effort of this pointless fake banter and sank down on a bench. "Actually, I'm in a terrible mess," he said, burying his head in his beautifully manicured hands.

Toby slumped down beside him. "Same."

"Finances?" Kevin muttered.

"Yes. I'm in the shit. You?"

"Same. In a bit over my head, if I'm honest."

"Oh, God, so am I," Toby blurted. "Saul and I are supposed to be flying to LA on Saturday to start a surrogate pregnancy. But I haven't got the money. And I can't tell him."

"Christ!" Kevin pulled a sympathetic face. "Well, I suppose my baby is about to go down the plughole too. My project should have been home and dry by now. My investment was assured—the money was promised."

"Me too," Toby said.

Kevin looked at him. "Who did you invest with?"

"It doesn't matter," Toby muttered. "He's gone missing."

"Charlie," Kevin whispered as if to himself, and Toby turned his head.

They'd looked at each other for a long time before Kevin told him about the passport.

Charlie looked up at Kevin now, eyes flicking from side to side, looking for escape.

"Look, I'm not a well man—I'm dying," he croaked.

"We're all dying." Kevin pulled the shed door closed and rang Toby.

FORTY-EIGHT

Four days earlier

Toby

KEVIN TOLD TOBY TO come straightaway.

"Why? What's going on? What have you found?"

"The main prize. Just get here. And, Toby, don't drive in. Put your car in the parking area down the road—there's a gap in the hedge in the far corner. You can get to the back door of the house from there."

Toby's face was clenched into a rictus grin and his hands were clamped onto the steering wheel as he drove. *This could be almost over,* he told himself. Kevin had said it was the main prize. He couldn't think further than that.

He shouldn't have worn his good shoes. The path was dusty, and as he stumbled over the rocks and tussocks, dirt swirled up onto his cream trousers. He swept his hand over his trousers but doing so made them worse, rubbing the dirt deeper into the material. Saul would see. How was he going to explain?

Kevin's face suddenly appeared at a window on the ground floor, and he pointed at a door farther along the façade.

It creaked loudly as it opened and Toby looked round to see if anyone had heard. He could hear distant music—a radio? Pauline must have been just on the other side of the building and he held his breath.

He was in a dark corridor. "Kevin," he called softly.

"Down here. Come to the end of the passage. We're down the stairs."

We. Had he found Charlie? Toby did an air pump in celebration and marched off to have it out with him.

He wasn't sure what he'd thought he'd find, but not this.

It was a scene out of *Reservoir Dogs.* It was some sort of kitchen—there were two stone sinks and a drain in the middle of the floor. It stank.

And Charlie was sitting on a kitchen chair with an old tea towel stuffed in his mouth. He had his eyes shut. Toby could taste the fear in the room when he licked his lips.

"What the hell's going on?" he blurted. "Why have you gagged Charlie?"

He lurched forward to pull the towel out but Kevin grabbed his arm.

"Hang on. He isn't playing ball. He needs to know we mean business."

Charlie looked at Toby, his eyes pleading with him.

"Business? What are you talking about?" Toby shouted. "We're not mobsters."

"Shut up, Toby."

"Take that gag out or I'm leaving."

Kevin leaned over and yanked the end of the towel, letting it unravel and fall from Charlie's mouth into his lap.

Freed, Charlie coughed and choked, his face turning puce. When he quietened, he looked at Toby again. "Thank you, old man. Things have got a bit out of hand, haven't they?"

"Not as out of hand as they will get if you don't start producing our money," Kevin said from the corner of the room.

"Look, Charlie," Toby said quietly. "It is quite simple. You took our money and we want it back. Just transfer it into our accounts and we will leave. No one wants it to get nasty. . . ."

He certainly didn't. He didn't really know much about Kevin Scott-Pennington—he'd had him down as educated, sophisticated, cool, but he could almost smell the testosterone coming off him. Toby felt like he was back at school, watching the big boys pulling the trousers off his writhing, sobbing friend, helpless, angry, afraid.

"Come on, Charlie, let's get this sorted out."

Charlie shook his head. "My dear boy, I have tried to explain to our friend here that it isn't that simple. I've been let down too. We are all in the same boat. I'm going to lose my house."

Toby looked over at Kevin.

"It's bullshit," Kevin said. "Tell Toby about the other people you've conned. Your former business associates in London—"

"I haven't!" Charlie tried to bluster it out. "There may have been a misunderstanding. An honest mistake. All resolved."

"Misunderstanding?" Kevin shouted, spit flying out of his mouth. "I've been making calls and that's not what they say. The only mistake here was us getting duped into your dirty scheme."

"Is there any money left?" Toby croaked.

"A few hundred," Charlie said quietly. "I made a chancy investment and it didn't pay off—you both knew there were risks involved."

Kevin flew across the room at Charlie. "You've stolen it, haven't you? This whole investment company is a fabrication. He's done nothing but lie to us, Toby, from the moment we met him. We've been had."

"I'm calling the police."

"No. Not yet," Kevin hissed. "He's stashed the money somewhere—I bet he was about to run off with it. He's got a bag with him. I think we should leave Mr. Perry to think things over for a while. Come to his senses."

Toby looked at Charlie. He'd stolen their future. "Nice little business you've got here," Charlie had said when he first offered to help Toby find the money for the baby.

Toby could see himself, excitement fizzing up his spine, as Charlie laid it all out. "It's by invitation only," he'd murmured, and winked. "But I think I could persuade the syndicate to allow one more in."

Saul would leave him when it all came out. He'd have nothing.

"We need to make sure he doesn't escape," he said now, and Charlie's head slumped onto his chest.

Toby crept back to his Volvo to find a strap he'd used to tie luggage down but came back with a giant roll of cling film he'd bought at the Cash and Carry instead.

FORTY-NINE

Charlie

T'D GOT DARK IN the basement. And cold. Charlie had struggled against his bindings as soon as they'd left, sure he could loosen them and get away. *Bloody amateurs,* he'd thought when they'd wound cling film round his body and told him they were leaving him to think it over. Not what he'd have done.

But the plastic film only got tighter as he pushed against it. Too many layers. Charlie was suddenly too tired to try anymore. The confrontation had exhausted him—fear did that. And he'd been afraid when Kevin had stuffed the towel back in his mouth. He struggled, fighting the wet material with his tongue and gagging. He knew he had to control his breaths, counting slowly in his head until the steel bands round his lungs started to give. Like his little girl must have done.

He let his body droop. He'd rest for a bit and then have another go. The light was fading, so he didn't need to close his eyes but he did anyway. To shut it out. To shut Birdie's terror out. And his guilt.

But the seed of his nightmare had germinated. Tendrils of dread wound themselves around him like another layer of cling film. The terrible images of that night played on a loop in his head.

He'd seen her in the ambulance and thought she was dead.

But it hadn't been him who'd done that to her. It was Stuart Bennett. An addict with a volatile temper who'd gone into the house where his daughter was sitting like a sacrificial lamb.

She shouldn't have been there. She shouldn't have bloody well been there, screamed in his head. But she had been. She'd let herself in with the key Charlie had given her. Pressed on her when they started seeing each other again. Their little secret.

It'd been a risky strategy but he'd been the instigator, waiting outside her school one afternoon, following her to the bus stop and sliding into the seat beside her.

"Hello, Birdie," he said. "I've missed you so much."

She didn't want to make a fuss on the top deck of a crowded bus and pretended to look out of the window while he quietly pleaded his case.

"Your mum and I fell out of love but I never stopped loving you. You are my little girl."

"I'm nearly eighteen. And you lied to us," she said.

"I never lied about how I feel about you."

He'd brought a present with him in case he needed a sweetener. A pretty silver necklace with a pendant. And her face softened.

"It's mistletoe," he explained as she opened the small box, "because you always loved Christmas—and kisses."

It swung things his way and they talked more and planned a second meeting before she got off the bus.

"Will you tell your mother you've seen me?" he said.

"I don't think so." Birdie smiled. "She might not understand. Let's keep it our little secret for the moment."

When Charlie had got fed up with taking bus rides, he'd given her a key to the house in Addison Gardens. "Give me a call if you're coming round so I can make sure to be there," he said. Later he wrote down the code for the house alarm "just in case I have to go out."

And he was congratulating himself on reeling her back in when he realized a small silver rabbit—one of his first purchases for his collection—had gone missing. He thought he was getting careless, but when, a month later, he couldn't find a favorite charm bracelet, he sacked the cleaner and was about to report it to the police. But then a silver pillbox disappeared. And one evening he came home early and found Birdie there.

"I tried to call," she said, eyes of innocence. "I didn't think you'd mind. I was just watching the telly and waiting for you to come home."

And she curled up beside him on the sofa, telling him about a university course she was keen on, calling him Daddy.

He tried to enjoy it—it was what he'd longed for, wasn't it? But he wasn't able to stop wondering how often she'd let herself in and out without him realizing.

Charlie had blamed Lila—he persuaded himself that she'd found out about him and told Birdie to steal from him. To punish him. And his old rage was exhumed and given fresh life. He planned to confront his ex-wife and give her the list of stolen items. Make her afraid that their daughter was about to be reported to the police. He could see the scene in his head. Lila in tears begging him to forgive them.

And he would be the big man and sort it all out; of course he would. And she'd be so grateful. And she'd know he couldn't be played.

But he had a bit of business to get out of the way first. A brilliantly simple plan he'd come up with to sort out a financial problem.

And suddenly everything came crashing down around him—plates skittering off their poles and smashing into tiny pieces.

The burglary had ruined everything. Bennett had ruined everything.

And you, Charlie, a voice whispered in his head. *What would Birdie say if she knew?* the voice said. Louder. *If she knew what you did?*

Now only Bennett knew the truth of that night. He was the final witness. And Charlie wondered how long he'd waited at their meeting place.

Charlie shuddered and it brought him back into the room. He didn't know how long he'd been sitting there. A fly was buzzing somewhere in the room. Landing on his face. Torturing him.

He was wasting time. He tried to jerk the chair toward the door.

The legs squealed against the tiles as he inched backward but he got too eager and tried to jump the chair farther. It lurched onto two legs and fell sideways to the floor. He lay there, moving on to plan B. He'd have to wait for his tormentors to come back and talk his way out, promise a bit of money. He was practicing his lines in his head when he realized the fly was no longer buzzing.

Someone must have let it out. While he was fighting to get free. Opened the door behind him. And come in. He tried to turn his head to see.

A torch blinked on and blinded him.

"Toby, old man? Kevin?" he gurgled through his gag.

Silence.

"Toby? Kevin?" He could hear the guttural tremble in his voice growing. It wasn't them, was it?

"Stuart?" he whispered.

FIFTY

Toby

TOBY WAS DRESSED IN black for the showdown. It had seemed appropriate as he pulled on black jeans that were slightly too snug and a polo neck in the dark as Saul slept in the next room. Kevin had clearly had a similar thought but his clothes fitted him. He looked the part but Toby just felt ridiculous—and sick—when he met him at the back door to Tall Trees.

"Come on," Kevin whispered out of the dark.

Toby could see a tire wrench in Kevin's hand. "What's that for?"

"Never mind that. Are you ready?"

Toby wanted to ask, *Ready for what?* but he didn't dare. He didn't want to know. He'd been so full of it earlier. Testosterone pumping as he'd helped secure their prisoner, and talking like a gangster. But he wasn't a gangster—he was a successful restaurateur leading a foodie revolution in Ebbing.

"Kevin," he said, but his partner was already leading the way downstairs and flinging the door open.

They both just stood there when Kevin's torch lit up the scene.

"Oh, God!" Toby breathed.

Kevin didn't speak. He walked forward into the spotlight and bent over the figure to slap him on the side of the head.

"Stop faking!" he shouted into the gray face. "Where's my money?"

The body on the floor didn't move.

"Oh, God, is he breathing?" Toby wailed.

"Shut up!" Kevin snarled. "Help me get him upright."

Toby didn't move. "I'm not touching him," he said.

"Get over here!" Kevin roared, and Toby jerked to attention.

He couldn't see any part of Charlie he was willing to get hold of. The dead man looked like a human chrysalis curled on its side, the torchlight bouncing off the plastic film that still attached him to the chair.

"He's a con man," Kevin said. "He's full of tricks."

"This isn't a trick. Can't you see he's dead?"

"He can't be. He fucking well can't be. I won't let him be. I'll wake him up."

And Kevin picked up the tire wrench. And stroked Charlie's face with the cold metal before raising it above his head.

Toby thought his chest was going to explode. "Stop! Stop!" he screamed. "We need to get out of here. They'll say we killed him. Oh, God, have we killed him?"

Kevin lowered the weapon and sank down on his haunches. "Shut up! Let's get the cling film off him. It'll have our fingerprints all over it."

Toby ripped through the layers with a small penknife on his key ring, gathering the plastic into a compact ball while Kevin paced the room.

Neither said a word as the seconds ticked by. It felt like days since they'd walked in, but when Toby looked at his watch, it was just fifteen minutes. Finally, Kevin spoke.

"We need to move him. We can make it look like he died in a fall. There's a coal cellar down the corridor. I was going to put Charlie in it first off but there was an open hatch and I thought someone might hear us. Where's the gag? He must have spat it out. And his bag? I thought I brought it in here. We'll have to get rid of everything."

Toby looked round and stuffed the filthy towel into the ball of cling film. But the bag wasn't anywhere and he couldn't remember if he'd even seen it. Maybe he'd just heard Kevin mention it.

"Forget it," Kevin said. "It must still be in the shed. Let's get on with this."

They both raced to take Charlie's legs. And Toby won. There was no way he was going to be at the head end. He knew it was a crazy idea but he didn't have an alternative. He just wanted to get out of there but he knew Kevin wouldn't let him.

He dropped Charlie's legs twice, his hands slippery with fear, but they eventually got him into the cellar. Toby smelled the dirt floor and the faint scent of diesel as they hauled Charlie under the gaping hatch, gasping for breath, the adrenaline beginning to ebb.

Kevin tried to arrange the legs and arms into a star shape—relying on comic book images of fatal falls, Toby thought—but they wouldn't budge.

"He needs an injury," Kevin muttered as if alone, and Toby wondered if Kevin even remembered he was there. "He needs a fatal head injury from the fall."

Toby squeezed his eyes tight shut as Kevin hit Charlie with the wrench. But he heard the blow, the soft thud of bone devastated by metal, and knew he would never unhear it. Neither said another word. There was nothing left to say.

NOW

FIFTY-ONE

Elise

ELISE SAT AT THE window with her one cup of decaf for the day. Mulling. The many faces of Charlie Perry. And she wondered if she was anywhere close to knowing who he really was. She wasn't alone. His neighbors had seen only what he'd allowed—the charming, twinkling version—and she wondered what he'd been like once the door of his caravan closed.

She looked through her case file, searching for him. And stopped at the black-and-white photo of Birdie. Charlie hadn't told anyone in Ebbing about the attack that had left her brain damaged. He'd let them believe it had been the result of an accident. But why would he hide that? It was a random tragedy. It wasn't as if it would make people think less of him, would it? But did he think it would?

She rang Caro.

"You're not supposed to be working today, remember?" Caro said. "You are way over your hours already. Get off the phone or I'll tell McBride."

"Shut up, Sergeant. Look, I want to talk to Charlie's old neighbors in London."

Caro sighed loudly. "But this case is all about Ebbing, isn't it? We've got the unfaithful wife and her lover in the frame—and now Pauline says Charlie had been up to his old tricks. We need to be looking for the people he's been conning to raise money, not digging into some ancient case that was solved twenty years ago."

"Yes, yes, but the bottom line is that our victim is not the man people thought he was. He had secrets and we're missing something. I just feel it in my waters."

"Thanks for that image," Caro laughed. "Okay, but we'd better get a wiggle on—the inquest opens this afternoon and the coroner will use Charlie's real name. I imagine the press will be straight on the trail. I'll pick you up in an hour."

"Lovely."

"IT'S GOT PILLARS," CARO said, standing in front of the black iron railings of 16 Addison Gardens and craning her neck to look right up to the roof.

It was four stories with a kitchen in the basement and two attic windows. It made Elise think of the Darlings' house in *Peter Pan*. *But no fairy tales here.* There was no one home when they knocked but Caro noticed a face at the window next door. The door to number 18 opened and a woman came out with a watering can. Elise would have put money on there being no water in it.

"Hello," she said. "Sorry to trouble you but I'm trying to find out about someone who used to live here."

"Let me guess. . . . Charles Williams?"

"That's right! How did you know?"

"Nobody has ever come looking for anyone else. It's always Charles and I've been here since the year dot."

"Who has come looking?"

266

She rolled her eyes. "People he owed money to, generally. There were quite a few in the beginning. It tailed right off but we still get the odd one. Some odder than others. He was a charming man at a drinks party but a bit of a rogue, our Charles. He moved years ago. So why are you after him?"

"We're detectives," Elise said, and produced her ID.

"Ah! What's he been up to now?"

"I'm afraid he has died. In unexplained circumstances," Elise said, and the neighbor put down the watering can.

"Goodness," she said. "Do you want to come in out of the sun?"

The house was shuttered and wonderfully cool inside and Mrs. Simpson introduced herself as she poured them cold, fizzy water that beaded the glasses. Elise could hear herself gulping it down but couldn't stop.

"This is a great house," Caro said. "Is next door the same?"

"Hardly; they've ripped everything out—months of building work, and the dust! It's nice if you like that kind of thing. No doors but very modern."

"How did Mr. Williams have it?"

"Oh, it was lovely—filled with beautiful things: antiques, silver, paintings. He was a collector, you know."

"Were you here when his daughter and her boyfriend were attacked?" Elise asked, pressing the glass to her cheek.

The neighbor sat forward in her chair. "I was. Those poor young people. He was beaten to death and she was smothered, you know? While we sat watching some silly Christmas film on the television. Afterward I kept thinking if we'd only turned the TV off, we'd have heard something. Could have prevented it, perhaps. The first we knew was when the police arrived. One of the neighbors saw the front door left wide open."

Elise nodded sympathetically.

"It was a terrible time." And Mrs. Simpson hesitated. The detective waited for the "but." "But we've always wondered about it. Sofia had a key and the code to the main alarm, but what about the other alarms? On the rooms with the collections? Charles boasted they were top of the range and linked to a private-response company. But nothing went off."

"Did you say anything at the time?"

"Well, we didn't like to. The boy was dead and Sofia was in a coma. Charles had that to deal with. And then he sold up and moved."

They sat quietly for a moment.

"You said there was still the odd visitor looking for Charles," Elise said. "Has anyone come recently?"

"Well, there was a man round Christmastime. He wasn't the usual—he wasn't banging on the door demanding money. He just loitered around in the street and I didn't like the look of him. You have to be careful round here—with the park just across the road. You get all sorts. Anyway, I sent my husband out to speak to him and he said he was just looking someone up. My husband said Charles didn't live here anymore. We'd heard he'd moved out of London. And the man walked off."

FIFTY-TWO

Kevin

K EVIN SCOTT-PENNINGTON SAT AT his laptop while the household whirled around him. The twins were struggling into their wetsuits and squealing about the sand they'd failed to rinse off them the last time.

"There's grit all over the floor," Janine shouted. "Do it outside."

He hunched his shoulders against the onslaught and pretended to study his screen.

He should have been back in the office, safely tucked away battling Frank Tenpenny in Los Santos on his Xbox—and batting away angry e-mails from his investors.

But Janine had refused to go back to London when she'd returned from the shop on Tuesday with her bottles of water and inside information. She'd begun with that passive-aggressive thing Kevin knew so well: "Well, we could go—I don't mind. The sea air is better for my head, and the kids want to do that kite-surfing course, but I understand if you've got to get back. Don't worry about us."

But when he refused to pick up the underlying message and carried on packing up the car, she went full frontal.

"Look, you can work from here and we'd be on our way back in a couple of days. We'd be doing a U-turn in London. Why do you want to sit in stinking city fumes? We should stay."

She didn't say she couldn't bear to miss a moment of the town's descent into depravity. The police were sticking to "unexplained," but "murder" was all anyone was talking about and Janine had found a new tribe—the women of Ebbing who'd always known this was coming to their town: Liz, who'd sold them the Gulls; Karen, who occasionally did her hair; and even flirty little Millie Diamond. The Sodom and Gomorrah girls, Kevin called them secretly as Janine recounted their latest inanities.

"Liz says Charlie always had a haunted look in his eyes. Did you see that?"

"No. And nor did you. You wouldn't have been able to pick him out in the street until this week."

"Rubbish. I definitely noticed him," Janine insisted. "The word is that the wife's involved."

"Oh, do stop this nonsense," he snapped. "Everyone in this town is suddenly Sherlock fucking Holmes."

"Kevin! There's no need for that sort of language."

THE TWINS HAD FINALLY gone and Janine sat down opposite him. *Here we go.*

"Look, I know things aren't right," she said. "Is it the business? Is there something I should know?"

"No, nothing," he said, slamming down the computer lid. "Look, everything's in hand. I'm going outside for a cigarette."

He could smell summer dying in the air as he stood looking at the sea. Autumn just round the corner. He'd kept the feeling that the year began in September from school days. All that bustle about uniforms and protractors had been about renewal and looking forward. Not like the dead hand of New Year's Day.

And drawing a line under things was his goal today. The money was gone. He would put the Gulls on the market next week. And then never come back to Ebbing. Janine would go mad but he could weather that—there'd be worse things to come. Bankruptcy. Having to ask his in-laws to pay the twins' school fees. The impending shame burned his throat. There had to be another way.

He pulled out his pay-as-you-go phone and dialed.

"Hi," he growled, and cleared his throat.

"Have you heard anything?" Toby croaked at the other end.

"No. You?"

"Nothing. How are you feeling?"

"What sort of question is that? Look, Toby, all you've got to do is hold your nerve. You'll be on a plane tomorrow."

"I'm trying." But the wobble in his voice told another story.

"You need to try harder," Kevin said, and ended the call.

Toby Greene was cracking up. Kevin wasn't going to stick around for that.

FIFTY-THREE

Elise

FEEL LIKE WE'RE just pulling at loose threads here," Caro said as she fastened her seat belt. "Where is this leading?"

"To Charlie. He was clearly bent. The people he scammed carried on looking for him for years. 'His old tricks,' Pauline called them, but he'd been at it before he even met her. But how does this tie in to the burglary? You heard the neighbor—there was something off about the whole thing. Could he have been involved? Who would know? There are no witnesses now. Birdie's memory was wiped by the attack and the boyfriend is dead."

"There's always the killer," Caro muttered, and swung the car into the traffic.

Elise slammed her hand on the dashboard and Caro did an emergency stop, shooting everything off the backseat and the dregs of a cold cup of coffee onto her feet.

"What the hell is it?" she shouted.

"Sorry," Elise said, feeling ridiculous. "I've just had a thought."

"A thought? You've ruined my new shoes. What?"

"It's eighteen years since Stuart Bennett went inside. He could be out. He could have been the man loitering in Addison Gardens."

Caro parked and pulled up the information on her tablet. "Okay, good call. He was released on license, December fourteenth, 2018," she said. "His current address is a hostel in Paddington, a couple of streets away."

"YOU'D BETTER COME THROUGH to the office," the duty manager said when they announced themselves and were buzzed in.

"Is there a problem?" Elise said.

"We haven't seen Stuart Bennett for a week. There's been no contact since he left here last Friday. He was supposed to see his probation officer but he didn't turn up."

Elise could feel her heart pick up the pace. That was the first night of the festival. The night Charlie went into hiding.

"Any family addresses? Do any of his mates know why he's disappeared?"

"He doesn't have any family listed—or mates. Bit of a lonely boy. He's had only one visitor since he came here."

"Was it an elderly man?" *Has Charlie been here?* Elise felt her fingers crossing.

"No—a young woman. She came a couple of weeks ago. She didn't stay long."

"Where is he? Where would he go?" Elise said when they got outside. "We need to talk to someone from the case."

One of the senior officers in the Addison Gardens case was still on the force, just. "I retire in three months—can't wait. The job isn't the same," he complained when Elise tracked him down.

"I just want a chat—I'll buy you a late breakfast if you like," she said. "I'm in the neighborhood."

DI Wicks had already ordered a full English before they got there—Caro said she'd have one too, and Elise whispered to the woman at the counter that she'd have wholemeal toast with avocado and a poached egg. When it arrived, Wicks looked at it as if someone had vomited on the table.

"What is that muck?" he said as he shoveled a whole fried egg into his mouth.

"It's good for you—eating this muck means I'll live longer than you." She laughed. But she didn't know that anymore. "Anyway . . . like I said on the phone, we're investigating the death of Charlie Perry—Charles Williams, you knew him as—and I'd like to find out a bit more about the attack on his daughter and her boyfriend."

"Horrible case," he said, wiping his mouth with a tiny serviette. "That Bennett was an animal."

"He's out," Caro said.

"Is he?"

"Yes, and missing," Elise said. "He went AWOL from his hostel over the bank holiday weekend."

"Well, he'll be straight back inside where he belongs when they find him."

"Could he have gone looking for Charles Williams? Did he know him? Was there any connection?"

"He burgled the man's house—that's the only connection I know of. Why?"

"A man turned up in Addison Gardens around the anniversary—days after Bennett was released."

"Right. Well, we never found any link." Wicks busied himself with his plate.

"But you looked?"

Wicks looked up and nodded slowly.

"Yeah. There were things that jarred with me. The alarms, for a start. There were two or three separate ones—but they didn't go off. It would've taken ages for anyone to disable them without the codes. Mr. Williams said his daughter knew where to find them—she'd seen him put the list in his desk drawer once and told him off for not locking them away. She could have told Bennett when he tortured her. The thing was, we couldn't ask her, could we? She was in a coma for weeks and then her injuries meant she couldn't remember anything."

"No, we've met her, poor girl."

"And there were some very valuable antiques and jewelry missing but we found only Mr. Williams's computer in Bennett's squat. My boss thought Bennett must have dumped the stuff in people's bins when it went pear-shaped. They were small items and he was an addict robbing to feed his habit, not a jewel thief stealing to order. We searched but never found anything. And he wouldn't say a word when we questioned him. The psychiatric assessment for his defense team said he was severely traumatized."

"He was? What about the victims?" Caro said.

"Quite. The father was destroyed when I told him what had happened," DI Wicks said. "He threw up in my car."

Elise put a serviette over the remains of her food.

"What do you think happened to the stolen goods?"

"I really don't know. We had our hands full with the murder and attempted murder, and as I remember, the insurance company was dealing with retrieving the stuff. I think the parties came to a settlement in the end. I could check."

"Please. Did Stuart Bennett do it alone?" she asked. "Did he have associates? Fences? People he could have stayed in touch with?"

"There was no evidence of an accomplice," Wicks said as he

wiped up the last of a yolk with a crust of bread. "But the squat where Bennett lived was full of junkies and no-hopers—there were even little kids living in that shithole. We questioned them all but got nowhere. I can have another look in the files if you like."

ELISE DROVE BACK. THEY were sitting in nose-to-tail traffic and Caro was checking her e-mails.

"There's an update from the lab," she said. "Results from the contents of Charlie's suitcase. They've found his fingerprints and the laborer's everywhere and—oh, hang on—a thumbprint on the phone matches a Philip Golding. He's on the system. Date of birth: October 1982. And a record for possessing and supplying cocaine and several drunk-and-disorderly offenses."

"Who the hell is he? He doesn't sound like Charlie Perry's type. Tell Wicks."

It didn't take him long to call back.

"I've found him," he barked down the phone. "Golding was living in the squat and questioned at the time but nothing stuck. I'm sending a photo of him. I expect he's probably shooting up in a park somewhere now."

He wasn't. A quick search on Caro's tablet showed that an inquest had just been opened into Phil Golding's death. Which was a shame on two counts, as he was also the man on Birdie's residential home CCTV.

FIFTY-FOUR

Elise

RONNIE WAS STANDING OUTSIDE her door, looking up the High Street, when Elise finally got home.

"Hi," she called, and Ronnie turned and half raised a hand. "Are you waiting for someone?"

"No, just getting a breath of air," Ronnie said, her voice flat and small.

"Ronnie? What's up?"

"Nothing." She plastered on a smile. "The heat and Ted are taking it out of me, that's all. How are you feeling?"

"I'm good, thanks. Just been up to London—come in and have a cup of tea." It was the last thing Elise needed but she was worried about Ronnie.

"I'll stick the kettle on," she said, dumping her work stuff on the sofa. "Or do you fancy a glass of wine?"

Ronnie followed her into the kitchen and leaned on the counter while she found glasses, opened bottles of Gavi and fizzy water, and rummaged for a jar of olives in the fridge.

"Come on, we'll sit outside, shall we?" Elise asked.

The garden table was crusted with salt, seagull droppings, and seeds from a bird feeder but they both pretended not to notice.

"So how is it?" Ronnie said.

"Exhausting," Elise said, kicking off her shoes and flexing her toes.

It was the first time she'd admitted it to anyone. The act of concentrating for long periods had run down her batteries like in an old mobile and she'd found herself zoning out during important conversations. Caro knew how tired she got but she hadn't let on and quietly texted Elise key points afterward.

"Perhaps you've gone back too soon?" Ronnie said.

"I hope not. But it's a bit more intense than our *Thelma and Louise* routine."

"I miss that." Ronnie drained her white wine.

"I know."

Elise knew she'd dumped Ronnie like a used tissue and the guilt sat in her throat. She wondered if Ronnie still had her incident room up in the kitchen.

"You must be dead on your feet, I should go."

"No, stay, Ronnie," she said. "Look, I could do with talking through some things."

"What things?" Ronnie sniffed. "To do with the case?"

"Yes."

Ronnie's eyes widened and she reached for the wine.

"Okay, I know who was trying to see Charlie's daughter, Birdie. A man who lived in the same squat as Stuart Bennett in 1999. And whose fingerprint was on a phone found in Charlie's bag."

Ronnie crashed her glass down dangerously and Elise discreetly screwed the top back on the wine bottle.

"Who is he?" Ronnie demanded. "Why aren't you questioning him now?"

"Because Philip Golding died two and a half weeks ago."

"Good God!" Ronnie said as she put another olive in her mouth. "Cause of death?"

"Don't get too excited—I'm waiting on the postmortem report, but he was an alcoholic found dead on a park bench. I need to find Stuart Bennett now."

"But he's in prison."

"Nope, he's out. And he hasn't been seen since the festival weekend."

"Could he have been involved in Charlie's death, then? That would be a fantastic twist."

"Hmmm. You do know that most investigations are not thrillers, don't you? Most of them are solved by good solid police work."

"Yes, yes. So could he?"

"We don't know. The Met has put out a warrant for his arrest for breaking his license conditions, so we'll see what they come up with."

"I bet Stuart Bennett's number is on Phil Golding's phone," Ronnie said, and sat back, closing her eyes in the sunshine.

FIFTY-FIVE

Elise

THE SATURDAY MORNING YOGA attendees were doing their usual competitive mat shuffle, trying to claim pole position in front of the bendy nymph about to torture them. Spinning was Elise's class of choice but her thighs weren't ready yet. Instead, she stood at the back of the hall, where tall girls always lurk, with the wrong clothes and attitude. She didn't own matching leggings, crop top, and *Oh, my God, Millie Diamond has got the barre socks as well.* But she noted that despite having the outfit, Mrs. Diamond still looked very subdued. Not chatting with the nymph or stretching showily.

Elise sat on her borrowed mat, which smelled of other people's feet, as the women talked among themselves about Charlie's death. Last week, he hadn't even merited an aside. Then it had all been about "that drug-stuffed festival" and the guilt of Pete Diamond. It had been loud enough for Millie to hear but she'd just hugged herself and swayed as if in a trance.

"They're still questioning Pauline," one said as she pulled off her sweatshirt.

"I know—I wonder if they'll charge her," the woman on the

mat next to Elise said. "They're calling her the Black Widow in the pub."

Elise studied a patch of stubble she'd missed when shaving her legs—she wasn't sure if the women knew she was in charge of the case but she wasn't going to engage.

The tinkle-tinkle music finally started and everyone was told to close their eyes and center themselves.

Elise tried but she was all over the place. The link between Charlie and Stuart Bennett was messing with her head. And what had St. Charlie of Ebbing been up to here?

She found herself still wobbling in a tree pose when the rest were lying prone under blankets to meditate. One of them was snoring.

"Er, Elise, isn't it?" The nymph came over quietly. "Would you like to do the Savasana now?"

She faked the relaxation and left as soon as was decently possible, changed, and headed for her office.

The flicker of the grainy CCTV images in the darkened room was making Elise's eyelids heavy. She steadied herself with one hand on the back of the officer's chair as he watched for vehicles visiting the Perry property.

"How are you doing?" she asked a world-weary sergeant apparently infamous in the station for his tea intake and cast-iron bladder.

"Slowly," he sighed, and pushed away his tannin-stained mug. "There were hundreds of cars on the road that weekend. It was a bank holiday and the sun was shining. People were pouring down to the coast and the music festival."

"Nightmare. Where are the cameras on that stretch?"

"There are three: at the Shell garage as you leave Ebbing; at the entrance to a parking area down the road from the property—the farmer who owns the land put it up after someone damaged his fence; and at the pick-your-own farm a mile beyond Tall Trees. I'm tracking vehicles that don't reach the pick your own."

"Anything yet?"

"Apart from Mr. O'Dowd's truck?" The officer switched screens to the images of the gardener's truck he'd flagged up. "I'm working backward from Sunday."

"What about the parking area? Someone could have walked to the property from there."

"Yep." He pulled it up on the screen. A dusty corner of a field with a hedge down one side and a fence on the other.

"It's smaller than I remembered," Elise said. "What does it take? Twenty cars?"

"About right. But one hundred and sixty-three vehicles went in and out of it on Sunday. It was a hot day, lots of families and dog walkers. The camera's up high to catch the whole area—it's not a number-plate recognition setup like in a council-car-park one—but we're going through the registration numbers we can get."

"Okay, can I see the cars that arrived after eight p.m.? When it was getting dark. They won't be walkers, will they?"

"The snoggers and doggers." He grinned. "I've just been going through them."

Elise pulled up a chair. "Show me."

"This one," the sergeant said, clicking on a still of a black SUV, "arrived at eleven forty-nine that night. Left thirty-six minutes later. We can't read the number plate because of the angle of the camera."

"Do we have the occupants?"

"Have a look," he said and flicked back to the live screen.

Elise leaned over his shoulder to watch. There was no lighting in the car park. The only illumination came from the headlights sweeping round as the SUV parked, causing the camera to flare and images to disappear. Then the interior light came on as the door opened.

"What do you think? Looks like just the driver inside." Elise squinted at the shadows inside the vehicle and watched as a figure got out and closed the door. "Male or female?" she said. "I'd say a man. Would a woman stop in a dark car park at midnight on her own?"

"Yeah, most likely a bloke. Might have stopped for an emergency pee? But it would have been one hell of a pee. And in the meantime, another car arrives."

The second car, a light-colored estate, swung into the area five minutes after the SUV.

"It looks like a Volvo to me but we're checking. And they park in the same corner as far from the road as they can and you can see the second driver gets out. Looks like date night to me."

"Have we got them returning to the vehicles?" Elise asked.

The grainy footage ran on in silence.

"That's the SUV driver," the sergeant said, stopping the film. "He gets in quickly and doesn't turn his lights on until he reaches the entrance."

The car swept out onto the road, turning back toward Ebbing, followed seconds later by the estate.

"Where do we see the cars before the car park? Did they come from Ebbing or outside the area?"

"Thing is, there are loads of these SUVs—it's the sort of Chelsea tractor weekenders use," the sergeant said as he pulled up the other cameras.

"I know. My neighbors have got one." She'd meant to have a word about it blocking the light when they parked outside her window.

"But we've got a vehicle the same color driving past the Shell garage three minutes before our one turns into the car park. See?"

A black car sped past the brightly lit forecourt and the officer's finger hovered over the fast-forward button when Elise leaned even closer.

"Go back," she said.

The black car reversed at speed and stopped.

"Look," she said. "Going the other way, it's Liam Eastwood's white van. It's got his logo on it—a dripping tap. He said he was at the Old Vicarage fire that night. Go back to the car park footage—was there a white van there? Was he there too?"

She could feel her face flushing. Liam had taken Charlie home two nights earlier. He'd known where Charlie was. Had he gone back to try to get his money?

"No white vans, boss. But he must have seen that SUV. He might have recognized it. Worth a tug. I'll sort it out."

"Actually, leave it with me. Look for the Volvo's journey and keep me updated," she said as she picked up her bag from her desk.

The phone started to ring as she walked back into her office.

"Afternoon!" DI Wicks sounded perkier every time she spoke to him. "Wasn't sure if you'd be in today."

"Couldn't keep me away and sounds like it's the same your end."

"Beats admin," Wicks said. "Anyway, I've been looking back over all the files and updating. And I think I've found an item from the burglary on a specialist website—a silver pillbox. We set up an alert at the time for the stolen goods in case any came on the market."

"When was it put on the website?"

"Three months ago. It was on a list to be looked at."

"Bennett had been out a while by then—is he selling stuff he stashed at the time?"

"That was my first thought but it's all a bit complicated. It was sold by an antiques dealer in Hamburg."

"And who sold it to him?"

"A local man who'd inherited it from his dad. He's looking for the paperwork but he thinks his father bought it in November 1999. A couple of weeks before the burglary."

"Before? Are you sure?" Elise's mind was racing.

FIFTY-SIX

Elise

HER DS LISTENED IN silence as Elise spelled out the CCTV evidence and DI Wicks's discovery.

"Well, you've been busy for someone who was supposed to be doing yoga," Caro said.

"I did do yoga, but it was all niggling at me. Where are you? I need to go and talk to Liam Eastwood about the black SUV and what he was doing up there that night."

"I'm at home. I'm supposed to be taking my little girl to ballet."

"Right."

It sounded like the seventh circle of hell to Elise but they'd taken different paths after Caro took a career break to have a baby. Elise had gone to the hospital with a present and a pink balloon that was already beginning to deflate, and had known as soon as she saw her partner that there'd been a fundamental shift. For a start, she'd hugged Elise. A first. And there'd been a softness about the way she moved and spoke that Elise had never seen before. Caro had been all edges at work—"the sharpest tool in the box," she used to joke—

but she hadn't been able to focus on anything Elise said about cases or the team. Elise had tried not to judge.

"Are you all right?" she'd asked one day after Caro came back off maternity leave. They'd been sitting in the locker room after her friend had stormed out of a team meeting over a stupid remark about breast-feeding.

"What do you mean? That new bloke was totally out of order."

"Agreed. But walking out? Not your style." *Well, it wasn't.* "What's happening?"

Caro laughed. "You have no idea, do you?"

"Well, tell me."

And she tried but she got all choked up. Elise had never seen her cry before—not even after the date-stamping—and she put her hand on Caro's back and patted it awkwardly.

"Sorry to cry on you," Caro said, "but you'd be in bits if you'd had to change a toxic nappy just as you were leaving the house. Jessie was in her all-in-one and everything. When I got her out of that, it was everywhere. On her, on me, up my nails, on my bag. I had to change every item of bloody clothing. God, that child can shit for England. And then I couldn't find the car keys."

"Christ, what a nightmare! Are you sure you can cope?" *Wrong thing to say . . .*

"Don't you start. It's bad enough with the blokes. They're calling me Mum now—have you heard? I'm not their frigging mother. I'm their colleague, their superior in some cases. I can cope. I've just got to be organized. Like you."

"It'll settle down," Elise said.

And it had. Well, Caro had.

"ACTUALLY, SOD IT," CARO suddenly said now. "My old man can take her for once—Baz, you're on tutu duty! I'm on my way."

When she arrived at Elise's, she was starving and Elise had nothing she wanted.

"Halloumi? Avocado? Seeds? Bloody hell. I'm not a vegetarian budgie. Let's go and get a ham sandwich over the road while we talk it through. And see what the locals are saying."

Doll Harman was behind the bar and nodded a greeting as Elise pulled up a stool and let Caro do the honors.

"Two Cokes and can we see the menu?" Caro asked.

"We're not doing food," Doll said. "Kitchen's closed—I'm giving it a deep clean."

"Shame," Caro chirped. "I'll have two bags of crisps instead. Meat flavor, please."

"We don't see you in here much," Doll said to Elise as she poured the drinks and deliberately blanked Caro.

"No, I've not been well."

"I heard—I'm sorry about that." And she smiled in sympathy. "How are you doing now?"

Doll leaned her bosom on the bar and winced in commiseration as they passed ten minutes discussing women they knew who'd had breast cancer, implants, bra fittings, and other hilarious moments in changing cubicles.

"When are you back at work?" Doll asked, idly sweeping crisp crumbs off the bar.

"I went back this week," Elise said. "Hard to sit at home when there's been a death on my own patch."

"Ah, Charlie," Doll said quietly. "To be honest, I thought the booze would kill him. Brandies at lunchtime! Madness. Dave had to ban him when he started to get nasty."

"Goodness! He was always so lovely when I spoke to him."

"That's what we all thought but we saw a very different side of him. He turned on Dave. Effing and blinding like a laborer. And he was very rude about me."

"No!"

"Said I was a ball-breaker because I wouldn't let Dave invest his pension in some scheme. Well, it was a bloody stupid idea. I put my foot down straightaway. 'That's our old age,' I told Dave. We're planning to buy a house in Spain when the time comes, put up a couple of deck chairs, and pickle ourselves in G and Ts. That's the plan, anyway."

"Sounds perfect."

"It is. I think we had a lucky escape. I bet others haven't."

Bingo!

"I bet. Look, we'd better get off," Elise said, sliding off the stool. "It's been lovely to chat."

"Same." Doll smiled. "Come back anytime."

"UP TO HIS OLD tricks! Wonder if that was Charlie's first try in Ebbing," Elise said when they got outside. "God, Mrs. Dave really hates you!"

"Ha! She'll hate me even more when I rearrest her son," Caro said. "But Dave didn't give Charlie his money, did he? Who else in Ebbing has got money to be conned out of?"

"Pete Diamond? And the local business owners? What about the Lobster Shack man? Toby something? His website's quite flash. We can go and see him after we've been to the Eastwoods'."

"It'll have to be quick. Baz will kill me if I'm not home for feeding time at the zoo. I said I'd be gone for only a couple of hours."

They were climbing into Caro's car when Ronnie suddenly shot out of her door and flagged them down.

"Elise, have you heard? The police were at the weekender's cottage next door to yours earlier. Suspected drowning. It's the husband. Val's heard that the coast guard got a call early this morning about a swimmer who'd disappeared from sight, and a pile of clothes was found."

"Seriously?" Caro said, scrolling through her phone. "Yep. At seven this morning. Who goes swimming at that hour? Is this him?"

She showed Elise and Ronnie a photo on her phone of a good-looking man in ridiculous swimming trunks.

"Yes. That's Kevin Scott-Pennington," Elise said. "He and his family come down most weekends."

"Perhaps he didn't know about the riptide," Ronnie said.

FIFTY-SEVEN

Dee

ELISE AND DS BRENNAN have come to see Liam. I can see it's a bit awkward for Elise but I do it every day—acting as though I don't know people when I see them in different circumstances.

"Mr. Eastwood," she says. She talks different when she's being a police officer. Her voice goes deeper. "We'd like to talk to you about sightings of your van."

"Look, I thought all this had already been cleared up," Liam says. "I told you I took Charlie home in it. On the first night of the festival."

"Yes, you did. But we want to talk about where you were on that Sunday."

"Er . . . I told you I was at Cal's football training."

"Yes, we've checked with the other parents and they've confirmed your presence. But later?" Elise says to Liam, and I try not to hold my breath. "You told me you were at the Old Vicarage fire until the early hours of Monday morning."

"I was!"

"But your van was captured on CCTV going past the Shell garage on Sunday night, just before midnight."

Liam stares at her. I hate it when he does that gormless face.

"Midnight?" he says. "That can't be. I walked up to the Vicarage—I'd had a couple of beers, so I didn't want to drive—and got home about one thirty. I woke you up, didn't I, Dee?"

"Can you confirm that, Mrs. Eastwood?" Elise says, and looks right at me.

The "Mrs. Eastwood" wrong-foots me. It feels like she's talking to my mother-in-law.

"Er, yes," I say.

"I think you must have made some mistake," Liam says. "My van was outside the house when I left and when I got back."

After Elise leaves "to make further inquiries," I turn to him and grip his arm. "Why did you ask me to confirm where you were? I didn't wake up when you got home. You had to tell me about it in the morning."

"To make them stop asking stupid questions. I was worried I'd say the wrong thing. How could they have seen my van? They've probably got the wrong night or something. Those cameras aren't reliable."

I nod. "Well, someone's got it wrong."

ELISE AND DS BRENNAN come back half an hour later, when Liam and Cal have gone to the park for a kick about.

"He's not here," I say.

"That's all right," Elise says. "It's you we want to talk to. We've checked the footage, Mrs. Eastwood, and it's definitely your husband's van. But we can't get a clear image of the driver. You appear to be the only other person with access to the keys. Could it have been you?"

"I doubt it. I was in bed. Are you sure you've got the right date?"

"Quite sure."

"Well, I mean, I sometimes go to the garage or the big supermarket to buy biscuits or something for Cal's packed lunch. I pop up there last thing for bits I've forgotten. They're both open all night."

"Why didn't you say before?"

"You were asking Liam. Anyway, I can't remember every time I go to the shop. Why are you asking, anyway?"

"We are looking at vehicles that drove past Tall Trees that night. And talking to people who might have seen something. Or someone."

"I'd have said."

"Right. Perhaps you could look at your bank account and see if you spent money at the garage or supermarket that night? It's important. You do understand?"

"Of course, Elise. Sorry, DI King. I want to help."

FIFTY-EIGHT

Toby

SAUL WAS FUSSING OVER last-minute adjustments to the luggage while Toby stared into his coffee.

"We're over the weight limit, so I'm taking out jumpers—you've got your cream jacket if it's cooler in the evening. Can you wear it on the plane?"

Toby nodded but he didn't really know what he was agreeing to. Things had been better between them since the row about his walks last week. Saul had got hysterical, accusing him of seeing another man when he disappeared off on his own even though Saul knew he wasn't the type. He'd never been on the scene, just quietly queer in the Essex town where he'd grown up. Saul had been his coup de foudre—an exchanged glance at a party had sealed the deal—and he'd never strayed once.

Toby had reached for his husband, pulling him in. "There's no one, I swear. I love you. I'm just a bit stressed. There's a lot going on, isn't there?"

"Why have you been going to the Perrys' place, then?" Saul's voice was muffled in Toby's shoulder.

Toby's whole body stiffened.

"I . . . I haven't. . . ."

"You have. Let's stop the lies now. You owe me that." Saul looked up at him, his face tearstained.

Toby pulled him even closer so he didn't have to look at him. "I've been going on walks near there to try to get my head straight, that's all," he whispered into his husband's ear.

"But you hate walking. . . ."

"There's so much going on in our lives at the moment and I've needed to find a moment to myself. I've been driving up to that car park by the footpath."

TOBY COULDN'T BELIEVE HE'D bought it but Saul had been so relieved—it meant he could get back to full-on packing for the trip.

Toby had wanted to cancel the whole thing but Kevin told him he should go ahead with it.

"Don't do anything to draw attention. And being away is a good thing."

But he should say now. Stop all this. Just say it. *We haven't got enough money to pay for a baby, Saul. It's all gone.* He practiced it as the cappuccino froth collapsed in front of him. He should say now. Now.

"Saul," he managed before his treacherous tongue stuck to the roof of his mouth.

"What? Come on, haven't you finished that coffee yet? It's two thirty! Go and get ready. I've never been in the VIP lounge at Heathrow—think of all that free champagne. I might have a massage. Come on!"

Toby was hauled out of his chair and into the nightmare to come. "Saul," he tried again but he said it so softly that his husband didn't seem to hear. He was already out of the door, wheeling the new suitcases into the hall and laughing about something.

Toby couldn't remember the last time he'd laughed. Or slept. He'd tell Saul when they got there. It was too late now. He'd tell Saul the first evening in LA. That their plans had to change. But he knew he wouldn't. How could he? What would he say about the money? Where it had gone. Why he couldn't get it back.

It was his fault. He should never have booked the flights. He'd jinxed it all by buying two first-class tickets to Los Angeles. It'd been a special offer in his inbox in June—too good to miss, he'd told himself. He'd have the money to pay for them in plenty of time with his investment due to pay out. But he should never have gone ahead.

The thing was, he would have done anything to make his husband happy. And all Saul wanted was to have a child. "It would complete us," Saul had announced from the other pillow on Toby's birthday just over a year ago.

And Toby had been thrilled initially. "A family . . . I'd love that." It would mean adopting or finding a surrogate and he wondered if his sister would do it. Or Saul's old friend from school.

"We could ask Joanie," he said.

And Saul laughed. "I'm not being funny but we don't want Joanie's DNA anywhere near our baby. You haven't met her parents. . . . Anyway, this isn't going to be a DIY project. No turkey basters, thank you. If we can afford my plastic surgery, we can afford the specialist clinics in America. They're the go-to. Five-star reviews."

When Toby had looked, the prices had literally winded him. "You're talking about a hundred grand," he gasped.

"We are talking about our child. It'll be worth it. You'll see."

And so he'd booked. And kept it from Saul. It was to have been the big reveal—a limo pulling up at the door, bags secretly packed by him, a bottle of fizz in the car. He spent hours planning every detail. He wanted to see Saul's face when he opened the front door to the chauffeur, and feel the surge of joy when he told his husband they were on their way. He'd be the happiest man in the world. But Saul had been on his own when the travel company had rung with a query and Toby had had to tell him everything. Well, almost everything. Saul had been bowled over and it'd been a wonderful day.

But the money hadn't arrived. And then Charlie Perry had stopped taking his calls.

The limo parked outside was a gleaming black monster that could take an entire school prom.

Toby picked up his jacket with the boarding passes in the inside pocket and walked out into the sunshine.

Saul was already in his leather-upholstered seat, holding a champagne flute and looking for the cheesy biscuits, when the car drew up and two women got out.

"Mr. Greene? We are police officers," one of them said.

Toby sat down hard on the pavement. The chauffeur jumped out and ran round the front of the car just as the officers reached him.

"Are you all right, sir?" the driver said, squatting down and fanning him with his peaked cap.

Toby couldn't breathe. Didn't want to breathe. He closed his eyes and let himself slump over.

Saul was now shouting. "Oh, my God! What's wrong with him? Speak to me, Toby!"

The police officer who'd called his name knelt beside the prone figure. "He isn't a good color," she announced as she checked his vital signs, then spoke softly and slowly. "Mr. Greene, Toby, I'm DS Brennan. Can you open your eyes? Tell me if you feel any pain anywhere?"

Toby's eyelids fluttered and he put his hand on his chest. "Can't breathe," he wheezed.

"Ambulance, pronto, boss."

But he could hear the other woman already talking to the 999 switchboard.

"Could you get a blanket or something to make Toby comfortable?" DS Brennan asked Saul, who was buzzing like a wasp in a glass.

Toby knew he didn't really need a blanket—the sun was beating down on him—but she probably wanted to get rid of his husband for five minutes so he could rest quietly until help arrived. Saul ran inside sobbing. When he came back, he'd brought a throw with the message *Cuddle and Chill Blanket* scrawled across it.

"It was all I could find. We've only got duvets. Oh, Toby! Don't leave me!"

The ambulance loaded Toby into the back and Saul pleaded to be allowed to go too. The last thing Toby heard before the doors shut was the chauffeur telling the officers they were supposed to be on a flight to Los Angeles.

"Do you think I should follow them to the hospital? I've got their bags in the boot."

"I honestly don't know," one of the officers said. "But I don't think Mr. Greene will be traveling anywhere today."

FIFTY-NINE

Elise

THEY HAD TO RING the doorbell twice before the door was opened. Elise had dragged Caro with her. "Look, we've got a wealthy man who has left his clothes on the beach before disappearing. A bit of a cliché, isn't it? Perhaps he had money troubles? It's got to be worth a knock?"

"A quick knock."

The missing man's wife was still in her nightclothes and looked like she'd been crying for hours.

"Mrs. Scott-Pennington? Could we come in for a moment?"

"Have you found him?" Janine gasped.

"Not yet, I'm afraid," Elise said, and watched as her neighbor tried to place her.

"I know you," Janine spluttered.

"Yes, I live next door. In number five. I'm DI King—I don't know if you knew I was a police officer. . . . I was so sorry to hear about your husband's disappearance."

"I don't understand," Janine said. "Kevin's such a good swimmer. He went in every day. I can't see how this has happened. I've just had to tell his mother." And she broke down.

Caro helped her to sit.

"We wondered if your husband had been worrying about anything?" Elise said as she pulled out a stool and a notebook. "Anything weighing on his mind?"

"No! Well, he's been busy with work. He's organizing the refinancing of a major project at the moment. He's developing new digital technology for the banking sector."

"I see. I'm sorry to be blunt, Mrs. Scott-Pennington," Elise said, "but when you say 'refinancing,' are you saying your husband has money problems?"

"He didn't kill himself," Janine blurted. "Kevin would never do that. He'd have found a solution."

"But he did have money worries . . . ?"

Janine drooped in her chair and nodded.

"Does Kevin know Charlie Perry?"

"Charlie Perry?" she shrieked. "Why are you asking that?"

"We understand that Mr. Perry was offering to help people locally with financial advice, talking to people in the Neptune about investing in a scheme. We wondered if your husband was one of them."

"My husband doesn't take barroom advice," Janine snapped. "He's a professional. A very successful man in his field."

"Of course. Did he take his phone?"

"No, he left it here. When he went out. He never did that. It was in his hand every waking moment."

"We just need to see who he was in touch with before he disappeared."

"Oh, God, he's been disappearing for weeks," she said, wiping her eyes with her hands. "It's been such a tense time. He kept saying he was swimming but his trunks and towel weren't always wet. I checked. I thought it might be another woman—but who could it possibly be? In Ebbing, for God's sake?"

"Did you argue about it?" Elise said.

"I tried to talk to him but I couldn't get anything out of him when he was here. He was always on his computer. For hours."

"Perhaps we could take that with us as well as his mobile?" Caro said.

Janine got up and fetched the phone and laptop from another room. She was followed back in by two tearful teenagers in their pajamas. "My children," she indicated. "They're very upset. We all are. My parents are on their way to pick them up."

"We're not leaving you," her daughter sobbed, and her son threw his arms round her.

"Do you know the password?" Elise said.

"No," Janine said.

"I do," her boy said quietly. "Dad let me use it for gaming sometimes."

Caro wrote it down.

"Thanks so much. We'll be in touch as soon as there is news," Elise said as she stood to go. "We'll see ourselves out."

"Refinancing?" Caro said in the hall. "I smell Charlie Perry."

SIXTY

Toby

TOBY FELT SAFE FOR the first time in weeks. Kind people were talking to him, asking him questions he could answer without double-checking his story. Saul stood at the head of the bed, as white as the sheets, murmuring he loved Toby and taking his hand every time they were alone.

When they sat him up, the doctor told him he was still waiting on some results but he was pretty sure he'd had a panic attack. "Is it your first? Are you under a lot of stress at the moment?"

Toby wanted to laugh but it came out as a sort of scream and the doctor nodded sympathetically. "Let's see what the final tests show. You get some rest."

"But we're supposed to be catching a flight to America," Saul said. "Aren't we?"

Toby nodded.

"What time?" the doctor said.

"Six thirty," Saul said, looking at his watch. "We've checked in online but we've got security and everything to get through."

The doctor sighed and turned to Toby. "I think you might be wise to see about changing your flight."

"I think that's a good idea," Toby croaked. "I still feel very shaky."

Saul kissed his head and swished aside the curtain to go and make the calls. "We've got insurance," Toby said to the nurse who was adjusting the monitor. "It should be okay. . . ."

"Just try to relax," she said, and smiled.

HE'D ONLY JUST GOT out of bed and dressed to go home when Saul tore aside the curtain.

"I've just had to spend an hour on hold, listening to 'Fly Me to the Moon,' before being totally fucking humiliated," he spat. "My card was refused by the airline and the bank said there are no funds in any of our accounts. How can that be?"

Toby put out a hand to stop the onslaught. "I'm not well, Saul," he gasped.

"Never mind that," his husband whispered fiercely. "Where is all our baby money?"

THEY HAD TO GIVE him more sedation after Saul left and he was in a sweaty doze when DS Brennan and DI King appeared at the foot of the bed like angels of death.

"Mr. Greene?" DS Brennan said softly.

"Yes," he murmured, trying to remember where the hell he was.

"How are you doing?"

The heart monitor at his side started accelerating and he tried slow breaths.

"You certainly look better than the last time I saw you."

"Thank you for looking after me," he managed.

"It's what we're here for." She smiled. "Well, among other things."

Toby took another deep breath.

DI King came round to the side of the bed. "We need to talk to you, Mr. Greene, because we're investigating the death of Charlie Perry. And I understand he'd been asking people to invest in a scheme. Were you one of them?"

The alarm suddenly shrieked on the monitor and a nurse came rushing in.

She laid Toby back down and silenced the machine. "I'm sorry. Mr. Greene isn't up to talking at the moment. Perhaps you could come back later to ask your questions."

DI King looked at him and nodded. She looked as if she'd already got the answers.

SIXTY-ONE

Elise

SHE RANG THE HOSPITAL for an update first thing and was told Toby Greene had just been collected by a friend. Elise pulled on clothes, wrestling with her bra and the stupid insert that kept falling out. She left it on the floor in the end. She couldn't fanny about—no one else was going missing in this case on her watch.

The relief manager at the Lobster Shack had pointed Elise out the back. "I went and got him this morning. They said he could come home but he's not in a good place. There's been a terrible row and his husband's gone."

Toby was sitting in the restaurant courtyard, shoulders hunched against the world. He tried to get up when he saw her but got his leg tangled in the bench.

"Hello," Elise said, noting the complete collapse of Toby's gelled spikes and the blue smudges under his eyes. "How are you doing today?"

"Not good," he said weakly.

Same, she wanted to say. She'd had a bad night; cancer demons had plagued her, preventing her from sleeping and leaving her feeling as though she might crumble at any moment. But Elise hadn't been about to let it stop her.

"I need to have that chat with you about Charlie Perry. Are you up to that?"

He nodded and led the way back inside and upstairs.

"Did you have financial dealings with Mr. Perry?" Elise said as soon as they sat down at the kitchen island.

He laughed silently. "You could call it that," he muttered. "Charlie stole every penny I had. He took it all."

"How did he do that?" Elise said.

"A scam," Toby sighed. "You think these things only happen in e-mails from Nigerian princes or fake Microsoft phone calls. But he sat at my bar and said he was helping me raise the money for our surrogate baby. Then stole from me. I invested money in a scheme he said he'd set up with some City friends. Chums, he called them. And it paid out the first time."

"But not the next?"

"No."

"When did you last see Charlie Perry?"

He looked up at the ceiling while he considered. "Not for weeks—I phoned every day and he kept saying the money was coming, that there'd been a slight delay but it was coming. And then he stopped taking my calls. I went up a few times to try to talk to him but no one ever answered the door."

"That must have been very frustrating," Elise said. "Do you know Kevin Scott-Pennington?"

Toby swallowed hard. "Er . . . he's got a holiday home on the High Street, hasn't he? He comes in the restaurant sometimes."

"We think he may also have been conned by Mr. Perry."

Toby looked at Elise, his eyes sliding around.

I hope you don't play poker.

"I don't know," he said slowly as if he didn't trust himself to say the words. "You'll have to ask him."

"I'm afraid we can't. Mr. Scott-Pennington disappeared while swimming in the sea yesterday."

Toby put his head in his hands.

"I'd like to continue our discussion at the station, Mr. Greene. And we're going to need your phone."

THERE WAS A BUZZ in the incident room when Elise stepped in on her way to the interview. Atkins practically bounded over and the younger ones on duty scraped back their chairs to stand.

"Toby Greene's husband has called in," DS Atkins said. "He says Toby gave Charlie Perry all their money and was regularly driving to the Perrys' place. He'd put a tracker on his phone because he thought he was cheating on him. We've got the data, and some days he makes the same journey four times."

"What car does he drive?" Elise interrupted. "Is it a black SUV?"

"Er, hang on. Right, so no. It's a Volvo estate. Silver."

Elise smiled. They were on their way.

"Okay, let's get that car in pronto. I've had the same story from Mr. Greene—that he was being scammed out of thousands of pounds by Charlie Perry and made repeated unsuccessful attempts to confront him about it. Did his husband say anything else? About how Toby was acting?"

The wind temporarily went out of Susie Atkins's sails.

"Er, distracted. But, hang on, according to this data, Toby Greene carried on visiting after Charlie was reported missing. Not as frequently but we've got him driving up and down the road from Saturday morning until just after midnight on Monday morning. Then he stops."

"Brilliant. Well, we'd better ask him why, hadn't we? What time was his last visit?"

"Er, twenty-three fifty-one."

Elise smiled. "Excellent. Come with me Atkins—and someone give the CCTV team the new information."

She noted the ubiquitous Mr. Grimes looked a lot less pink-cheeked sitting beside his new client. No knee patting or exchanged glances. Toby Greene was the color of the magnolia walls and she hoped she wouldn't need the first-aider.

"Why were you driving to the Perry house four times a day the week before the Diamond Festival, Mr. Greene?"

"I don't think it was that often," Toby stuttered. "But as I told you, I was trying to see Charlie Perry. To find out what he'd done with my money."

"Even after he went missing? You carried on, didn't you? Your last visit was just before midnight on Sunday, the twenty-fifth. Just hours before Mr. Perry's body was found."

"No, I didn't. I wouldn't have gone at that time of night. . . ." He dry-gulped.

"I see. We also know that you stopped calling his mobile on Sunday afternoon. Why was that, Mr. Greene?"

Toby tried to shrug but the tension in his body made his shoulders jerk as if he'd had an electric shock. "I gave up. It was obvious there was no point," he croaked, and reached for the plastic cup of water in front of him.

"Why was it obvious? What made you so sure? Was it because you'd found him?"

"No," he moaned to himself. "I can't remember."

DS Atkins produced a printout from her file. "Let me help you. We have data that shows your regular trips took a maximum of fifteen minutes door-to-door," she said. "But you changed your routine on Sunday. You didn't drive up to the caravan. You arrived at the car park near the Perry property at five ten on Sunday afternoon and stayed forty-two minutes before returning to the Lobster Shack. You made the same journey again at eleven fifty-four that night. This time you were recorded staying for thirty-one minutes."

"Data? Recorded?" Toby looked dazed by the detail. "What do you mean?"

"CCTV—and there was a tracker app on your mobile phone," Elise said.

"Saul." Toby crumpled in front of them.

"What were you doing on those final visits, Toby?" Elise pushed a box of tissues over the table. "Who was driving the black SUV that arrived at the same time? And what did you do to Charlie?"

His whole body shuddered and Mr. Grimes laid his hand on Toby's arm.

"I would like a moment with my client . . ." Grimes started, but Toby couldn't be stopped.

"We didn't kill him," he said. "He was dead when we found him."

" 'We'?" But she knew. Her view of the High Street had occasionally been blocked out by his monster car.

"Me and Kevin."

"Kevin?"

"Scott-Pennington. We'd both been conned."

"Did Charlie Perry have a head injury when you found him?" Elise pressed on.

Toby closed his eyes.

SIXTY-TWO

Elise

"WHAT'S HAPPENING?" ELISE SAID when Caro appeared at her office door. "What's the news on Toby Greene?"

The restaurant owner had collapsed sobbing on the table after his admissions, and Mr. Grimes had insisted on a medical assessment of his client.

"He's not up to any more questions at the moment," he'd said firmly. "He's getting chest pains. He's going back to A and E."

"Update in an hour," Caro said. "No sign of Kevin Scott-Pennington's body but the digital forensics team has found a cache of interesting images on his phone. He likes a bit of violent assault, our Kevin. He spent hours—and I mean hours—playing brutal video games."

"There's no law against it, unfortunately," Elise said. "What about his calls and e-mails?"

"Regular calls to Charlie but the calls to Toby Greene start only on the Sunday. E-mails to Charlie got increasingly threatening and none were answered. It all matches with e-mails on Charlie's laptop. We've cracked his main e-mail account but the techies are still working on passwords for some old ones. The latest e-mails in Kevin's inbox are from a law firm saying he's about to be sued for half a million pounds. That didn't stop him spending, though. He was burning through his credit card."

"So he was under huge pressure. People do stupid things when they are under that sort of strain. Sometimes terrible things."

"But from what I hear, Toby Greene insists that Charlie was already dead when they found him," Caro said. Elise could hear she was still sore at missing out on the interview yesterday.

"Look, I didn't call you in because I didn't want to eat any further into your family time," Elise said quietly. "You and I will push Greene further on that when we get him back in. The data and CCTV show they'd been there earlier that day. Greene said they were looking for Charlie but didn't find him. What if they were having their little talk about the money? Those sorts of conversations rarely go well, do they? What if they frightened him so badly on that first visit that he had a heart attack?"

"But why go back later? Surely, they'd have done their attempt at a cover-up straightaway? They wouldn't have risked going back a second time, would they?"

"We need to push Greene harder. . . ." Elise felt like tearing out her new hair. "When we get him back. What are we doing now?"

She suddenly wasn't sure and took a quick look at her list. "The call history on the phone in Charlie's bag? The one linked to Phil Golding?" she asked Caro.

"Chasing but it's a sideshow, isn't it? The priority's nailing Toby Greene and Kevin S-P, isn't it? We're very close to cracking this."

"Yes, yes, of course . . ." Elise knew she was right, but as soon as Caro left, she rang the forensics lab. *Just tying up loose ends.*

"I'd been told to concentrate on Scott-Pennington's phone," the officer grumbled. "But I can send you what I've found so far."

It pinged up in her e-mail seconds later and she sat down to plow through a list of numbers. The last text Golding received had arrived after his death. **Hello, mate. Why aren't you picking up?**

She searched the case files for the sender's number and whooped when it came up.

"Stuart Bennett! It's bloody Stuart Bennett!" she shouted.

"Are you calling me?" Caro put her head round the door.

"No. Come in. Stuart Bennett got in touch with Phil Golding on August the fifteenth." Elise slapped her hand down on the desk. "Were they planning something together— planning to get Charlie?"

"Well, if they were, it didn't happen, did it?" Caro said. "Phil Golding was dead on August the fifteenth. And it looks like our pair got there first."

Elise waited for Caro to leave and dialed DI Wicks to see if he'd found anything else. *Just dotting the i's and crossing the t's.*

Elise held for what felt like an age while someone went and found him.

"Elise? Sorry to keep you but I was tracking down the postmortem report," he boomed down the phone. "It got stuck in what is laughingly called the system. Anyway, you'll be glad you waited. Phil Golding died of ethylene glycol poisoning."

Elise gripped the phone harder. "Poisoning?"

"Yes. He drank vodka with an antifreeze mixer."

"Bloody hell? Was it suicide? Or did someone give it to him?"

"We don't know yet. We're opening an investigation and examining the bottle found by his body. I'll call you as soon as I've got something."

"Right—and what about Charlie's stolen pillbox? Have you got anywhere with the previous owner in Germany?"

"Bloody hell! Am I the only one working on this case? You've got a roomful of young coppers!"

"Okay. Calm down! Send me the contact details and I'll push it along."

Elise walked too fast to the incident room.

"We've got another death linked to the inquiry. It's Phil Golding," she told Caro, and knew she sounded breathless. Like a new girl. "He died after drinking vodka and antifreeze the week after attempting to visit Charlie's daughter."

"Bloody hell, that's a turnup," Caro said.

"Quite. The receptionist at Birdie's residential home said Golding never came back," Elise went on. "But let's get the security tapes for the days until he died. Charlie may have been involved in more than fraud."

Elise realized she felt good for the first time in ages. This was what made her happy. The hunt, the rush to the finish line.

Everyone was busy, so she picked up a ringing phone.

"We've got into another of Charlie Perry's e-mail accounts. An old business one, it looks like—for Williams Rental Properties," the voice on the other end said. "Can you tell the boss there's something of interest?"

"I am the boss," Elise said, trying not to smile. "Tell me."

"Sorry, ma'am. There has been nothing but junk mail for years but Charlie got an e-mail on Wednesday, August twenty-first, asking him for a meeting."

"Who from?"

"Addison1999@yahoo.co.uk."

"You are kidding! Is it signed?"

"No. No names used but they arranged to meet on Sunday the twenty-fifth. In Ebbing. I'm sending you the thread now."

Elise called Caro over.

"It looks like Charlie was on his way to meet someone from his past when Toby and Kevin grabbed him," she said, trying not to sound smug.

"But it was them who grabbed him, wasn't it? Do you think this is from Stuart Bennett?" Caro said, reading the exchange. "Why would Charlie invite him to Ebbing?"

ELISE WENT DOWN TO the local coffee shop to take some deep breaths and buy herself the sort of decaf tea the canteen staff had never heard of. But as she walked back in DC Chevening called her over.

"I think I've got something, ma'am. I've been going through Phil Golding's records and he was put on the at-risk register in 1996. When he was living here."

"Here?"

"In town."

Caro was right. It was all about Ebbing.

SIXTY-THREE

Elise

HER OTHER SECOND-IN-COMMAND'S PHONE was answered immediately when Elise rang.

"What's up?" Ronnie said.

"How old is your daughter?"

"Er, thirty-six. Why?"

"Good. Can you get in contact with her and ask her if she knew a Philip Golding when she was thirteen?"

"Phil Golding? The dead Phil Golding? How would she know him?"

"He was here in 1996. On the at-risk register—neglectful mother, it says. I need to find out why he and his family came and why they left Ebbing. I know it's a long shot but worth a go."

"It's late in Sydney, but Meggie will be up."

Half an hour later, Ronnie was back on. "He was in her class! Just for a year. She remembered him because he had the same birthday as one of Meggie's friends and they had to share a cake because he hadn't brought one in. His mother hadn't known—or hadn't bothered—and everyone felt sorry for him. She doesn't know why he was in Ebbing. Phil never talked about life at home. Meggie thinks he just disappeared during the school holidays."

"But did he come back?" Elise said, noting it all down.

CARO WAS STANDING IN the door of her office when Elise put the phone down, head on one side.

"Ronnie's just helping with a bit of background," Elise said quickly. "Her daughter's the same age as Phil Golding—they were in the same class."

"When? Could he have known Charlie here?"

"No, the Perrys didn't move here until 2013. But Phil's link to Ebbing must mean something. There's something there."

"All very fascinating but I still think you're chasing ghosts. We'll find the truth a lot closer to home. I've had a call from Dover. We put out a missing-person alert on Scott-Pennington when his clothes were found and he's turned up at the port, trying to hop a ferry. They're sending him back to us."

"Wow! His wife will be relieved," Elise said. "For five minutes, anyway. Until she hears what he did in Charlie Perry's basement."

"I'll ring and tell her he's alive," Caro said. "And check with the team on the forensics."

"WE'VE GOT MATCHES FOR Toby Greene's and Kevin Scott-Pennington's DNA in the cellar and on Charlie's clothes," she told Elise when she joined the team. "But negative for Bennett. If he was there, he left no trace."

It'd been a long shot, Elise knew, but she had to push back against the disappointment that instantly clouded her mood. She'd been so sure the roots of the crime went back to the burglary.

"Come on, we've got our men," Caro said. "Greene is on his way back in for an interview."

"SO, MR. GREENE, HOW are you feeling now?" Elise asked.

"Terrible," Toby murmured.

"Well, the doctors have discharged you, so I take it we can pick up where we left off? With Charlie Perry's head injury?"

"My client would like to make a statement to help your investigation," Mr. Grimes said, and Toby looked at his solicitor and took a breath.

"Kevin did it," he said quickly. "He said it had to look like Charlie had fallen, so he hit him with a wrench."

"A wrench? Was the weapon there in the cellar?"

"No, he brought it with him."

"You saw it? You knew he was intending violence to Mr. Perry?"

"I told him not to do it." Greene looked away.

"When? When did you tell him? When he came armed to do grievous harm to Charlie?"

"It was just to frighten him. That's what Kevin said. He wanted to show him we meant business. But Charlie was dead. And when I realized what he was going to do, I told him to stop."

"But he didn't."

"No. No, he didn't. It was awful. . . ." He faltered.

"I imagine it was," Elise said. "Did Kevin have the weapon when you visited the Perrys' house the first time that day?"

"I got there after him. I can't remember seeing it," Toby stuttered.

"Try," Elise said. "I would have thought the events of that day are etched on your brain. You saw your first dead body. You saw Charlie's head being bashed in."

Toby's mouth trembled.

"Inspector," Mr. Grimes chirped his warning.

"Okay, let's try again. Why did you go to Tall Trees on Sunday afternoon?"

"Because Kevin rang and told me to come. When I got there I realized he'd found Charlie. I wanted to ask him for my money. I just wanted it all to be over."

"Where had he found him?"

"At the house. Kevin told me that someone had seen Charlie's passport in the caravan that morning, so we were taking it in turns to watch the place in case he came back for it. Kevin caught him trying to leave and took him in the basement—in a little kitchen. He had him in there when I got there."

"What state was Charlie in when you saw him?"

"He was a worried man," Toby said quietly.

"Worried or terrified?"

"Ummm . . . he was upset. He kept saying all the money was gone. That he'd been let down like us. But Kevin didn't believe him. He said we should leave him there for a few hours to think about the trouble he was in."

"But why didn't Charlie escape when you left?"

There was a beat before Toby whispered, "We tied him to his chair."

"What with?"

"Well, we used cling film. It was all I had in the boot of the car—one of those catering rolls. We just wound it round him."

That's why there were no marks on his body. Elise couldn't wait to tell Aoife.

"Did you gag him?"

"Kevin put an old towel in his mouth. And when we came back, he was dead," Toby carried on. "He was still sitting in the chair but it had toppled over. We couldn't believe it. We just couldn't believe it. . . ."

KEVIN SCOTT-PENNINGTON TOLD HIS own version when he arrived in Southfold, handcuffed and huddled in a thin T-shirt and jogger bottoms.

"It was Toby's show," he said immediately after the recorder was switched on. "He was driving the whole thing and he brought the wrench to frighten Charlie, and then hit him with it. I was shocked."

"That's interesting," Caro said, "because we know from your phone records that you rang Toby Greene on Sunday afternoon while your car was parked near the Perry property. You summoned him, didn't you? And a wrench was bought on your wife's credit card between your two visits to the Perry house. That's some coincidence."

Kevin's solicitor, a severe-looking young woman imported from a big Brighton firm, scribbled something on her yellow pad and whispered in her client's ear.

Kevin's chin sank and he went to "No comment" as the questions continued to pile up in front of him.

But when they got to the attack on Charlie, he blurted, "I didn't hurt him—he was already dead. There's no specific offense of assaulting a dead body."

He's been googling, then, Elise thought.

"What about kidnapping and imprisoning him in the basement?" Elise said. "Those are specific offenses."

"He had stolen our money," Kevin muttered, and his solicitor tutted.

"We're also looking at charges of manslaughter, based on your actions that night."

That shut him up.

"Why did you put Charlie's bag in the skip?"

The question clearly knocked him off guard because he forgot the instruction to stick to "No comment."

"I didn't. Which skip? He had it with him when I took him into the house—he was about to go on the run. But we couldn't find it later and I didn't want to spend time looking."

"And then you rang his widow on Charlie's phone, pretending to be him? To hide what you'd done. To give yourselves time to leave."

"No comment."

"Where is the phone now?"

"No comment."

"I see. I think we are finished here for the time being. Take him back to the cells, please," Elise said.

Kevin sat with his eyes screwed shut as his solicitor packed her briefcase.

SIXTY-FOUR

Dee

THEY'VE PUT ME IN the interview room with a young copper and a cup of weak tea while they go and get Elise. I've told them I've got something to tell them. About Liam.

It shouldn't take long. He'll confess. He's right at the tipping point. And then they'll charge him.

Look, it's got to be done. Some people might say I'm throwing him under the bus but I've got to think about me and Cal. Liam is dragging us down. I can't have him around our child, bringing drugs and the police into our lives like this. I can quietly move away now. No one will blame me for making a fresh start. Maybe I'll try Devon or Cornwall. It's pretty down there. I can find a new place and begin again.

I wonder when they'll arrest Dave. I'd give anything to see Doll's face when they do.

When Elise and DS Brennan come in, Elise looks dog-tired. Her eyes are sinking. She's overdoing it.

"Mrs. Eastwood," Elise says like she doesn't know me. Well, that's fair. She doesn't really. "I understand you want to help us with our inquiries relating to the drugs circulating at the festival."

I'm sweating and I can feel my hair sticking to my head. I wonder if Elise has noticed.

I take a deep breath and she leans forward.

"Liam helped Dave Harman get hold of the ecstasy," I whisper. Like I don't want to say. "From an old mate in Brighton to get Pete Diamond into trouble. And that poor girl nearly died."

Elise looks at DS Brennan.

"Mrs. Eastwood, how do you know your husband was involved?" Brennan says.

"By accident. I found out he'd gone to meet that scumbag Spike Jefferies in Brighton. Spike was always bad news. They knew each other back in the day when Liam was into drugs—when we first got together. But . . ." I close my eyes. *Take it slowly. . . .* "But Liam told me he'd done Dave a favor by putting him in touch with Spike and helping him buy a hundred Es. Dave was going to give Liam some work if he helped him close down the Diamond Festival. He got Liam and Ade to smuggle the drugs into the event. They were going to plant them on Pete and call the police. But it all went wrong when Ade and his girlfriend took one."

Brennan writes it all down.

"Do you know where the rest of the drugs are now?"

"Under our dog's kennel in the yard. I heard Liam telling someone on the phone. I haven't touched anything."

Well, it's almost true. I had to check they were there after I heard Liam telling Dave he'd hidden them last night. I had to be sure before I went to the police. But I wore my rubber gloves.

"I won't be a minute, boss," Caro says as she skips out of the room, and I expect she's gone to arrange for Liam and the ecstasy to be picked up.

I'm ready. I made sure Cal was at his babysitter Jenny's before I came in.

"I'm just going to talk to the police about something," I'd crouched down to say to him. "Nothing to worry about. I need to help them and then I'll be back and we'll go to the beach and get an ice cream. Okay?"

Cal hadn't looked convinced but Jenny told him he could play on her laptop.

"Twenty minutes' screen time only, Cal," I'd said. I don't let him play those horrible video games.

ELISE IS LOOKING AT me hard.

"We will need you to make a formal statement about your husband's activities and all the information you can give us about Spike Jefferies."

I hesitate, dig my nails into my palms and blurt, "I can't. Liam and Spike will know it was me who shopped them, won't they? They'll come and find me. I'm frightened about what Liam would do." And I touch the old bruise on my face.

"Has your husband hurt you?" Elise says carefully, and I look away. "Has he?" And I nod.

"Look, it's essential you give your statement. This was a very serious offense. You do see that, Dee?"

I'm Dee now. And I nod again.

"But you may need to go and stay with someone. Is there family who could help?"

"No, they're all dead."

"I'm sorry. Friends?"

I shake my head. I need to think. "Can I have a glass of water?" I say.

After I've sipped the cup of tepid water brought in by the young constable, I say, "There's something else."

"What?" Elise says.

I hesitate, just long enough for her to lean forward to push me. Letting her think she's got the power.

"About the Sunday after Charlie went missing. The night you say Charlie died. I don't know where Liam was that night, or when he came home, so it might have been him in the van. We're sleeping separately, you see. Things have been tense at home—he's been very jumpy lately, what with Charlie owing him all that money and then the drugs investigation."

Elise is lapping it up and I hope it'll mean Liam is kept in custody. Just long enough for me to get away. She takes me through the whole thing again and then smiles at me.

"Thank you, Dee. I know how hard this must have been for you."

"Okay. But I need to go home now to pick up Cal—and our things. While Liam is being questioned. I've got to make arrangements."

"Of course—I'll give you a lift if you like."

I try to smile my thanks but it's the last thing I need. I want to be on my own to plan my next move.

SIXTY-FIVE

Elise

CARO HAS GOT HER confession from Liam by the end of play.

"He broke down and cried like a baby. Said it was a stupid practical joke that had gone wrong. That no one was supposed to take them," Caro told Elise afterward. "Ade Harman planted them in a bag Pete Diamond was carrying around that night—but after Ade collapsed, Liam went and found them to make sure no one else took any and hid them in his van. When he got home, he says, he pushed them under the kennel until the fuss died down and he could get rid of them."

"And lying about his whereabouts on the Sunday?"

"He says he panicked when he said Dee could confirm it but claims everything else he said was the truth. And at the moment, we've got no forensic evidence to put him in the basement."

"Not yet. But tests are still ongoing."

"Okay, but in the meantime I think Dave Harman is ready to talk, boss," Caro said.

"Great," Elise said.

The pub landlord and his legal adviser were seated side by side, heads together, when the detectives marched in. No sliding into chairs, feeling their way, winning confidence this time.

"Mr. Harman," Caro said, "we have evidence that you bought one hundred tablets of MDMA from a known dealer in Brighton and that you were part of a conspiracy to supply those drugs at the Diamond Festival."

"No comment," Dave said, his face porridgy gray with fear.

"Liam Eastwood introduced you to the dealer, didn't he?"

"No comment."

"And you conspired with Mr. Eastwood and your son, Adrian, to smuggle the tablets into the festival?"

"I am not a drugs dealer!" Dave Harman banged a hand on the table, spilling water from a plastic cup.

"You did this in order to get the festival shut down, didn't you?"

"No comment." Spit was gathering in the corners of his mouth.

"In order to plant the drugs on Pete Diamond."

There was a beat of silence. "No comment."

"What is your evidence that my client had anything to do with this conspiracy?" the solicitor said. "An earlier accusation against his son was dropped after the police acted improperly in interviewing a vulnerable witness—"

"We have recovered a number of MDMA tablets," Elise addressed Dave directly, "and we have a new witness."

Dave Harman groaned and put his meaty hands on the table.

"Liam?" he said.

Elise nodded. "Mr. Eastwood has made a full admission to his part in the conspiracy."

The solicitor whispered something urgently into Harman's ear but he shook his head. "It's over. We need to sort this out."

ELISE AND CARO STEPPED out to allow the solicitor to take fresh instructions, and walked back to the incident room. On the way, Caro was stopped by a uniform in the corridor and was grinning when she hurried to catch up with Elise.

"Shouldn't laugh but we've just been called to a punch-up at the statics. Seems Pete Diamond discovered his daughter was still visiting. He went up there and got hold of the lad she's been sleeping with and someone called the police. They're on their way in."

"God, I'm glad I don't have kids," Elise said before she could stop herself.

Caro gave her a look but didn't say anything.

"I'm going to treat myself to a proper posh coffee," Elise went on. "Do you want one? We deserve it."

She was walking through the car park when Pete Diamond stumbled out of the police van with a tissue held to his bloody nose. He saw Elise and looked like he was going to involve her, so she picked up speed. His daughter's love interest was behind him, head down until he stumbled and looked up. Elise stopped in her tracks. That face. It was on the whiteboard upstairs.

"Hello, Stuart," she said. "We've been looking for you."

SIXTY-SIX

Elise

STUART BENNETT WAS STARING at his bruised knuckles, refusing to engage with the detectives.

"Why did you text Phil Golding after he'd died, Stuart?" Elise asked, and Bennett looked up, startled by the question.

"Well, I didn't know, did I? We were supposed to be meeting for a coffee. But he went back on the booze. It was a real shame. He was trying to make something of himself."

"You should know that the police are looking at evidence of foul play in connection with his death."

Bennett stared at her. "No! What do you mean? Did someone kill him?"

"It's being investigated. When did you last hear from him?"

"We saw each other a couple of times after I got out of prison."

"But when did you first meet?"

"Years ago. We lived in the same squat for a bit. We were just kids and we all helped one another out back then."

"When was that?"

"Nineteen ninety-nine," Bennett muttered.

"Why did you get back in touch?"

"Phil came to see me in prison last year. It was completely out of the blue but he said he wanted to say he was sorry."

"For what?"

"For sending me to do the burglary at Addison Gardens."

"So it was a setup?" Elise asked. "Was it Phil's idea?"

"No, he was made to do it by the man he worked for. He threatened to plant drugs in the squat and call the police on Phil. He said he'd go to prison and his little sister would be taken into care. So Phil got me to rob the house."

"Who did he work for?"

"Charles Williams—the man who owned the house."

There it was. The final confirmation. Elise felt a bit teary and put her head down, pretending to finish making a note. When she looked up, Bennett didn't seem to have noticed.

"He was a rich bloke who owned lots of the old properties round Paddington. Phil collected rent for him. He told me the best way to get into the house and said the alarms would be fixed. It was all going to be so easy. All I had to do was take the stuff out of the cabinets, bring it back to the squat, and I'd be paid my cut. Look, you have to understand I was injecting back then—I would've done anything for my next fix."

"But it didn't go according to plan?" Elise said quietly. Nudging him along. He was ready to tell the whole story.

Bennett rubbed his eyes as if he couldn't bear to see what had happened.

"Everything was wrong. I thought I'd broken into the wrong house. There was nothing there to steal. Just empty cabinets. And the girl and her boyfriend were there. It was like I was in a bad dream."

"Why didn't you just make a run for it?"

"They'd seen us."

"'Us'? Who else was there?"

Bennett's head went down. "Phil's kid sister," he whispered. "I was minding her for him but he didn't come back. I would never have taken her with me. But she made me. She kept crying and stuff. She wouldn't stay on her own. I forgot she was there after we got in. But then—"

"What? What happened?"

"She was seen by the girl in the house. I heard her shouting. That's when it all went to hell."

"Did she see what you did? When you killed the boyfriend? And put the bag over Sofia Nightingale's head?"

"I was off my face. I didn't know what I was doing." He broke down in dry sobs. "I can't remember all of what happened."

"That poor child," Caro said. "Let's hope she can't either. How would you ever get over that?"

"Did you come to Ebbing to have it out with Charles Williams?" Elise asked when Bennett had finished blowing his nose.

"Williams? No, I didn't know he was here. I went and asked around his old place in Kensington but he was long gone and no one had an address."

"That's not true, is it? You had an arrangement to meet him here on Sunday evening. You and Charlie had been e-mailing."

"What are you talking about? I didn't have any arrangement."

"You used the e-mail Addison1999@yahoo.co.uk," Elise pushed on. She was so sure it was him. Who else would have chosen that incendiary address?

"That isn't me. You can check on my phone."

"We are. So why did you come?"

"Phil Golding's sister."

"The girl you took to the burglary?"

"Yes, she lives here. She told me when she came to see me."

The young woman at the hostel.

"I couldn't stop thinking about her. I just wanted to say sorry for taking her that night, for getting her mixed up in it. She was really upset when she left my place the other day and I wanted to tell her we had to let it go. Get on with our lives. But I couldn't find her. And then I thought I saw Williams in the street going into the festival. He was an old man, but I'd looked him up online. Seen his photos from when he was the big businessman. I couldn't believe it. Just couldn't believe it. But I had to be sure—I told myself this was my chance to confront him and tell him what he did to me, to his daughter, Phil, and to everyone who was involved. I slipped over a fence at the side of the venue and he was there, a few yards away, in the crowd. I think he saw me but I didn't get to speak to him. He just disappeared."

"Did you go looking for him? To confront him away from the crowds?"

Bennett shook his head. "No. It really upset me, seeing him. I just stood there. It brought it all back, you see. And I couldn't even move. I went and got wasted—this girl had some coke she'd found in her old man's wardrobe."

"Was that Celeste Diamond?"

"Celeste, yeah. She's lovely. It turned into a bit of a big night, really. The thing was I knew I'd be banged up again if I went back to the hostel. They do drugs testing and I wasn't going to pass that. A lad at the statics said I could stay with him if I gave him some money. I was working things out. What I should do. And Celeste kept coming back with food and stuff."

"So you never saw Phil's sister again?"

"No, I wish I had."

SIXTY-SEVEN

Elise

ELISE PACKED UP HER bag slowly. There'd been no sign of the Addison1999 e-mail exchange on Bennett's phone. And they had nothing to hold him.

It was a sideshow like Caro had said. Charlie's criminal past had been catching up with him but it'd been his new con trick that had brought death to the basement. Bennett was out of the frame and on his way back to prison. And Phil Golding was dead.

They'd got the right people in the cells. There was a heady buzz in the incident room—the sound of people who knew it was done and dusted. They had the men who had held Charlie prisoner, bound like a joint of meat in Tesco's, and left him in that stinking basement, knowing his reckoning was coming.

"No wonder he had a heart attack," Elise had said to Caro. "I probably would have had one too."

And the cast of *Breaking Bad* had been charged with the drugs conspiracy.

And everyone was happy with the outcome. Aoife the pathologist had been quietly pleased with the cling film angle. "Clever," she'd said. "Leaves no marks but it's a very effective binding material. You try it—it's impossible to get off."

"Well done, Elise," DCI McBride had said. "Straight out of the traps and two cases sorted. Great police work."

She'd smiled and said it was the team who'd cracked it. And she should have been happy too—it was all neat and squared away. Just as she liked it. But she'd known—her waters had told her—there was unfinished business here. In Ebbing. The little sister. *Someone who lived through a terrible thing and didn't tell a soul.*

Elise had run through her yoga class and all the women she knew in the town in her head, looking for her.

But in the end she'd gone into the corridor and rung Ronnie. "What time is it now in Sydney? Can you give your daughter another call and ask her if Phil had a sister?"

Fifteen minutes later, she had her answer. "She was a lot younger, Meggie thinks. Not at school," her other second-in-command bellowed down the phone. "Sorry to shout but Ted's playing Bill Hayley at full volume upstairs."

"Do we have a name?"

"Hold on. . . . Turn that bloody racket down! Right. Yes. Diana, like the princess."

And Elise nodded. *Of course it was.*

ELISE PULLED UP OUTSIDE the Eastwoods' little house as Cal practiced penalties with a friend in the front garden.

Dee came out and stood in the doorway. Watching her.

"Can we talk?" Elise said as she got out of the car.

"Sure. Come in. Play nicely, boys."

They sat down at the kitchen table, opposite each other. Dee fiddled with her necklace while Elise took her jacket off.

"I think you used to be called Diana Golding," she said.

And Dee nodded slowly.

"Nobody's called me that for years. Mum named me Diana because she loved Princess Di—she still had an old video of the wedding when they cleared her last flat," she said, not taking her eyes off Elise. "It was in the box I was given. No video player. Just the tape. Anyway, I stopped being that girl a very long time ago. When I was eight."

But she came back, didn't she? Dragging all her baggage behind her.

"Charlie Perry did a similar thing, didn't he?" Elise said, watching her cleaner for a reaction. "He stopped being Charles Williams the crooked businessman when he fancied a fresh start down here. When did you realize who he really was?"

"Not until I read it in the paper," Dee said. "When his real name came out at the inquest."

Elise looked for the lie but didn't find it in the fragile eyes across from her.

"Stuart Bennett didn't tell you when you went to see him?"

Dee's mouth flew open.

"We know you went to see him the week before the festival," Elise cut her off. "But why? Why did you want to see him?"

"I . . . I knew he'd been in touch with my brother, Phil, before he died—I was told he'd been at a vigil for his death—and I just wanted to talk about Phil. I loved him so much when I was a kid—he was my hero but I was put in care and couldn't find him again when I was old enough to look. That's what we talked about—Stuart didn't tell me anything about Charlie."

"Did you know Stuart came down to Ebbing the weekend Charlie went missing?"

Her eyes widened. "No. He knew I lived here but he never said anything about coming. Did he see him? Charlie said he'd seen someone, didn't he? He told Liam that in the van. It could have been Stuart."

"Stuart says he saw him at the festival," Elise said.

"Did he have anything to do with his death?" she whispered.

"No. There's no evidence that he was there when Charlie died. Stuart says he didn't even speak to him in the end."

"But it must have frightened Charlie," Dee said. "I'm glad. I'm sorry but Charles Williams was a terrible man. Nobody here knew—they all loved Charlie Perry. I did until I realized who he really was. He was always so nice to me. Some clients don't even say thank you but he took the time and spoke to me like I was someone, not just a cleaner."

Dee looked at her rough red hands. "But he was a fraud, wasn't he?" she said. "Pretending to be someone he wasn't. That's what they do, con men, isn't it? Put it on, to trick you and rob you and wreck your life without a second thought. And I've heard he was still doing it. To Toby and Kevin. He's ruined so many lives. Including my brother's. Phil drank himself to death in the end. He was so eaten up by what he'd done all those years ago."

"Charlie used him to set up the burglary, didn't he?" Elise said.

"That's what he told Stuart. Poor Phil. He was just a kid. And frightened. Out of his depth."

"He never knew you were there that night, did he?" Elise said. "That Stuart took you with him?"

Dee looked at Elise, tears forming in the corners of her eyes.

There was silence in the kitchen. Then the thud of a football hitting the wall outside.

"Not until Stuart told him when he went to see him in prison. Stuart said he was absolutely shattered."

"And what about you? Were you shattered?"

"I was only eight. I told myself it was like one of the horror films I used to watch with Phil. I could pretend it wasn't real. I was so young. I put it away somewhere I couldn't find it. But then it all came back. Here, where I thought I was safe from my past."

"But it's all over now, Dee," Elise said as if to the child Dee had been. "We know how Charlie died."

Dee's chin trembled and her hands wove a knot of fingers.

"The two men he owed money to tied him up and threatened him and he had a heart attack while they weren't there. When they came back, they moved his body and tried to fake a fall."

Dee closed her eyes and didn't speak for a long time.

"I know I shouldn't say it but I'm glad he's dead. He can't hurt anyone else now."

"What would you have said to Charlie if you'd had the chance?"

"That his greed and lies had cost lives. Not everyone died right away but people were destroyed by him. My brother was destroyed."

Elise hesitated before she spoke. "I don't know if you have been contacted yet, Dee, but it appears the vodka your brother was drinking was contaminated with antifreeze."

Dee closed her eyes. "Who would have done that?" she whispered.

"We don't know but we think Phil tried to go and talk to Charlie's daughter. To apologize for his part in the burglary. Charlie may have found out. The Met police are investigating."

"People will know, then, won't they?" Dee said slowly. "What a monster he was. I'm glad."

She was getting a glass of water when she turned.

"Will you tell people who I am?"

Elise shook her head. *What's the point? The little girl who cowered in terror deserves peace—and to know it's all over now.*

RONNIE MUST HAVE BEEN listening for her because she appeared at the door within seconds of her arrival home, armed with a bottle of prosecco.

"We should celebrate you catching all the villains and putting them away—or whatever it is you do with them."

"Thank you, Watson."

BEFORE

SIXTY-EIGHT

Charlie

WHEN THE MUSIC STARTED at the festival, it hit Charlie like a wave, making his head ring and his pulse race. He clapped his hands over his ears and shut his eyes. He was in a nightmare.

It was all Phil Golding's fault. He'd lit the fuse to all this with his pathetic attempt to confess his sins. He certainly hadn't been who Charlie had expected to be standing outside Birdie's residential home. He'd thought it would be Bennett trying to track him down. Not this sad specimen. Phil Golding had never been much of a human being but he looked terrible standing there, framed by the delicate wisteria. It emphasized his yellow-tinged skin and Charlie noted the distended stomach and the flaking skin. He'd seen it before. Advanced alcoholism was never pretty.

"What are you doing here?" he'd asked.

And Phil had gone on about doing the right thing. Some Alcoholics Anonymous nonsense about making amends. And he thought he could just say sorry and have his slate wiped clean. Phil seriously thought he could get forgiveness from Birdie if he pitched up and apologized.

"That's why I need to talk to her," he said. "I've already made amends to Stuart for sending him. I explained it all to him. How you wanted the burglary done to get the insurance money. How it wasn't his fault your daughter was there. He was very decent about it, considering."

Charlie had pretended to listen to the rationale but all he could hear was his darling girl's hurt and horror when she found out her father was a cheap criminal who had ruined her life through greed. She might forget the details quickly but she'd know who her dad really was.

He'd lose her again. And everything else he'd worked so hard to build.

Phil become distraught and Charlie put him in the car and drove him home. Charlie told Phil they'd go to see Birdie the next day. Together. On the way, he stopped for a pee and fetched the vodka the policewoman had donated to the raffle out of the boot. He'd added only a touch of antifreeze to seal the deal. Charlie left Phil with it at a park near his hostel and let nature take its course. The man was killing himself already. It was just hastening the process—it'd been a kindness really.

But, of course, it wasn't over. It was just the first step. Phil Golding had told Bennett everything.

But Charlie thought he'd sorted it—he was going to get the money and shut Bennett down for good.

And it had all been falling into place until Bennett showed up early and Charlie had to run for it.

Charlie was hiding in the trees when the girl drifted into sight. A girl with her hair in plaits. And he thought he must be back in his nightmare. Back in Addison Gardens.

There'd been a girl there that night. He'd seen her when he'd done a quick drive-by in the interval before dessert was served. It was only ten minutes down the road from the dinner in Mayfair and he just wanted to check things were going to plan. For a moment, Charlie thought she'd come out of his house. But afterward, he told himself he must have imagined it. She was on the steps but he didn't see the front door open. And he watched her skip away. She looked as if she was off to school. But it was nighttime. She was far too young to be out on her own. But he stopped thinking about her when minutes later Stuart Bennett ran out of the house like he was on fire.

The street was lit up with flashing blue lights a couple of hours later when he came home from the event. He had the number of the insurance company in his pocket and the list of his best pieces—the Georgian silver pillboxes, the Art Deco jewelry—in his head. Phil was picking it up later that night from his man. Everything was in place for him to collect the insurance and then quietly sell the pieces to discreet collectors who would not ask questions if the price was right. Double bubble. And he could keep his house.

He was astonished by the number of police waiting for him. He'd been expecting a couple of cops, a bit of sympathy, a business-like account of the break-in, and an invitation to see what was missing. He was ready. But not for this.

Charlie threw open his car door and almost fell out in his haste.

"What on earth's happened?" he said to the small crowd of neighbors held behind black-and-yellow tape, but no one would look him in the eye, not even the Simpsons from next door.

An officer walked toward him, took his arm, and led him gently to a police car. "Mr. Williams? Could you come and sit in here for a moment," he said. "I'm DI Wicks. Can you tell me where you've been this evening?"

"Er, a Rotary do at the Park Lane Hotel." And he fished the invite out of his dinner jacket pocket. "I'm on the committee. What's happened? Has there been a break-in?"

"Who lives at this address, Mr. Williams?"

"Me."

"Just you?"

"Yes, I live alone. What is this about?"

"Well. I'm sorry to have to tell you that two people were attacked at your address tonight. One person has died and the other is critically ill."

And the world stopped. He stared at the detective for what felt like an age. "Died? Critically ill?" he managed to croak. "Who?"

"We are still in the process of formal identification of the deceased but we have a witness who says the survivor is your daughter."

His stomach heaved and he spewed the last course of his meal, filling the police car with the sweet-and-sour stench of undigested tiramisu.

"Christ! Sergeant," DI Wicks shouted out the window, "get some wet wipes pronto."

Later, at the police station, they'd taken his soiled clothes away and given him a paper overall to wear. But he could still smell it.

He wept as he told them about Birdie. How she and her mother had moved out. "She'd only recently come back into my life. I'd given her a key to the house—and the code to the alarm in case I wasn't there to let her in."

"But you didn't know she would be there tonight?"

"No, no. Oh, God, why was she?"

"We don't know. A neighbor saw the door was open when he walked his dog. When we arrived, we found the victims in the living room."

Charlie wasn't able to bear to hear the details of what had happened then, but the detective carried on, punctuating each horrific point with a small apologetic cough.

"A plastic bag? What sort of monster would do that?" Charlie sobbed.

Birdie had been asthmatic as a child, struggling to breathe some nights. He and Lila had had to sit with her, watching her fight, trying to decide whether it meant a trip to the hospital. He could still hear the slow rasp and wheeze of each breath.

"Have you caught the bastard who did this?" he shouted to stop the sound.

The inspector shook his head. "But we will," he added. "We'll get whoever was responsible."

And they thought they had, of course.

THAT NIGHT AT THE festival, he heard himself scream, "Birdie!" over the music and the girl whirled round.

And he screamed again, the shock rattling his jaw.

"Are you okay?" The girl crouched beside him and took his hand.

"Why are you here?" he said, his focus slipping off the face in front of him. He must have been hallucinating.

When he saw the mistletoe necklace round her neck, Charlie tried to grab it.

"Birdie . . ." he gasped.

But she pushed him back and ran off. He heaved himself onto his shaking legs and threw himself into the crowd to follow her, ricocheting off the dancers.

NOW

SIXTY-NINE

Dee

WE WALK CAL'S FRIEND Mikey home after a bit. It isn't far and I need the air. Liz wants to chat but I tell her I've left something in the oven. She hasn't heard about Liam being charged yet but she will. She won't want anything to do with us then.

On the way back, we go on the beach and throw pebbles into the sea. Cal loves doing that. And I throw my necklace in as well. I should never have kept it. Should have thrown it away years ago. I knew that. But I had nothing when I was little. I wanted one thing to keep. I made a hole in my little anorak and pushed it inside, in the stuffing. I started to wear it only when I got back to Ebbing. When I felt safe.

But I'm not now. Elise says she won't tell anyone but she's a cop. She'll tell someone one day. We need to move. I'll have to tell Cal tomorrow. There's too much going on.

I'll just pack up and go. I can now that I know they've arrested Toby and Kevin for what they did to Charlie. And I've said as much to Elise. She won't come looking. She's got her story now. About

Dee the victim. I dreaded it but it was easy in the end. I told her what I wanted her to believe and she heard what she wanted to hear. Lots of it was true. The stuff about Phil and Stuart being way out of their depth.

And I told her enough so she didn't feel she had to press me on what had happened that night.

I shouldn't have been there but Phil had left me with the boy in the next room that night. Stuart, the boy who let us boil water.

"Can you watch her for an hour, mate?" Phil said. "I'll be back in plenty of time for tonight."

I remember we sat on the floor in the dark and I watched Stuart messing around with his phone.

It got late and I started looking at the door. I was hungry but Stuart was sniffing stuff. He suddenly stopped and stood up. He looked like he was standing in a big wind, swaying all over the place.

"I've got to go to work," he said. "Where's your brother?"

"I don't know."

"Well, you'll have to wait here for him."

"No," I said, and started to cry. "Don't leave me on my own. Please."

"For fuck's sake. Okay, put your coat on."

I ran after him, clattering down the stairs, and walked in his footsteps. He didn't speak to me. I think he forgot I was there.

He climbed through a window at the back of the house and I did the same. It was all dimly lit and so warm. I remember the carpet felt like a mattress under my feet. Stuart went into a room off the hall and told me to stay quiet until he was done. But I got bored and wandered farther down the big hallway. I wanted to see. And I heard a voice—a girl's voice—and followed it.

She was lying on the sofa when I walked in. I'd never seen such a beautiful room—it had a glass chandelier and everything was shiny. And the girl shouted when she saw me. "Christ, what are you doing here?"

And Stuart came running in and tried to grab me to go but she started screaming and he got hold of her. And it was too late to leave.

She was shouting for someone to help her. And we heard a door slam and someone running. And yelling, "Sofia." Stuart picked up a poker from the fireplace and hit the man when he rushed in. I stood in a corner and saw it all playing like a video game, the blood splashed in neon colors, the screams digitally manipulated. The man didn't say anything after that. Stuart tied up the girl with her belt and sat her on a chair. He kept shouting, "Where's the silver stuff? The jewelry?" And there was spit coming out of his mouth. But she wouldn't say. He put a clear plastic bag over her head and said he would take it off if she told him. And he got me to hold where he'd twisted it while he put a computer in his backpack. I was supposed to stand at the back of her but she twisted her head and I could see her face through the plastic. She was wearing a really pretty necklace and I reached to touch it. Her eyes were bugging out, her mouth sucking the bag in. "Tell him," I whispered to her. But she didn't. She just stopped sucking the bag in.

"Stuart," I remember saying. And he came over and pulled the bag off.

"Fuck," he said.

"Can we go home now?"

"Go, get out of here!"

And I went out the front door and stopped at the bottom of the steps. I couldn't remember where I was for a minute. Then I saw the gardens opposite and ran.

Phil wasn't there when I got back to the squat. He crawled in beside me later. He smelled really badly of drink and wasn't making any sense. I clung to him as he snored and tried to go to sleep.

When I woke up, the police were all over the squat. Stuart had gone—he'd been captured on CCTV on the way home. Phil couldn't look me in the eye. He said he'd got drunk with mates and forgotten the time. He'd been blind drunk when he'd rolled in. He'd fallen on the bed and gone to sleep.

"Just keep quiet about Stuart babysitting you here last night or they'll take you away, Diana," he said.

Being taken away was what Mum used to threaten me with when I talked back or came in late from playing. So I didn't say anything. But they took me away anyway.

A nice lady asked me how old I was and where did I live. I said with Mum, like Phil had told me to say. But she went to see Mum and came back very angry.

"We're going to go somewhere nice," she said in the car. She'd held my hand on the long journey to Wales until it had got sweaty and uncomfortable and I pulled away.

I'd locked all that in a box, deep in my head. It was one night in my whole life, I told myself when I got old enough to think like that. I had to forget it and get on with living. I called myself Dee and grew into another person.

But I looked online later. Of course I did. The press coverage said that a teenage burglar, high on drugs when he broke into the million-pound house, had found Sofia Nightingale and her boyfriend there, bludgeoned him to death, and tied the girl up. He'd put a plastic bag over her head. "It was just to scare her," Stuart had wept in his police interview. "She should have told me where the stuff was."

She should have, I thought.

The girl wasn't dead when we left. She was in a coma in hospital.

Then I couldn't find anything else. I thought she must have died. It was weird reading about it. But good weird. It felt as though it had happened to someone else. Not me. A story I'd heard somewhere.

Until Phil died. And I went to see Stuart. And saw Charlie's passport.

I couldn't quite believe it at first. Could it be him? Here in Ebbing? Someone I worked for? And liked?

I sat and wrote down what I knew: His real name was Williams, the same name as on the rent receipt I'd found in Phil's notebook. But lots of people were called Williams.

The brain-damaged daughter in the home. He never said what had happened to her, did he?

And why had he taken a new identity? What was he hiding?

I had to be sure. I set up a new Yahoo! account—calling myself Addison1999—and contacted him anonymously. And he replied a couple of days later, asking for a meeting. And I knew. On the Sunday, I got the e-mail telling me to be in the car park. And I wasn't sure at first. But I told myself it was in a public place where I'd be safe. And I wanted him to know he'd been found out.

That's all. But he never came.

BEFORE

SEVENTY

Birdie

BIRDIE WAS LAUGHING AT how clever she'd been when she saw the child in the doorway. It made her scream. A spooky child. Just standing there looking at her.

"Christ, what are you doing here?" she shouted.

But a man suddenly appeared and ran past the child and into the room. It was all going to shit.

Birdie had been stealing from her dad for months. First it was the occasional tenner, a packet of cigarettes, a bottle of Scotch. It'd been a game, really. She'd loved seeing how easy it was to trick him. He didn't know her—he pretended he did with all that "darling Birdie" stuff but he'd lied to her and Mum. He needed to know he couldn't just buy his way back into her life. But she'd liked the lovely things in the cabinets. Loved the mistletoe necklace he'd given her. So she tried it. A small silver rabbit. He'd never miss that. And she'd taken more. One thing at a time.

Until she'd overheard her father talking to someone on the phone while she waited to be taken out for a meal.

"Is it set up for the Saturday before Christmas? I'll sort out the alarms when I leave for the dinner. He'll have time. Tell him not to take the pictures. Harder to shift without drawing attention. Don't screw this up!"

She'd known he was planning a burglary. An insurance fraud. Still conning people.

So she'd decided to stage her own. She'd done her research—seen how easy it was to sell pretty things. She'd sold a small silver pillbox she'd already taken. It had taken only twenty-four hours to find a buyer—a man in Germany. She'd DHLed it with a receipt signed with a scrawled "C Williams."

Her new boyfriend had been a bit worried about it but she told Adam it was a practical joke on her Dad—she'd take it all back in the morning. She hadn't needed to use the codes she'd found in her father's desk to open the cabinets. The alarms were already switched off. They took everything they could fit in their pockets. She'd already rented a locker at a corner shop down one of the backstreets to stash it.

She and her boyfriend had still been laughing when they got to the shop. It was he who'd suggested going back for more.

The last thing she remembered was the child's face. The spooky child staring at her through the plastic bag. And reaching for her necklace.

NOW

SEVENTY-ONE

Dee

WE'VE CAUGHT AN EARLY coach to Truro. Cal thinks we're going on holiday. He was excited when I told him, then went quiet. "What about Dad?" he whispered.

"Dad is going to try to come and join us later," I said. One more lie among so many can't hurt. We just need to get away.

He falls asleep after Stonehenge and I sit back and try to empty my head. But it's all still there. Of course it is.

I can see myself slipping out of the house when I heard Liam leave. He'd whispered to see if I was awake. Whether I wanted to go and see the fire at the Old Vicarage.

I'd just pretended I was asleep. Couldn't even speak to him, I was so furious. Running around the town, sightseeing other people's misery, when our lives were falling to pieces in front of us. The land-lord wanted to evict us—throw us out on the streets—because Charlie wouldn't pay what he owed us. He was still ruining my life all these years later. And I hadn't been able to tell him. Why hadn't he come that night? He must have chickened out.

I don't know how long I lay there after Liam had gone. But I suddenly got out of bed and started pulling on my clothes. If Charlie wouldn't come to me, I'd go to him. I could be there and back before Liam got home.

I know who you are, Charlie. And where you are.

It was breathing I'd heard that Sunday when I looked through the letter box. Tall Trees wasn't haunted. It'd been him hiding.

I DROVE HALFWAY TO the house, left the van outside a weekender's place where I clean, and walked the rest. I didn't want to alert Pauline—she might not have taken her sleeping pill that night. I'd got a key to the back door of the big house—it was on the key ring that Pauline had given me originally. I'm sure she didn't even realize. It'd taken me a while to work out which door it fitted but I'd got to it eventually. But I didn't need to use it. The door was on the latch. I pushed it open and used my mobile phone torch to light the way.

I can still hear the scuffling sound I heard that night, when I told myself it was only mice. *You can do vermin.* I decided to start at the top of the house—that's where I would hide—and began picking my way up the wrecked stairs, listening to myself breathe.

But the scuffling got louder. Then there was a bang somewhere below me. I ran down the stairs, trying to follow the last echoes of the sound. Down and down. Until I was there. My torch flashed onto the floor. And Charlie looked up at me.

I felt as if I stood there for hours, but when I looked at my watch, it was minutes. I was trying to make sense of what I was looking at. Charlie was on the ground. There was some sort of material in his mouth and he was stuck to a chair with what looked like layers of plastic. There was a giant roll of cling film on the floor beside him. I couldn't move. He was trying to shuffle toward me, humping his body across the floor.

"Stop!" I commanded him. And he did.

I bent to take his gag out—a disgusting rag of a tea towel—and tried to right him but he was too heavy. I needed scissors to cut him free but there was nothing in the room.

"Thank God it's you," he croaked. "I need a drink." And I brought him water in my hand from the sink. He looked so helpless.

"Who did this to you?" I said.

"Never mind that," he moaned.

He was too busy slurping to ask why I was there. *But he will.*

"What on earth did you do to make them tie you up?"

"A horrible misunderstanding over money. Can't you get this stuff off me? I can't feel my legs."

"No, it's wound too tight." I tried slashing at it with my keys but it was hopeless.

"Go and get a knife from the caravan."

"And wake Pauline? What would I tell her?"

"I don't care. I need to get out of here."

There was a beat and he asked the question I'd been waiting for.

"Why are you here?"

"It's a bit of a long story."

His face clouded and he was staring at me intently. It was putting me off, so I said it quickly.

"You owe my husband four thousand pounds and we'll lose our home if you don't pay him."

"I haven't got it," he said. "Why do you think I'm in this state?"

"And I know who you really are," I said.

He looked at me from the floor and groaned. "Who?"

"Charles Williams. You staged a burglary at your own house, didn't you? And ruined all those lives."

He closed his eyes and muttered, "Please, could you give me another drink? I don't feel well."

I fetched a handful, the water dripping between my fingers. As I leaned toward him, he caught my cheek and some of my hair in his teeth and bit hard. Like a dog. I screamed and pulled back.

"I know who you really are, girlie." And he kept on staring at me. "You were there, weren't you? You were there that night. When my daughter was being suffocated. You were the girl on the doorstep."

"I don't know what you're talking about." I was holding my cheek. It felt wet. He'd drawn blood.

"Yes, you do," he said, and his eyes flicked to my necklace. "That's hers. I saw you wearing it on Friday night."

My hand went straight to the chain. "It was a present," I said, backing away.

"No, you stole it from Birdie. She always wore it—"

"No," I said, but my voice faltered.

"You're not very good at this, are you? Look, girlie, get me out of here and I won't tell the police about what you did."

I just stood there. It was surreal that he'd taken charge of the situation, lying there on the floor, tied to a chair. I felt like I was in a dream. But I pushed my nails into my hands to wake myself up.

"Shut up!" I shouted at him. "I didn't do anything. I was eight years old. I just stood in the room while Stuart did it."

"I don't believe you," he said.

I bent down so I was on the same level as his face but far enough away from his teeth.

"I don't care," I said quietly. "Phil knew. And Stuart knows. We all know you set the whole thing up."

"What are you talking about?" Charlie hissed at me. "Your brother set it up. He employed a junkie who stole to feed his habit."

"He was made to do it. You forced Phil to fix it. Told him you'd make sure he'd go to jail for supplying drugs. And I'd be left on my own. You told him you'd turn the alarms off."

Charlie's eyes were bulging and he spat as he shouted, "Phil? Fucking lies! I had nothing to do with it! Anyway, he's not around to tell anyone anything, is he?"

"How do you know that?"

"Can't remember who told me," he said but couldn't meet my eye. "They said he was a piss head who drank his last drink. Look, I gave him a job, paid him a good wage. I was looking after him."

"Of course you did," I said. "Good old Charlie Perry, always doing someone a favor. People think you are a real sweetheart, don't they? But you're a coldhearted, greedy fake. You destroyed all our lives—mine, Phil's, Stuart's, and your daughter's."

"No one's going to believe you, you little bitch," he hissed. "But they'll believe me. They trust me."

I laughed in his face. And then realized he was right. I had no proof. Phil was dead. No one would believe Stuart. Charlie was going to brand me a monster. Of course he was. He'd seen the necklace. *Do something,* echoed round my head.

And I reached for the cling film and began to wind it round his mouth.

IT TOOK ONLY HALF an hour to clean up the mess. A tenner's worth of my time. I picked up Charlie's bag and checked that the passport was in there. I should have thrown it in the sea but I didn't have time. I needed to get home before Liam missed me, so I dumped it in a skip. Anyway, it doesn't matter now.

We stop at Exmouth for yet another comfort break and I wait for Cal, crouching down by a wall out of the wind. Make myself small while I decide who I'm going to be when we get to Cornwall. The front I'll put on before I disappear. And start cleaning again.

SEVENTY-TWO

Elise

EVERYONE WAS BUSY COLLECTING and collating evidence, cross-checking statements, when Elise quietly backed out of the incident room. She closed the blinds in her office and eased off her shoes.

DC Chevening appeared round the door. "Sorry, ma'am. Is it okay to disturb you?"

"Yes, come in. What have you got?"

"I'm putting together the forensic documentation—we've just received the full report—but I've found something I don't understand."

"Right. Go on." Elise tried not to sound irritated. She'd been a newbie once.

"So we've got Phil Golding's DNA on the phone and on the zip fastener."

"Zip fastener? Show me."

It was there in the section of results for the exterior of Charlie's bag. A smudged print the SOCOs couldn't lift but the microbeads of sweat from the finger that had touched it had been a partial match for his DNA. "Twenty-five percent," the lab technician had written beside it.

"But he was dead," Elise said.

"That's what I thought," the young officer said.

The explanation from the forensic scientist on the end of the phone was long and unnecessarily detailed, but when Elise ended the call, she was clear.

"The best hypothesis is that it is from a half-sibling," she breathed. "Dee.

"Can you drive?" she said to DC Chevening.

"Yes. Where are we going?"

"To find her."

ELISE RANG CARO AS she walked, breathlessly talking her through the new evidence.

"Phil's sister was there. Dee Eastwood. My cleaner. In the basement. Kevin said the bag was there when they left and gone when they came back."

"Dee is Phil's sister? When did you find that out?"

"Er, yesterday. Stuart Bennett put me onto it."

"And you think seeing her made Charlie have a heart attack?"

"I think she confronted him about what he made her brother do. She told me yesterday she was glad Charlie was dead."

"Did she? So you've spoken to her?"

"I went to tell her about the police investigation into her brother's death."

"Right—so I suppose it could have terrified Charlie. He was wrapped up in cling film, so completely vulnerable."

It stopped Elise in her tracks and DC Chevening crashed into her. "Sorry, ma'am."

"You go and pick her up, Caro. Take DC Chevening with you. I need to call Aoife and then speak to Toby Greene. About the plastic in Charlie's gut."

"What?" Caro said. "Oh, okay. On our way."

AOIFE MORTIMER DIDN'T SPEAK for a full three minutes when Elise asked the question. She thought the line had gone dead and had been about to redial when Aoife cleared her throat.

"The shreds in the stomach could be from a cling film gag," she said carefully. "If it'd been loose enough. He could have fought to get it off. And smothering him with a bag or film could certainly produce a heart attack, especially in someone with his medical history. And would leave no evidence."

"Toby, did you gag Charlie with the cling film you used?"

Toby Greene shook his head. "No. I told you, Kevin used an old tea towel. But Charlie had managed to spit it out when we found him. I couldn't work out how. I wrapped it up with the cling film and threw it away."

"I see. And you are sure you never put cling film near his face?"

"Of course not. What kind of monster would do that? He wouldn't have been able to breathe."

"DEE EASTWOOD LEFT HOME this morning with her son," Caro said when she called in. "She asked the babysitter to look after her dog and said she'd be in touch. She hasn't taken her car—she must have thought she'd be too easy to find. I'm getting a warrant to check movement on her bank account. Shouldn't take long."

It didn't. "She bought two tickets for a coach to Truro. One way," Caro said. "We're a good hour behind her but the coach stops a few times along the route. I've asked the local police to be there in case we don't manage to catch up."

In the car, Caro put her foot down hard and Elise closed her eyes and reran the conversations she'd had with her cleaner. Looking for the signs she'd missed. But Dee had been clever. *The invisible cleaner who sees everything. Who cleans up everything. The messes, the filth. Charlie.*

She wondered what it had felt like to have him at her mercy. To watch him die. Dee had been a child when she'd seen Birdie fight for breath in Addison Gardens. But she wasn't anymore. She had known exactly what she was doing when she put that cling film over Charlie's face.

"I should have pushed her about the sighting of Liam's van the night Charlie died," she said almost to herself.

"Stop beating yourself up, boss. Look, we're at the turnoff. We're there now."

They were waiting when the coach pulled up. Seagulls screeching overhead and diving for half-eaten burgers in the bins.

Elise got out and scanned the faces in the windows of the bus. The excited people going on their holidays. Pulling bags off the racks above their heads.

Dee was at the back. Talking to her son, smiling, and buttoning his jacket when she caught sight of Elise.

She put her hand to her mouth and the boy turned to look. She pulled him in close and nodded at Elise. Then sat, waiting for her to come and get her.

She hardly said a word when they put them in the police car. But she started to weep when her son said: "Can we go home now?"

ACKNOWLEDGMENTS

I owe a huge debt of gratitude to the many people who have supported, prodded, soothed, and encouraged me in the writing of this book.

I'll begin with my brilliant editors, Frankie Gray and Danielle Perez, who never faltered in their support despite false starts, and everyone at Transworld and Berkley who helped get the book on track.

Heartfelt thanks to my wonderful agent, Madeleine Milburn—the best possible person to have in your corner—along with Liane-Louise Smith and the rights team.

As always, there were specialists who helped prevent me from making a complete fool of myself:

The endlessly patient Home Office Forensic Pathologist Dr. Debbie Cook, who introduced me to the enduring properties of sweet corn in the gut—and so much more.

Detective Superintendent Tara McGovern and DC Polly Gallacher, who talked so frankly about the impact of breast cancer on women in the police and introduced me to the work of the inspirational breast cancer charities Breast Mates (https://breastmates.org)

and Future Dreams (https://futuredreams.org.uk). Thanks also to my friend Helen Turner for guiding me through the treatment.

And retired murder squad DCI Colin Sutton, who took time out of his own hugely successful writing career to guide me on some police matters.

As always, any mistakes that lingered are my own.

Thank you to the wonderfully generous Fiona Doyle, who made the winning bid to name a character in *Local Gone Missing*. I'm sorry it has taken a while for Dave Harman to see his name in print but he and Fiona helped raise more than £7,500 for children and young people with cancer in the CLIC Sargent Good Books auction (https://www.younglivesvscancer.org.uk).

Finally my brilliant family and friends who kept me going—my husband, Gary; children, Tom and Lucy; mother, Jeanne; sister, Jo; brother, Jon; and BFs, Carol and Rachael. I couldn't have done it without you.

This book is dedicated to my dearest dad, who died in January 2021. He was a writer, a journalist, and a champion of his children in whatever we decided to do. This is for you, Dad.